To Charley,
Can this truly be
the end?

BOOK 5 OF

THE YEDS

THE DAY
THE SKY FELL

[signature]

AN EMERGENT STEAMPUNK SERIES
BY ADAM DREECE

ADZO Publishing Inc.
Calgary, Canada

ADZO Publishing Inc.
Calgary, Alberta, Canada
www.adzopublishing.com

Printed in Canada

This is a work of fiction. Names, characters, places, and incidents are a product of the author's imagination. Locales and public names are sometimes used for atmospheric purposes. Any resemblance to actual people, living or dead, or to businesses, companies, events, institutions, or locales is completely coincidental.

Library and Archives Canada Cataloguing in Publication

Dreece, Adam, 1972-, author
 The day the sky fell / by Adam Dreece.

(The Yellow Hoods ; book 5)
Issued in print and electronic formats.
ISBN 978-0-9948184-8-5 (softcover).--ISBN 978-0-9948184-9-2 (Kindle)

 I. Title. II. Series: Dreece, Adam, 1972-. Yellow Hoods ; bk. 5.

 PS8607.R39D39 2017   jC813'.6   C2017-900768-8
                                        C2017-900769-6

1 2 3 4 5 6 7 8 9 2/26/17 64,319

DEDICATION

To my daughter, whose simple request to have me capture a silly story I told her at bedtime one night turned into this amazing series,

To my wife who has been my rock every step of the way,

To my sons who remind me of unrelenting imagination every day,

And to every supporter, fan, and friend, you made me believe that this was possible.

PREVIOUSLY

Don't remember exactly what was going on in the last few books? Then this section's for you! Otherwise, skip on ahead to Chapter One.

We last left the Yellow Hoods (Tee, Elly, Richy, and Mounira) at the ruins of Kar'm, a secret base for inventors and rebels under the leadership of Christina Creangle.

Caterina, also known as the Lady in Red and the Regent Catherine, had sent her ground forces and Skyfaller airships to attack, aided by secret agents of the Fare loyal to her.

The Yellow Hoods, with the help of Bakon and Egelina-Marie, as well as fellow inventive teen, Alex, brought down the Skyfallers before all was lost.

Tee's grandfather, Sam Baker (the Baker), and Elly's grandmother, Eleanor DeBoeuf senior (the Butcher), made a desperate deal with the Moufan-Men to repel Caterina's ground forces, saving many lives but at a cost of dissolving their secret society, the Tub.

Marcus Pieman, who had been captured by Caterina (along with Tee's other grandfather, Nikolas Klaus) at the end of Book 3, has avoided execution at Caterina's hand and has played the Great Game masterfully. Now, his guilt or innocence for crimes against his fellow continental leaders will be determined at the first Trial by Royals in more than a century.

And Nikolas Klaus, who was captured along with Marcus, is being held in Relna's keep in the kingdom of Belnia as a political prisoner tied to the Trial by Royals.

EORTHE

Cartographer: Driss of Zouak, 1793
Created at the behest of the Council of Southern Kingdoms

CHAPTERS

CHAPTER ONE
LIDDEL PROBLEM

The shepherd stretched out his arms and yawned at the cloudy, late-summer sky. "Time to go home," he said to his sheep that were milling about on the grassy mountain plateau.

He pulled his grandfather's old crook out of the ground and cleaned off the bottom with his hand, just as he had for his father. The hooked staff and the trade that came with it, had been passed down for centuries from one Liddel to the next. It was for good reason that they were trusted with all the sheep of the village.

"Go," he urged a sheep that stared at him blankly. "Can you not see the smoke rising from the chimneys? It means our day is done." He pointed, but the sheep seemed unconvinced. "This is not one of my stories. Can you not feel it in your belly? Surely, you're full, and I can have my dinner."

After a look of contemplation, the sheep nodded, turned, and started trotting away.

"Listen to Chikahn, my friends. It is time for us to get home, eat, and rest. We will be back tomorrow." He used his crook to get the stragglers moving, and gradually they all headed down the mountain.

Arriving at the valley floor, he corralled the sheep and counted them quickly. He checked the eyes of two of them and the hooves of another. The Liddel family was known for their meticulous care of animals in their charge and their passionate storytelling around the dinner table.

As Chikahn was about to get the sheep moving again, he noticed something in the sky approaching the village in the distance. Putting his free hand over his eyes to block the late afternoon sun, he wrinkled his face at the sight. "Is that an air balloon? I haven't seen one in years."

He smiled and patted one of the sheep. "Can you believe that? An air balloon. This is a sign of something. Maybe we will have good fortune on this day! Wait... It looks like two... Two air balloons? Unbelievable. They are strangely close together, though. Something is connecting them like they have one huge basket or... it almost looks like a ship's body connecting them. This doesn't look like the one used by the Official Cartographer of Teuton. Maybe it is new?"

Clapping his hands, he stirred the sheep to get moving. He glanced up at the sky periodically as they approached the village. "What an odd air balloon ship."

Bat-like wings came out of the sides of the airship, catching the wind and propelling the ship quickly forward.

"What further strangeness is this? Unbelievable. What a story it will make for dinner: a wind ship. I wonder where it's..." His heart skipped a beat. "It's heading for our village."

Chikahn nudged the sheep anxiously with his crook and swallowed hard as his heart sped up. His eyes fixed on the airship. "There is something evil about. I can feel it. We must go. Go my friends! Go! Go! Go!"

As the airship pulled in its wings and slowed over the village, Chikahn abandoned his position behind the sheep and rushed to the front. His ears filled with the sound of his blood pounding.

"Leave!" he yelled, waving furiously. "Go away!"

Glancing back at the sheep, he threw his crook and bolted down the dirt path. "The sky! Everyone, look at the sky!"

Tripping on a small hole, he slid on his hands and knees. Brushing off his bloody, dusty hands, he watched as fiery streaks fell from the airship onto the unsuspecting village. The pastoral silence was shattered as explosions filled the air.

Chikahn fell backwards, his hands over his ears. "What are you doing? Who are you? Leave my village alone!" He scrambled back to his feet and ran for all he was worth.

As he came upon the white post in the road telling him the village was only a half-mile away, the world fell silent. He slowed to a walk and then dropped to his knees. There wasn't a building left standing. Everything was on fire that hadn't been destroyed, and he couldn't hear the cry of a single child. His blood ran cold.

The airship put out its wings again. The wind passed no judgement on it and gave it a strong push.

"No!" he yelled, standing. "You do not get to float away!" He turned about, his hands outstretched. "Where is the justice in this? My village did harm to no one! Who will right this? Who?" He lost his words as he noticed a strange cloud floating the wrong way. Squinting at it, he shook his head. "Am I dreaming?"

The cloud then lowered in the sky and accelerated towards the escaping airship. The air filled with the sounds of a hundred windmills.

"Are you... the god of the sky?" he asked.

The strange cloud maneuvered behind the airship, and then two claps of thunder erupted from it. The airship's balloons, and parts of its body, blew apart. As pieces tumbled towards the ground, the mysterious cloud sailed up and away, the sound of a hundred windmills going with it.

Chikahn's hands wouldn't stop shaking. "What... what miracle of justice have I just seen? An airship destroyed by a cloud..." He glanced at his village and then at the sky again. "Thank you! I shall never forget."

With a deep breath, he forced himself to look at the smoking remains of his village. "I will seek not vengeance, for as my grandfather said, it only consumes a man. No, instead I will tell the world of this miracle."

He stared up at the sky, turning about. "Do you hear me? I shall tell all of this day: the day that a piece of the sky fell to vanquish evil. You have the promise of Chikahn Liddel."

CHAPTER TWO
AIR APPARENT

"Slowly!" yelled Abeland to his crew through a bullhorn as the Hotaru lowered. "Keep those turbines synchronized. We don't want to lurch to the left like we did the last time we landed. After a perfect combat test like that, I'd like a perfect landing. Everyone ready?"

"Aye!" yelled back his crew.

"Cheeky monkeys," replied Abeland with a laugh. "Are you all pirates now? Stay focused." He put the bullhorn aside and placed his leather-gloved hands on two longer, bronze levers among the dozen before him. Then he looked over his shoulder at his crew of eight, everyone at their positions, each by a turbine or large, magnetic-coil gun. The engineer sat at the back, an array of silver bells and levers similar to Abeland's in front of him and a cabin door behind him.

The Hotaru eased below the tree-line and wobbled delicately over the railroad platform, its turbines still belting out a deep, rhythmic thumping sound.

Abeland pulled one of the levers and grabbed his bullhorn, which was roped to the console of meters and gauges above the bells. "Are we ready to drop the ropes?"

A member of his crew peeked over the bow of the Hotaru and gave him a hand sign of two fingers straight up.

"Good. Then ropes away!" Abeland pulled the lever.

The crew below grabbed the ropes.

Abeland looked at the silver bells and their cryptic labels. He plucked out one and gave it a ring.

The engineer rang his confirming bell, and the turbines slowed even more.

"While the Skyfallers are clumsy and sluggish, the one thing I'll give the Lady in Red," said Abeland to himself, "is that it was genius to move airships by rail. I don't mind stealing that, given that we built the yigging rail system."

The Hotaru banged back and forth as it fit into place.

He smiled at the sound of the engines shutting down, and the wub-wub of the turbines slowly giving way to the sounds of people working furiously. With a satisfied sigh, he bent down and picked up his metal-and-glass breathing helmet and detached its hose from the deck floor.

"All clear?" called someone from the ground.

"All clear," yelled back Abeland.

A second later, ladders were leaned against the Hotaru and a team of engineers and support staff climbed aboard.

"And?" asked the chief engineer, suddenly appearing in front of Abeland.

"You know, if I didn't know better, I'd think you were

trying to give me a heart attack."

The short, grey-haired man smiled. "You Piemans are hard to kill."

"That we are," replied Abeland with a smile. He handed over the helmet. "On the positive side, the breathing apparatus worked beautifully this time. I had no problem getting air from the tanks below deck. Check with everyone else that they found it better, but I believe we've solved the problems of altitude. Now, if you could do something about the glass before my eyes fogging up when we go into the clouds, that would be wonderful."

"You what? You're... I'm sorry, but these aren't designed for that purpose."

"How will we know our limits if we don't test them?"

"Is plummeting out of the sky to your death a reasonable outcome, then?"

Abeland raised an eyebrow and slapped a hand on the man's shoulder. "Isn't science about learning from what we do and engineering about ensuring we don't die while we do it? And are you not my chief engineer?"

The man glared at Abeland.

"I'm glad we understand each other." Abeland offered a half-grin.

"Any other impossible tasks you'd like me to contend with?"

"We need to boost the speed of the Hotarus. Maybe by... twenty percent?"

"Why not just say a thousand?"

Abeland gave the man a sharp look. "Because I know you can do twenty percent. The steam engine's not at maximum efficiency. I can feel the vibrations and loss of energy when we try to give her all she's got. Also, I think that finding a way to rotate the turbines, so they can push us along, not just give us some lift, could go a long way. It doesn't need to be much, just a bit more. It would do wonders."

"Hmm..." The chief engineer scratched his head. "I'm not promising anything, but I'll give that some thought."

"That's all I'm asking for."

The chief engineer grumbled and marched off.

Abeland took off his gloves and stuffed them into the pockets of his long, brown coat. After a satisfied glance at all the activity, he disembarked and started walking southward along the rail lines.

As he left the bustle behind him, he thought about Caterina, also known as the Lady in Red. Recent reports about her steam engine trains and new Skyfallers were disturbing and indicated potential to reduce the Piemans' advantage significantly. Worse was the news that the Lady in Red had not only had the Council of the Fare murdered, but Caterina had managed to get most of the Fare's factions to pledge themselves to her. Her forces and spy network were quickly matching that of the Piemans, and her financial resources were significantly stronger.

He stared up at the sky, thinking.

"You have that sour face, Uncle," said Richelle, stepping off a rail-raft and waving off her four soldiers. She was wearing a dark brown jacket and pants, with black boots and her trademark red hood.

"Did I really not hear that approach?" he asked, surprised, as the soldiers pumped the rail-raft off to join the Hotarus' train.

"It's not the first time I've caught you lost in thought lately."

He grimaced. "It doesn't matter that the Hotarus are still a hundred times better than the Skyfallers. The only captains we have are you and me. Everyone I've tried to train has nearly cost us a Hotaru. They just cannot think in three dimensions."

"Hmm," said Richelle.

Abeland kicked at the ground. "Even if each Hotaru can take out a dozen of Caterina's airships, she'll overwhelm us given the latest numbers I received."

"Well, I have a lead on someone I think might be able to be a third captain," said Richelle. "They've proven themselves to be… very adaptable."

Abeland raised an eyebrow.

"I won't be saying a word more about it until I know that they are on board." She started walking back to the Hotaru; Abeland followed. "How did the ship handle this time?"

"Honestly?" he said, looking back, "I'm rather pleased.

The latest set of changes had exactly the effect we wanted. The MCM engines now provide the extra boost we need to get in the air more quickly, and once the steam engine takes over, the MCMs allow our weapons to fire and reload quickly."

"I still think the single best improvement was painting the bottom to look like a cloud in the sky," said Richelle. "You are aware I originally meant it as a joke, are you not?"

"Some of the best truths lie in jest. On another note, we downed an actual Skyfaller," said Abeland.

"Pardon?" said Richelle, stopping in her tracks.

"We found it and followed it from a distance until it bombed some small mountain village a few dozen miles from here. We blew it right out of the sky before it even knew what was happening."

A huge smile crossed Richelle's face. "So the magnetic coil weapons work?"

"Magnificently." He motioned for her to continue walking. "Now, you find us some captains, and I will get more Hotarus ready. Then when we hear back from Father, we'll be ready."

Richelle took a deep breath. "Are you worried about this Trial by Royals? It's been more than a hundred years since leaders from throughout the continent have come together to judge another leader's crimes. There are no real rules, from what I hear. Never mind that Opa has a lot of enemies these days. The Lady in Red's got some serious influence over many royal families, as well as the entire original Fare under her command."

"Concerned, yes. Worried, no. I've learned never to underestimate my father. He's already caused Caterina no end of frustration. First, she tried to execute him, but he forced a trial. I suspect next he'll find a way to avoid the trial altogether."

"She won't lose well," said Richelle, evaporating Abeland's good mood.

He glanced about. "No, so we'll need to be ready. Any word about the remains of the Tub?"

Richelle shook her head. "There are rumors that the Butcher and Baker have been active near Relna, but nothing significant. Maybe it's the last, desperate flail of a dead secret society. Like Caterina's will be soon enough."

CHAPTER THREE

WHISPERS TO FEAR

Tee peeked out from behind a big pine tree. She pulled her yellow hood back down over her face. "I don't see them," she whispered to Alex.

The fifteen-year-old towered over her, standing right beside her.

He was dressed in his daily garb of a worn, green, long coat and high-collar shirt. The cuffs and elbows of their clothes were threadbare, and the stains and small tears told much of the story of the past two months since Kar'm.

The dense forest was carpeted with autumn leaves of all shapes and colors. The majestic trees seemed innocent of it all, with the canopy high overhead still thick and blocking some of the afternoon sun.

A rifle crackled in the distance.

"That was further away than the last time," said Alex, his Enderian accent crisp and sharp. He tugged on his cuffs and pulled up his coat's collar. His chin raised, he scowled at the landscape.

"See, I told you they'd go the wrong way," said Tee,

leaning against the trunk of the tree. She pulled back her yellow hood and put down the leather sack. She slid her backpack to the ground, rolling her shoulders in relief. "I have to admit that was more of a chase than I was hoping for."

Alex grumbled, running a hand through his short, tight-curled, black hair. "These missions the leaders of the Tub have been sending us on are getting more and more dangerous. We shouldn't be doing them." He gave Tee a sideways glance. "There's no Tub, so why are we doing their bidding?"

"Because that's the only way we're going to get my grandpapa back or see any of our families again."

Alex bristled. "If they wanted to save Nikolas Klaus, then I believe they would have already done so. That Madame DeBoeuf, Elly's supposed grandmother, she has many plans."

Tee raised an eyebrow. "What are you talking about?"

His face tensed, and he turned away. "Nothing. I'm sure she promises everyone something to keep them in check."

"Alex, what's going on?"

He shrugged.

Tee shook her head. "I don't like that they've been keeping us all apart. Madame DeBoeuf, in particular, has been preventing any of us from having any time alone, but I think it's because she's worried about our safety."

"Are you that naive?"

"Excuse me?" snapped Tee. "I'm going to do whatever it takes to save my grandpapa, and I have complete faith in my other grandfather, Sam."

Alex licked his lips and looked at Tee. "I would like Nikolas Klaus to be free; I do. He sounds like a splendid man. But I am not sure I'm willing to risk my life for his."

"Ah. Wow." Tee checked the cable that ran from her armband grapnel device to the backpack. "We're all on the same side you know."

He slowly shook his head back and forth. "I'm not sure. I believe if the Butcher and Baker wanted to save Nikolas Klaus, they would have done it weeks ago."

Tee's face twitched. "Is it true that when you were paired with Elly a few days ago, you basically sat out and she had to do everything? She mentioned it quickly before we left, but I couldn't quite believe you'd do that, until now."

Alex nervously brushed his sleeves. "We were asked to break the law, to steal maps from a cartographer. And those maps didn't seem to have anything to do with freeing your grandfather. We didn't even leave any money to pay for them. That's wrong." He gestured about. "Don't you see how they're warping our sense of what's right and wrong? I mean, you still have not said anything about regretting killing those men at Kar'm." His eyes welled up. "How can you live with yourself?"

Tee stood up and shoved Alex with one hand. "You've got some nerve."

"It's the truth, Tee. I haven't said anything because I hoped to hear it come from you, but I no longer believe it will. I thought you were an honest and honorable person. But you killed those men when you threw them off that airship."

She glared at him and went nose to nose with him. "They were killing good people. They were going to kill us. I did my best to make them stop, and if some of them died in the process, that's what happens."

Sorrow was written all over Alex's face. "How can you be okay with that?"

"I don't know what life was like growing up with your uncle as king, Alex, and I'm sorry you had to flee your homeland, but where I grew up, if a wolf attacks you, you do what you must to survive. If there's no cruelty or malice in your heart, then you didn't do anything wrong."

He bit his lip and looked down.

Tee took out a thin leather strip and tied her hair back. She stared at him all the while. "So, you think I'm a killer? Or is this a twisted-up sense of being homesick?" She slid her backpack on again.

He stared quietly at her.

She took a big breath. "I'm going to pretend this conversation didn't happen. I'm going to pretend that you're just freaked out because there are men with guns hunting for us."

Tee pulled back the white sleeve of her blouse. Studying the gauges on her grapnel-armband, she turned a dial until she was happy with the readings. "Give me a second to finish recalibrating this."

Alex shrugged. "Anyway, shouldn't we be scurrying along to the rendezvous point? We're supposed to meet Monsieur Baker and Richy a mile or two from here, aren't we?" He pulled out a compass. "It's that way."

Tee picked up the leather sack and slung it over her shoulder. "You don't want to wear the yellow cloak, fine. But don't judge what I do from your moral tower. You're down here with me, and if you've got any better ideas, then share them." She wrinkled her nose.

"I thought you were going to pretend many things?"

The edge of Tee's mouth curled into a snarl. "Now I will. Let's get moving."

After walking in silence for several minutes, Alex broke the silence. "As the King of Endera, my uncle avoided wars with his neighbors despite the often prodding from war-mongers and the nefarious secret societies. He said they whispered poison and could spin one's moral compass."

Tee cleared her throat, her fists tightening around the sack and the strap of her backpack. "Drop it Alex. You have no idea what you're talking about."

"Then what's in the sack? Where did they send Amami? Why did Madame DeBoeuf send Mounira off to stay with Christina Creangle and the Moufan-Men?"

Tee glared at him.

"It was like when she sent Bakon and Egelina-Marie out

west. She did it then told us. She claims it was because she didn't want a little child getting hurt, but Mounira was the only one hitting the Butcher with questions."

They jumped as a shot rang out.

"That was close by," whispered Tee, pulling her hood up and crouching down.

Alex leaned against a tree and pointed. "Did it come from that direction?"

"I don't know." Tee squinted and surveyed the area.

The air crackled with another rifle shot.

"That was even closer." Sweat beaded on Alex's forehead.

"Where are they?" Tee's leg bounced with anticipation. "They're probably a hundred and fifty yards or so. Let's go this way." She stood up and took his arm.

"How can you estimate like that?" asked Alex.

"We did it in our lessons. Didn't you learn that in—what's it called?—school?"

"No."

She scoffed. "Well, maybe we're not the barbarian brutes you secretly think we are."

Two more shots rang out, one taking a chunk out of a nearby tree.

"Let's get out of here," said Tee, running and pulling him along.

Alex looked back over his shoulder. "I can see something moving."

"Eyes up ahead. Run and live, look and die. That's what Amami says."

"I don't think we're going to outrun them this time. We had the rain last time to help us lose them," said Alex, his voice laced with panic, his hands slick and shaking.

Tee changed their course sharply.

"Why this way?"

She craned her neck to stare upwards. "Do you see something shiny up there?"

"What are you looking for?" Alex glanced about.

"I think it's a canopy bridge. Elly, Richy, and I found some a while back when we dealt with the Ginger Lady. Grab on to me," said Tee, pulling back her sleeve and fidgeting with her armband.

"What are you doing?"

"We're going to test out the latest edition of this contraption of mine and hopefully not die. How strong is that belt of yours?" She pointed her armband upwards.

"I don't understand," said Alex, his arms outstretched, his eyes wide and wild.

Tee pulled him right up to her and glared. He grabbed on to her, and she fired the grapnel up into the air. "Hang on!"

They zoomed through the air until they came right up to the metal canopy bridge. It was covered in leaves and branches.

"Climb around the edge and onto the bridge."

"What are we doing?"

"Please, just do what I'm asking."

"Is this safe?"

"Now's not really a great time to be asking that," said Tee, looking below for their pursuers.

"This is what I'm talking about. How is this the type of thing that a young lady should be doing? This is lunacy. The Tub makes you think this is normal," said Alex, getting a firm hold of the metal slats and carefully making his way up and over the side of the canopy bridge. "How do you even know about this thing?"

Shaking her head at him, she freed the grapnel. "Good, it's still usable." She then turned two knobs on her armband, and the cable started reversing. Sliding her backpack off, she began feeding the cable carefully back into it.

"What are you doing?"

"Getting it ready in case we need it again. By the way, we have company." She pointed downwards at the confused Red Hoods who were walking about, weapons out, cursing.

Alex looked at the fifty yards of bridge that headed off to the east, and then the same distance to the west. "This is huge."

"Yeah, pretty big," she said, finishing up with the cable and closing her backpack.

"Which way are we supposed to go?"

"Shh. Nowhere, yet. We don't want to make noise and tell them where we are. Also... I don't know anything about this bridge. For all I know, it could fall apart as we run on it. I've done the dangling in front of bad guys thing before, not my favorite moment."

"What?" Alex put his head in his hands. "Can you just be serious?"

"I could, but since Elly's not here, someone needs to be snarky," said Tee, watching the Red Hoods below.

One raised his pistol and shot into the air randomly. He waited then fired another shot in a different direction.

Tee glanced at Alex, whose face was flush and whose head kept shaking back and forth. "We're going to be okay." She put a hand on his arm. "Really."

"This isn't what I was raised for. I'm supposed to be in a royal court. I'm supposed to be studying and inventing, maybe leading conventioneers someday. Not hiding in trees and running from agents of the One True Fare." He stared at her, tears of terror in his eyes. "What are we even doing here?"

"You flew in the air to save me, remember?"

"I wasn't thinking then; I am now."

"Then just stop thinking. Breathe, and just be. We're here and we're going to be okay." She pointed to one of the ends of the canopy bridge. "Over there is either a ladder down or another bridge and then a ladder down to the ground. In two minutes, we're going to be on our way."

Alex tapped his fingertips on his forehead.

"Okay?"

His eyes met hers. "I am okay. What do we need to do?"

The Red Hoods fired another shot, this one ricocheting off a nearby piece of the canopy bridge.

Tee and Alex froze, staring at each other. They could hear the confused Red Hoods below.

"I can't understand what they're saying," said Tee.

Alex put a finger to his lips, his eyes moving side to side intently.

Tee waited anxiously, scouring the landscape for more signs of trouble. After a minute, she pulled out the pocket watch her granddad, Sam Baker, had given her.

Alex put his hands over the pocket watch as he continued to listen intently.

Glancing down, Tee noticed one of the Red Hoods pointing a rifle in the air. She grabbed Alex, making sure her yellow cloak was underneath them.

"What?"

A shot rang out.

"Yigging pargo," cursed Tee, letting Alex go. She rubbed her back. "That stings."

They peeked down and watched as the Red Hoods threw up their hands and started walking off.

Tee patted Alex on the sleeve. "See, we're okay." She groaned. "Not great, but okay."

"Yeah," said Alex, standing and holding on to the tree-branch-covered railings of the canopy bridge.

"What did they say?" asked Tee, standing up and motioning for him to start moving.

"They said some things that didn't make sense. I think they were mixing in a language I didn't recognize—or maybe they were military words? One thing seemed important to them: having seen a Yellow Hood. There's a bounty from someone named Lou."

Tee grabbed Alex's arm.

He turned to see her face was pale. "What is it?"

"LeLoup. Did they say LeLoup?"

He shrugged. "Maybe. Why? It doesn't matter; they're gone."

"No. It matters. Did they say LeLoup?" she asked, her face inches away from his.

Alex frowned at her and peeled her fingers off his sleeve. "I don't know. I'm perplexed why this is so important to you."

"He's the guy who shot Elly. Who Richy, Elly, and I first tangled with."

Alex straightened his collar and shook his head. "It's most likely someone else. You are simply paranoid."

CHAPTER FOUR

MADNESS IS KEY

"How come we have to be the lunkers to deal with this guy?" asked the first guard, staring at the prisoner villa before him. In his arms was a silver domed tray of food. "I swear I caught him making sense once when no one was looking."

The political prisoner compound was in the heart of Relna, the capital of Belnia, and was connected to the southern end of the main keep of the royal castle. The perimeter of the rows upon rows of prisoner villas was marked by an eight-foot fence made of black metal rods.

"What?" said the other guard loudly, leaning in. The rain drummed on his pointed helmet. "You want to steal something from this guy? He doesn't have anything. Trust me. I've looked. Crazy old bat, this one."

The first guy shook his head. "You need socks."

"I what?"

"No." The first guard put his mouth near the other guy's ear. "You should stuff socks in the top of your helmet. It absorbs some of the noise."

"You like socks for toys?"

"Gah! Oh, for the love of… Just unlock the yigging door!"

The second guard stared at him, annoyed. "What'd I do?" He shifted his grip on the backpack slung over his shoulder.

"UNLOCK IT!"

The second guard looked at the door and pointed at the lack of lock on the outside of the door. With a smile, he went to open it but found the door wouldn't budge. "Ah, I think he locked it from the inside."

"I swear you're doing this on purpose." The first guard, balancing the tray of food, kicked the door.

"Never seen a porpoise."

Waiting, they stared curiously at the wooden nameplate that hung to the right of the door.

The first guard shook his head again. "How can this guy be so important and not have a proper name? What kind of nickname is Saint Nik?"

The second guard knocked insistently on the door. "The captain uses saint for the jerk ones."

The door creaked open.

In a blink, Nikolas' eyes went from sharp to dull. "Nibbles? Nibbles!" He rubbed his hands together and ushered them in. His white beard was big and bushy, and his bald head shone in all the crank lantern light from inside.

The first guard stepped in and stared at the sea of papers everywhere between him and the table, which itself was covered in a dozen piles of paper. Only the comfy chair that stood two yards away was empty of paper.

"How did he make it to the door?" asked the second guard with a laugh.

Nikolas took the silver tray, removed the dome, and put it on the head of the second guard. Then, like an expert dancer, he made his way to the table without touching a single sheet. Putting the tray down, he made his way right back before the guards could understand what they had just witnessed.

"Blurff?" asked Nikolas, his eye twitching.

"What's wrong with this guy?" asked the first guard.

The second guard took the dome off his head. "I heard he took a nasty smack to the noggin and lost his marbles. He's a weird one. I swear he did something to the door last week. I got the shock of my life; my fingers still hurt. I heard the door fell on someone once, came clean off the hinges."

"I heard he throws things if you get him too mad." The first guard glanced about the little room. It had three small cabinets, a wood stove, and stairs up to the bathroom and bedroom. "He has a place that's nicer than mine. That's not fair."

"Mine? Mine?" asked Nikolas tapping the backpack.

The second guard glanced over his shoulder. "Yeah. It's paper. Apparently, someone asked that he get as much paper as he wants."

"Yig, look at this place! It's almost wall to wall paper."

"Gazoo!" said Nikolas, taking the backpack and opening it up. "Ha! Ha!" He took a few sheets and threw them at the guards, then danced over to his chair, perching himself on it like a gargoyle clutching a treasure. "Garlic bees need to dance."

"Let's go," said the first guard.

Nikolas narrowed his eyes at the guard. "Nana bezel your underpants." He wagged a finger at the men.

"Don't make me break that off." The first guard turned to the second. "Let's just get out of here. He's freaking me out."

With a smile, Nikolas raised a finger getting the men's attention. "Prezzie!" He then pointed up the stairs. "The poops! Lots of the poops!"

The second guard bowed his head and rubbed his face with both hands. "Why today? Why my shift?"

"What?" asked the first.

"He's made a mess again. I heard he's done this a few times."

The first guard reached for the door. "Let's just go."

"But the poops?" Nikolas motioned for them to go to the stairs.

The first guard opened the front door. The sound of the pummeling rain filled the room. He gestured at his colleague. "Come on. The crazy guy's got his food, he's got paper, so let's go. Let the next guard shift deal with the mess."

The door slammed shut.

Nikolas waited, his fingers drumming on the backpack. His eyes shifted from the door to the clock hung above the door. After two minutes, he let out a satisfied sigh, put down the backpack and stood up. He stretched his back and walked over to the door, locking it. With a coy smile, he reached into his pocket and pulled out his new treasure: a set of keys he'd taken off the first guard.

"Well, good thing you gentlemen didn't call my bluff, yes? There were no poops for you today." He rubbed his face with one hand. "I need to get out of here or I won't be pretending to be crazy, I will be." He stopped, shaking his head. "And now I'm talking to myself."

Turning his attention to the keys, he studied them carefully. "Hmm, I think this one might be for the western gate out of this compound."

CHAPTER FIVE

RENDEZVOUS

Sam Baker sat on the back of the horse-drawn cart, his grey hood pulled over his eyes and his short legs dangling off the edge. He glanced over at Richy, who was pacing about madly. He pulled out his pocket watch and grimaced.

"They're late, aren't they?" said Richy.

"Rendezvous aren't an exact science. You know that, Richy." Sam scratched his brown and white beard.

They both watched as another two-horse carriage came past, waving at the driver who sat up top. Sam watched until it rounded the corner, leaving him nothing to look at but forest.

"You're grumbling again," said Richy. "You don't like that Eleanor has us in such a high traffic area."

Sam looked at Richy, a dark sense of amusement on his face. "You, Tee, and Elly, you truly were made for this. And no, I don't. This is one of the main roads to Relna. We've only been here for two hours, and how many royal caravans and merchants have passed? It baffles my mind that she'd have us here. It's almost like she wants someone to notice us." He squinted at the afternoon sky; there were only a few wispy clouds. "Makes no sense at all."

"At least that last carriage didn't stop and ask me if my little brother and I were okay."

Laughing, Sam got off the cart. "True. One of the benefits of being a dwarf is people often see what they want, and their assumptions play against them. Others just underestimate me. Being a spymaster, you use whatever advantage you have. Take Eleanor. She's never taken me seriously." He chuckled and shook his head. "And I am talking too much. Another sign of old age."

They smiled and waved as a caravan of carriages and carts, flying various flags, came by.

"I'm going to need to do some shopping again; there's too much going on. I feel... detached from it all."

Richy frowned at him and then snapped his fingers. "It just dawned on me. When you say shopping, you mean getting information, don't you?"

Sam replied with a blank look.

"Nice try. You certainly are sneaky, you spymasters."

Returning to his perch on the edge of the cart, Sam pulled out a paper from under his cloak and re-read it.

"I know I've asked you several times, but where's my sister? Did the Butcher send her away like Mounira?"

"No, she didn't," said Sam, putting the paper away. "And I would know, this time. She'd doing something of paramount importance."

"Have you heard anything from Bakon and Egelina-

Marie? The Butcher said she sent them westward, but we haven't heard anything, have we?"

Sam stared at Richy and shook his head. "There are a lot of things bothering me, and once Eleanor stops having us run around and I can do some proper shopping, I'll get some answers." He smiled and pointed. "Finally, they're here."

CHAPTER SIX

LIDDEL SHOP

A dark-grey-cloaked woman put her hand up and held the bell above the door as she walked into the store. Despite the sign in the window saying closed, a man was sitting at one of the two small tables, reading. The unmanned counter behind him was covered in objects wrapped in paper and set in wooden crates. The walls were lined with canned goods and jars of various preserves.

She walked over to the counter and leaned against it, watching the man out of the corner of her eye. He wore a beige shirt and brown vest that were a bit small for him and pants that ended early with socks pulled high to meet them.

"Is that the Wizard Killer?" she asked the man, her face hidden in the shadow of her hood.

He flinched, staring wide-eyed. "Sorry?"

"The book," she said pointing. "Is that the Wizard Killer? I can't see the cover from here. I know she keeps a bookshelf in the back for slow days."

"Oh." The man turned it over and looked, running a hand through his shoulder-length, curly hair. "No. I finished those yesterday. This story is about a man and nine clouds. It's good." He held the book in both hands. "In my village, we would only have books when traders came through, and then everyone would read them, and by the end, the books were so worn that they were unreadable. This place... it is a magical land."

"Ah ha, well, you might be surprised what the world has to offer. Are you from Teuton? Northern mountains, I would hazard to guess?"

"How did you know?"

"Your accent, your word choice. I've spent a good deal of time in the Republic of Ahemia."

"Yes, we are right on the border."

"Beautiful countryside."

His eyes welled up, throwing her off.

"Sorry."

"I will return to my book now if you do not mind."

"Please."

"I thought I heard someone talking," said an old, bald woman as she came from the back. She had on a brown apron and skirt and a stained, dark blouse. Staring at the bell, she raised an eyebrow at the woman. "I should have known I hadn't missed it; you didn't let it ring, did you, Alisson?"

A smirk appeared on the woman's face. "It's Alice these days," she replied, pulling back her grey hood. "I got your message. Good thing it found me when it did; I was nearby, heading westward to repay a debt."

The woman came around the counter. "Let me look at you. Sam always said if there was anything out of the ordinary, to let you or him know. And the word is the Tub's gone and him with it. I'm not sure if that's the Fare spreading rumors or not, so I figured I'd get your attention."

Alice frowned and whispered. "Shouldn't we talk somewhere else?"

"Oh, don't pay him no mind," she said waving at the man. "Chikahn is dead to the world when he's got a book."

"I'm assuming that this has everything to do with him."

"It does," said the storekeeper, folding her arms. "He showed up in town about two weeks ago hoping to find some work. One of my regulars was in here and noticed his accent, then started talking to him. Before I knew it, Chikahn was going on about seeing his village destroyed by air balloons which were, in turn, destroyed by clouds. He then started ranting about how the sky will rain down on evil doers and that..." She rubbed his face. "No one would come in the store until I found I could feed him books."

"Now was it air balloons he saw or something else?" asked Alice.

"I heard someone say that they'd seen something like that in Staaten and northern Brunne. Something called a Skyfather?"

"Skyfaller?"

"That might be it. Have you heard of it? They said

things like that destroyed the royal palace at Myke a while ago."

Alice nodded. "I hear all sorts of things." She smiled warmly. "And so you took in this lost soul?"

"I couldn't leave him wandering around, talking about things that could get him killed, now could I? Wouldn't be right."

"You are an utterly fantastic person, you know that, right?" said Alice.

The bald woman shifted her stance. "Well, I might need reminding every now and then. Anyway, I'm not sure what to do with him. I hoped you'd have an idea. Every time he's out on the street, it doesn't take long before he starts going on about the miracle of justice. If there's any truth to what he yammers about, someone from the Fare's going to find him and put a knife in him. I'm sure of it."

Alice reached into a pocket on the back of her belt and pulled out a purse. It thunked as it landed on the counter. "I'll take him and some supplies."

The shopkeeper picked it up, weighing it in one hand. "This feels a bit much," she said with a frown.

Alice smiled. "Anyone who remembers him, do something nice or distracting so that they forget. Tell them a different story about him enough times until they think that's what happened. I'm sorry to impose, but it's for his own good."

"Hmm."

"Did I mention how you are utterly fantastic and have a huge heart?" asked Alice.

The shopkeeper tucked the purse away under the counter. "He's all yours."

Alice sat down in front of Chikahn, who kept reading. She pulled down his book, finally getting his attention. "My name is Alisson Vundalun, but you can call me Alice. I heard you saw something miraculous."

"I did!" He put the book down. His eyes lit up and his fingers started to twitch with anticipation.

Alice raised a hand. "I know it's exciting, but you need to wait. I need you to come with me as I have a friend near Relna who needs to hear what you have to say."

Chikahn nodded. "I will go to the ends of Eorth to tell everyone, everywhere, of what I have seen." He leaned forward. "We must all worship and praise the sky."

"Yes, well," said Alice flashing a momentary smile, "we all have things we should do in life. Now, if you'll come with me, we must get a move on."

CHAPTER SEVEN

GAMES NEED PAWNS

Standing in the shadows of an alley's tall, brick buildings, Elly peeked out from under her black hood at the bustling, wet cobblestone street ahead. The smell of fresh rain and autumn molds danced in the air, and leaves choked the gutters.

Elly folded her arms for warmth and rolled her shoulders, forever uneasy with the weight and feel of the black cloak. She'd asked her grandmother what the shiny embroidery meant, but had been rebuffed. Few, if any, questions ever received any semblance of answer.

"Hurry up, Eleanor," she muttered to herself, glancing at the tavern door that opened into the alley. "Get your meeting over with and let's go. You promised I'd finally get to spend time with Tee. It's been weeks since I got to spend any time with her." She looked at the sky. "And I have had enough of you hammering on me."

A flash of color caught Elly's eye. She looked and sighed at the sight of yet another young woman in an elegant, frilly skirt and smart jacket, sporting a brightly colored umbrella, going past. "The civilized world is so pretty."

Her hand ran along her rough, dark blouse and landed on her belt. She reached into one of the pouches and felt the throwing weights. "More? That's just not fair," said Elly as a gaggle of girls in striking dresses went past. "I find it hard to believe that they're as uncomfortable as Tee says. Maybe her mom or her Aunt Gwen just didn't want her to like dresses."

Glancing about, Elly stiffened as she caught sight of three guards talking to a Red Hood two blocks away. A guard pointed in her direction; she broke out into a sweat and quickly backed further into the alley.

She pressed herself against the northern wall and waited, her heart racing. "Go somewhere else. Go somewhere else…"

The Red Hood appeared on the sidewalk, across the street from Elly's alley.

Elly pulled her cloak closed and lowered her head, hoping to vanish in the shadows as her grandmother kept telling her to do.

The Red Hood crossed the street and stood at the mouth of the alley, waiting.

Elly reached into the cloak and froze. Her grandmother had taken away her shock-sticks. She'd called them crutches. Elly fumbled for the throwing weights. One dropped to the ground, immediately drawing the attention of the Red Hood.

Taking a step into the alley, the Red Hood looked about.

"You shouldn't even be here, according to Eleanor. All the Red Hoods are supposed to be in Relna, on the leash of their real master, the Lady in Red," Elly muttered to herself. "You're two hours away from there."

The Red Hood didn't move.

"What are you waiting for?" Elly wiped her sweaty hands on her blouse.

She swallowed hard as the Red Hood took another step into the alley. His hands disappearing under his cloak.

Elly looked at the tavern's back door, thinking of her grandmother's insistence that no one and nothing disturbed her meeting.

Someone whistled, and the Red Hood left the alley.

Letting out a sigh, Elly rested her head against the wall. "It's not the same without Tee."

All of a sudden, the Red Hood returned with another Red Hood.

Elly's blood ran cold as one of them pointed at her, and they started advancing. She noticed one of them had a bronze-colored gauntlet with a cable that disappeared under the red cloak, while the other had pulled an arms-length brown staff from beneath his cloak.

"Don't you think she's a little small for a Tubman?" He pulled his hood back, showing a scarred and pocked face.

"Doesn't matter, the pay's the same." The voice was that of a woman.

Elly stepped into the middle of the alley, a few throwing

weights in her hands. "I don't know what a Tubman is, but I'm not one. I'm a Yellow Hood. It's just... wardrobe problems."

"Did she say Yellow Guardian?" said the man. "She must like history."

"I have no quarrel with you guys, just leave." Elly lowered her stance, her hands shaking. "Now I'm seriously missing that daily training with you, Tee," she said under her breath.

"The bad news kid, is you are most definitely the one we're looking for," said the woman, her gauntlet crackling with electricity. "The good news is, we're being paid to leave you alive."

"But not by much," said the man, readying his staff.

"I wish I had my shock-sticks," said Elly, her eyes shifting between her two opponents as they moved about the ten-foot-wide alley.

Elly threw a weight at the woman's head. She dodged, and it hit the man on the side of his face.

"Ah!" yelled the man, dropping his staff.

Spinning around, Elly let another one loose at the door of the tavern, giving a deep thump.

The woman lunged at Elly, narrowly missing her with the gauntlet.

Dropping to the ground, Elly kicked at the woman's leg and missed. As she scrambled to her feet, the woman landed a punch on the side of Elly's head, knocking her to the ground.

"Who paid you?" said Elly, scurrying backwards and then to her feet, more throwing weights in her hands.

The woman laughed and glanced at the man. "You should clean that up."

He touched his face and looked at the blood on his fingers. "Meh, I've had worse. Let's get this over with quickly."

Elly's leg started shaking, and a weight fell from her hand. She stumbled backwards as memories of fighting off Franklin and then being shot by LeLoup started running around in her mind.

Suddenly Elly crashed to the ground as the man's staff swept her legs. Her head landed hard against the stone, and the world wobbled.

The woman hauled Elly to her feet. "We were expecting more of a fight." As she went to plant the gauntlet on Elly's chest, she wiggled loose and fell to the ground.

Elly threw a weight at the man's face again, this time landing it squarely on his nose.

"Ah!!" He stumbled backwards.

The woman turned and laughed.

Dashing past them, Elly grabbed the man's staff and readied herself.

"Really? Staff versus gauntlet?"

"One down, one to go," said Elly, her voice shaky and her hands trembling.

"Suit yourself," said the woman. She leapt forward and spun.

Elly put her arm up to block the edge of the red cloak. She screamed as it cut right into her arm. Before she knew it, there was a hard punch to the side of her head. Elly dropped to the ground.

"You avoided the gauntlet twice. I'll give you that," said the woman, standing over Elly. "Time to end this."

Staring up, Elly watched as the woman inexplicably fell backwards.

"Who are you?" yelled the man, snatching his staff off the ground and pulling his hood down.

Something bounced off his cloak. Hauling the woman over his shoulder, he quickly exited the alley.

Elly rolled over, her world still wobbling.

A friendly face appeared overhead. "Hey, hope you don't mind some help," said Tee, her slingshot in hand.

Elly started to laugh but then to Tee's surprise, began to cry.

"Hey, everything's okay," she said, holding her best friend.

After a few seconds, Elly patted Tee. "I'm okay... sorry, I just... never mind."

"Okay," said Tee, helping Elly to her feet.

Elly leaned against the alley wall, her head down.

"Sam's across the street, keeping an eye out for any more goons."

The tavern door opened, and Eleanor stepped out. "What are you doing here? Where are they?"

"Who?" asked Elly, squinting.

Eleanor glared at Tee then shook her head at Elly. "Are you hurt?"

"Just a bit dizzy, that's all," said Elly.

"We need to talk, Eleanor," said Sam, entering the alley.

"We most certainly do. What are you lot doing here, Sam? Were my orders not clear? You could have jeopardized everything."

Sam bit his lip and glanced at the girls. "I think there are many matters we need to discuss."

"What's there to discuss? We need to get all the information we can to safely rescue Nikolas Klaus. Is that not your priority?"

Sam twitched. "What part of that mission has you here with Elly?"

Eleanor laughed. "So now you're going to ask questions and show an interest? Or are you doing this for Tee's benefit? Please. Now, before you do more harm than good, leave."

Scratching the side of his face, Sam put his hand on Tee's shoulder. "Let's get back to camp and make sure that Richy and Alex aren't getting into any trouble."

Tee studied the complex set of emotions on Sam's face for a moment and then nodded. "Yeah, who knows what they'll do if they run out of paper for their scribbled notes.

Without Amami there, they might try jumping off a cliff with their prototypes."

She turned to Elly. "Are you okay?"

Elly nodded. "Thanks, Tee."

"Yeah. See you soon," said Tee as they left.

Elly turned to her grandmother and pulled her hood over her face. "So, this was your doing?"

"For weeks I've been telling you that you need to rise to the challenge, and what happens? Once again you are in Tee's shadow. Let's speak no more of this and go. We cannot stay in the streets. Word will spread, and all of this will have been for naught."

CHAPTER EIGHT

PLANS TO COME

Caterina tapped the empty Neumatic Tube cylinder against the edge of the wooden table, lost in thought. At the back of her mind, she wondered when the glass would break. The message lay crumpled on the floor, her gaze so intent that it seemed as if it should burst into flame.

She gently put the cylinder on the table and pushed it to the perfect centre of the table. She turned to the maps and correspondence that were neatly piled on two other tables in the study. Underneath the tables were woven baskets filled with reports from the field that she hadn't yet opened.

The Belnian royal family had provided her with the largest of their guest suites. Caterina recognized this both as a show of respect to their neighbor and as a sign of strength on their part. It said to her that they viewed her as no threat whatsoever.

Connected to the substantial study were a large bedroom and a generous parlor with a balcony. Caterina looked at the outline on the study wall, a secret entrance for discreet needs, which she'd used for sending and receiving much of her correspondence since moving in.

She stood up and walked into the parlor, catching a glimpse of herself in a large, gold-framed mirror. Taking a deep breath, she looked at herself.

Her scarred, heart-shaped face still had some blotches from the failed assassination attempt a few years ago. "It's like my body is rebuilding itself the closer I come to claiming my own destiny."

Taking an apple out of the luxurious bowl of fresh fruit on the round table in the parlor, she turned and returned to the study, her eyes once again on the crumpled note.

"Did they honestly believe that I wouldn't notice that they haven't accounted for two Skyfallers? Do they think me so distracted?" She bit into the apple.

There was a knock at the secret door.

"Come in," said Caterina.

Zelda entered the room. She had her long, platinum-blond hair tied in a ponytail. She wore her white leather armor with metal plates in strategic places and a belt with a curved short sword and custom, repeating pistol.

"Any news from our red-hooded friends out and about Relna?"

"Nothing worth noting, yet, Your Majesty. I have vetted the new cleaning staff for you. This crew should be more… careful."

Caterina took another bite of the apple. "We cannot afford any spies in our midst, Zelda. No mistake. Marcus has tilted the board, but we won't have a single piece of ours fall."

"I have news from Alfrida."

"Oh? How is your twin sister?"

"She's doing well and has everything back at our capital well under control."

Caterina sat down, her eyes locked on Zelda. "Even High Conventioneer Watt? Franklin's temper seems to be as explosive as his defective train boilers." She pointed at the correspondence table. "Is it correct that the third of three steam engine trains is now marooned somewhere because of this boiler problem?"

"Yes, Your Majesty. Alfrida has informed me that she is applying all proper pressure to High Conventioneer Watt."

"Hmm. Sixteen-year-old genius or fraud? And what of Simon St. Malo?"

"He continues to stay locked up in the guest quarters on the palace grounds. Alfrida has hinted that there might be an opportunity for him, but nothing more."

Caterina tapped the table, staring out an open window. "That will only keep him in check so long. He's a liability that we need to address, one way or another. Remind me in a week to reconsider the matter."

Zelda nodded and pulled out a small booklet to make a note. "Will there be anything else?"

"Has there been any sign of that coward, Ron-Paul Silskin?" Caterina threw the remainder of the apple out the window.

"Not yet. As you know, there have been multiple sightings throughout Relna, but nothing conclusive yet. There is word that he has refused contact from any of the rebel factions of the Fare that serve the Piemans."

"Good. As long as he keeps out of our hair, then we'll focus on other matters." Caterina walked over to her wall of maps, her hands on her hips. "I find it funny how wearing a red hood has become a fashion statement. There are so many in the streets; it's hiding all of our agents."

Zelda was about to say something but instead looked out the window.

"But none of that matters, as the critical issue is the Trial of Royals and dealing with Marcus Pieman," said Caterina, massaging the bridge of her nose.

Zelda jolted. "Sorry, Your Majesty, I forgot to give you this." She handed over a folded note with the Belnian royal seal. "The King gave me this on my way over."

Caterina took it and broke the seal. "Anything else?"

In a rare look of discomfort, Zelda lowered her gaze. "He told me… to await your response."

"Response?" she replied with a raised eyebrow. Caterina read the letter. "What? Marcus Pieman's managed to convince them to have a full-length trial?" Her hands shook in frustration.

"Will you want to make an opening statement at the trial?" asked Zelda, gazing at the floor.

"This is a ruse!" yelled Caterina, throwing the letter out

the window. "Why do they listen to his verbal poison?"

"I don't follow, Your Majesty," said Zelda.

"He's pushing for a full-length trial, which will get agreed to on principal because he has enough supporters to endlessly delay any other decision. Then he'll undoubtedly get it deemed too expensive and time-consuming somehow." She clamped her hands on the back of a tall chair and shook it vigorously.

"And ultimately there won't be a trial."

Caterina glared at her, nodding. "When do they believe they're going to start?" she said, taking a calming breath.

"Within two or three days, I've heard. Do you want to push for—?"

"We aren't going to do anything other than smile, comply, and wait for our moment. You can tell the King that we will provide an opening statement; they'll all be expecting that, so let's not disappoint." She pushed her hair over her ears.

"But won't that leave them in command of the entire game?" asked Zelda.

Caterina smiled. "When everyone is focused on the King, you take out the rook and the rest, and then we topple the thing. If the trial doesn't ruin Marcus, then he'll be left with nothing, and Relna will be little more than rubble and memory."

CHAPTER NINE

TEA'D UP

"We'll go in here," said Eleanor, glancing about the busy street and then entering the shop.

Pulling back her hood, Elly looked up at the painted wooden sign that hung above the door. "Kai's Tea House? How many of these places do we need to go to?" She swallowed the rest of her words, knowing better than to question why they still hadn't returned to camp.

A trio of bells went off as Elly and Eleanor entered the humble establishment. A bouquet of fragrances brought a smile to Elly's face, as did the sight of a little, black creature with white paws sitting on a chair.

"What's that?" Elly pointed, her face alight.

"What's what?" asked the woman behind the counter, folding small towels. "The cat?"

"That's hardly a kitten. Cats aren't that small," said Elly.

"I don't know where you're from, but around here, he's a typical size for a cat."

"Wow, they're so small." Elly went up close to it. "Can I pet him?"

"Sure, he's pretty friendly." The woman turned to Eleanor. "Allow me." She took Eleanor's cane and waved them at one of the four small, round tables. "I'll be back in a moment."

"Hello," said Elly, her hand outstretched for the cat. They stared at each other until the cat decided it was time to give Elly's hand a sniff. Then, satisfied, he proceeded to give it a lick and seemed to wait for her thankfulness by positioning his head under her fingers. Elly obliged and gave him a scratch.

"I didn't know you like cats," said Eleanor, sitting down, the chair screeching sharply on the wooden floor.

"Oh, all animals. I used to have a dog, years ago," said Elly. "She died. She was sweet, about the size of a cat. Well, our cats, not this little guy." She noticed the astonished look on her grandmother's face. "Didn't expect that?"

Eleanor frowned in thought. "Your mother never liked animals."

"Pardon? My mom is the biggest animal lover I know."

"Huh," said Eleanor, turning to face the counter. "A small pot and some biscuits, please, Kai."

"Already on the way."

Standing up, Elly stared at the shelves of teapots and tea boxes. Careful not to be seen, she ran a finger along a mid-height shelf and then rubbed the dust off her fingers. She slowly turned, absorbing all the details she could about the strange, little store.

"Here you go," said Kai, putting down a full tea-tray.

Elly turned and noted that the Candlestick Maker's cane was now leaning against the wall behind her grandmother.

"Do you like sugar with your tea, Elly?" Her grandmother's hand rested on the spoon.

"I think Tee's sweet enough," she replied with a smirk. "But yes, please." She joined Eleanor at the table.

"This brings me to a point I wanted to discuss, and thus this little distraction." Eleanor folded her hands in front of her.

"Is this where you attempt to justify how you treat Monsieur Baker? Or why you've been keeping Tee and me separated?"

Eleanor touched her lips. "Anything else on your mind?"

"And this isn't an accidental little chat, is it? You planned on coming here." Elly pointed at the cane. "Its head isn't sitting quite right. I'm guessing that it's probably been screwed and unscrewed a hundred times, and the grooves are worn. I've seen that before."

The smile that spread across Eleanor's face gave Elly pause. She didn't recognize the look or the woman behind it.

"You know, your mother had so much potential. She was ready to take on the world, so much like you: observant, vibrant, smart. Like her, you've already seen that you can make a difference in the world."

Eleanor poured the tea. "She was naturally skilled at a few things, but brawling and fisticuffs weren't among them. She came a long way, but then... well, she just fell apart. She believed more in others than in herself, I think."

She picked up her teacup and stared at Elly. "I want better for you. There's a legacy for you, waiting, if you will only rise to the challenge."

Elly gently wrapped her fingers around the delicate teacup, her fingers appreciative of the radiating warmth. She was about to say something and shook it off. "What's a Tubman?"

"Oh," Eleanor said with a casual wave. "That's one of the elite guards of the Tub, a faction that reported to Anna Kundle Maucher until her demise, then to me for the short period before the Tub was decimated by Sam."

Elly sipped her tea and took a bite of biscuit. She stared at her grandmother then at the table. She rolled her shoulders trying to shake off the awkward tension.

"Sam may be able to accept a world without the Tub, where the Piemans are allowed to bring anarchy and steel-booted justice wherever they please, but I can't. The Bakers have always been meek and broken, a wasted chair at the leadership table of the Tub and of civilization. Sam's no different, and no better, than those who came before him."

Elly cocked her head to the side, her eyes narrowed. "Pardon?"

Her grandmother leaned back. "I saw you notice the things out of place in this little tea shop. The dust, the lack of personal mementos. You have a keen eye and a keen mind. What you did in Kar'm, making a rocket that took down a Skyfaller, was genius, but it takes more than that to lead an organization like the Tub."

"But the Tub's gone."

Eleanor raised an eyebrow.

Frowning, Elly leaned forward. "I never said I wanted to do anything like this. Where's my choice in all of this?"

"Elly, please. We all need to rise to our potential, we women in particular. Furthermore, when we become elders we need to make sure that the younger generation takes on the challenge instead of shying away from it. Do you want to sit idly by as the continent plunges into darkness, or will you help and fight back?" Eleanor's cheeks were flush, her eyes beady. "Marcus Pieman and his family will stop at nothing. Their hold over a piece of the Fare is crumbling. And the Lady in Red? She will drag all of us off the cliffs of chaos if she has half a chance."

Elly removed another cookie from the plate and shook her head. "So putting all of that aside: Why do you keep Tee and me separate? We're a team. We've been one ever since before we could walk. Together, we can do anything. Isn't that what you need? All of us working together?" She took a bite of her cookie, her eyes trained on Eleanor's.

Her grandmother poured herself another cup of tea. "Over the past few weeks, away from her, you have started to flourish. For all of Tee's... good qualities, she keeps you submissive. You need to have your own stage on which to perform, and that is what I'm giving you. With my tutelage, you can be the one casting the shadow, not standing in someone else's."

There was a sharp crack. Elly pulled her hands away from the remains of the teacup she was holding.

"Sorry," she said over her shoulder to the woman at the counter, who hadn't noticed. Elly glared at her grandmother. "I'm not in anyone's shadow. I don't know what happened between you and my mother, but I don't care. Don't you think I see what you're trying to do? You want to drive a wedge between Tee and me, and you're trying to appeal to some part of me that, I'm sorry to tell you, doesn't exist." She pushed her seat back and stood up. "I'm heading back to camp."

"Eleanor Junior, sit," commanded her grandmother.

"No! You are Eleanor. I am Elly. My mother calls me Elly, my father calls me Elly, and my best friend in the whole world, the person who was willing to throw her soul away to save me when I was bleeding in the middle of a forest, calls me Elly."

She went to the door and stopped. "That reminds me, you haven't given me a single word of what's happened to my parents. Every time you send me out, you promise that you will get some news, but then nothing. Do you know what my gut says? It says that you're holding back on me, on all of us. The next thing I know, you're going to tell me my parents are dead so that you can try and make me cling to you."

Eleanor lowered her eyes. "They are."

"What?"

"Your parents are dead," said Eleanor, taking a tea cloth off the tray and putting it over the broken tea cup.

Elly shook her head. "No way. You're messing with me."

Sitting up straight, Eleanor reached into one of the folds of her dress and pulled out a folded envelope. She dropped it on the table. "Here. Read it for yourself."

"I don't believe you," said Elly, taking a step towards the table.

"Then read it." Eleanor gestured at the envelope. "It makes no difference to the facts whether you want to believe them. Opinion and belief have no bearing on reality, but shaping those two things is precisely what the Tub is about." She leaned forward.

Elly ground her teeth and stared at the table. Her heart was pounding, and her eyes welled up.

"You're wrong," said Elly snatching the envelope and tearing it open. With a calming sigh, she dropped the paper back on the table.

"And what have you learned from this moment, Elly?" her grandmother asked, taking another sip of tea.

"That you're a cruel and twisted old woman."

"Please." Eleanor rolled her eyes. "Elly, some decorum. What have you learned?"

"That I could have walked away from this moment

thinking something that wasn't true."

"And in your heart, you would have taken it as truth, would you have not?"

Elly nodded.

"And yet, it said that your friends Egelina-Marie and Bakon are likely dead thanks to someone named Mister Jenny. But you feel better, don't you? Now let me ask you: Feeling better with that news, is it wrong?"

A tear dripped from Elly.

"No, it isn't. We live in a complex world, and it is our job to make the best outcome for history happen. You would have been devastated to learn of the death of your friends before believing your parents were dead. Instead you learned it second, showing that context and framing is everything. This is our role in society, and this is why we need to bring the Tub back. From the shadows, we shape opinions, shift beliefs, and serve the greater good."

"Alex believes that the Tub is as bad as the Fare."

"Well, some don't know that it's superstitious to rub a dub-dub for luck, yet they rub away on their wooden ducks hoping to keep spirits at bay."

Elly wiped her face.

"Sit," said Eleanor, her voice soft and soothing. "You've been through a lot, but these lessons are necessary. And, I have to say, I've learned something as well. I've learned that you have a steel to you that your mother didn't." She put a hand on the side of Elly's face. "I love your mother, but there's a reason she was sent away. You are different. You have a vibrancy and strength that can make a difference in the Grand Game, so learn to play it."

Elly looked at her grandmother, her face twisted in confusion.

"Now let us get going." Eleanor took out two large bills and left them on the table. "My apologies on the tea cup, Kai. This should more than cover it and some additional decorations." She turned to her granddaughter. "Shall we?"

Elly nodded.

"Good. There's much to do to stop this world from being plunged into the abyss by the Piemans."

"And we need to rescue Monsieur Klaus," added Elly, frowning.

"Yes, of course. That's important too."

CHAPTER TEN
FALLOUT

Abeland took off his thick cotton gloves and removed his brown leather long coat. "I agree with your assessment. This Hotaru can be returned to service. Good job," he said, slapping his grey-bearded chief engineer on the shoulder.

Stepping off the landed airship, Abeland eyed the team securing it to its wheeled brace. It looked very much like a strange ship in a mobile dry dock.

"Where to, chief?" asked someone.

"The barns."

"Now we have four ready," said Abeland.

The chief engineer looked at him and grumbled. "We'll get to that in a bit."

They opened the large mountainside door and walked down the long, lanterned corridor towards the cavern where the rest of the Hotarus were being worked on.

"I'm glad we were able to bring it back into service," said the chief engineer. "I understand your need for more captains, but I think you need to be a bit more selective. The idiot nearly destroyed one of the turbines. The last thing we need is another useless Hotaru."

"It boggles my mind how these people can understand getting the ship in the air, follow me through a simple set of maneuvers, but then as soon as I ask them to think for themselves, they point it at the nearest tree or simply the ground." Abeland bristled.

"It's painful to watch," said the chief engineer.

"I think it's worse to be in another Hotaru, seeing it happen. I almost want to blow them out of the sky just so that they don't dishonor all the hard work and money that went into making it." Abeland handed his coat and gloves over to an attendant and gazed out at row upon row of Hotarus below.

He held on to the metal railing of the stairs and motioned for the chief engineer to follow. "I thought it would be worth the risk to see if I could get us one more captain, just one. I think the locals are too used to horses. They're expert riders, but there are no oceans around here, so they are the masters at moving in two dimensions. But the third? That throws them. We'll need to consider finding candidates who swim."

"Fish that want to fly? Sounds like you might as well make dresses for unicorns."

"Gah. It certainly feels that way sometimes."

They left the stairs and walked along the metal walkway and then down to the cavern floor.

There was a dull roar of clanging, people yelling, and engines powering up and down.

Abeland took in a big breath. "Smells like progress, doesn't it? That oil, those fumes."

"Careful you don't collapse a lung."

He winked at the chief engineer. "I haven't felt this good in a long time. Modifying my breathing machine design to let us go up to the clouds was my sneaky excuse for needing to go high up every day."

"It wasn't very sneaky," said the chief engineer.

"No, I suppose not. But it was useful."

The chief engineer nodded. "Speaking of sneaky, I have something I should probably mention." He lowered his gaze and shuffled his feet. "Sir, I was in the nearby village yesterday when I recognized someone that I shouldn't have. Someone I knew back in Elizabetina. He was coming out of the general store and took off. I was unable to find him. I'm concerned."

"You're worried he's a spy?"

The chief engineer gestured indecisively. "I met him when I was a conventioneer. It was long before the Lady in Red came to power. I... never mind."

"No, what is it?" asked Abeland, folding his arms.

"I always suspected he was involved with something clandestine. I don't know if he was a spy for the crown or someone else, but... it made me nervous."

Abeland stroked his chin. "Did he see you?"

"No, I made sure of that. It's probably nothing. We've been so focused on Lord Pieman's capture, then his trial, and now getting the Hotarus in the air as quickly as we can, that maybe he's been here for six months and I didn't notice."

"Hmm," said Abeland gazing out at the Hotarus. "Maybe. You are right, though. We have been distracted of late. Hopefully, that doesn't come back to bite us. Thanks for bringing this to my attention."

Walking up to one of the Hotarus, Abeland ran his hand along the underbelly that was soon to be painted. "We need to get six more Hotarus ready by the end of the week and get them moved to our secret facility near the Teutonic palace. You've given me a bad feeling, and even if I have to travel back and forth by rail-raft myself, we'll get them moved." Abeland looked at his chief engineer. "Which brings me to my next point."

"The trains."

"Yes. Where are we with another steam train?"

"The second one is almost working, and a third is maybe three weeks away from completion."

Abeland scowled. "We need them faster than that. You know that."

"There's only so much time and more importantly, money. Since Lord Pieman was captured, we've been cut off from the Teuton treasury."

"And there's the real issue," said Abeland rubbing his face. "Everything's going to grind to a halt."

"I'm sorry to have to tell you, it's already started,"

replied the chief engineer.

The sound of light footfalls clanged on the metal walkway behind them.

Abeland turned to see a young girl, her hair in pigtails, emerge from the shadows. A Neumatic Tube cylinder was in her hands. "My Lord, a message!"

"Thank you," he said, bending down to look the girl in the eye and accepting the cylinder from her. He inspected it, making sure that the seal was unbroken. "You can't be more than nine years old."

She narrowed her eyes at him and leaned forward. "I'm ten."

"Well, I stand corrected," said Abeland standing up and giving his chief engineer a smile. "When did this arrive?"

"Just now. I was standing by the basket, on duty."

"Well, you take your job very seriously, then." Abeland cracked the seal on the cylinder and opened it. "Do your parents work here?"

"Yes, sir. My mom's one of the hull builders, and my father's one of the cooks."

"Ah, well, they both serve us very well then." He reached into his pocket.

"No, sir. Mom says you pay well, no need for tips. Most don't pay kids wages, but you do."

"Thank you," said Abeland as the girl ran off. He pulled out the letter and laughed. "Huh, well, that's who she thinks will make good captains? I wouldn't have guessed."

"Can they be trusted?" asked the chief engineer.

"You can't trust anyone quite like family, now can you?"

CHAPTER ELEVEN

WATT HAVE WE HERE

Amami watched from the shadows of the royal garden's bushes as two guards walked past her, less than ten feet away. She pulled out her pocket watch and shielded it from the icy, dark, summer rain. With a quick glance up at the moon, she flipped up its lid and noted the time.

"The patrol's right on time."

She studied the fifty-foot height of the royal library wall opposite her. The missions the Butcher and Baker had been sending her on over the past month had been getting increasingly dangerous, and their arguing only made her more and more concerned. Both thought she was on their side, but only one knew where she truly stood. Once again, she was walking a tightrope of loyalties.

Tugging her dark-grey hood down and pulling her cloak in, she took a steadying breath. Quickly, she filled her hands with two large, black sacks then lugged them over to the library wall.

She paused, her stomach tensing. Squinting into the

dark of the rainy night, she saw the shine of the camouflage tarp covering her King's-horse only a hundred yards away. Letting out a deep breath, she nodded to herself.

Scanning about first, she opened one of the large sacks and removed a long tube with a protruding spike. Raising it in the air, she then planted the spike firmly in the ground. Next, she pulled a lever bringing out three legs to hold it into position. Taking the rope from the other sack, she looped it around the bottom of the tube.

Carefully, she took out a copper coil and fitted it around the long tube and then attached a grapnel at the tube's top end.

She stepped back, her hand blocking the rain from her eyes, and muttered to herself about the angle and probable height. She held down the lever and gently adjusted the angle of the tube then adjusted it again.

"The Butcher was wrong about the height of the building. The magnetic push isn't going to be powerful enough to get the grapnel to the roof." Amami closed her eyes, her fingertips touching each other as her mind raced.

She opened her eyes and slid her backpack off from beneath her cloak. She rifled through its contents and stopped, pulling out her stopwatch. "Four minutes left."

Backing up several yards, she studied the wall. "Maybe I can climb it? No. What's causing that reflection? A window. I'll go in through the window, and hopefully no one hears the glass shatter."

She pulled the lever, bringing up the legs of the long

tube, and put it in a new position. With everything secured, she took out two potato-sized, black stones and crouched down. Glancing about to make sure the patrol wasn't early, she slapped them on either side of the bottom of the tube. The grapnel fired into the air, smashing through the top part of the window.

First checking that the grapnel would hold, Amami took out a knife from her belt and cut the rope off at the ground. She then hid everything back in the bushes and silently scrambled up the side of the royal library. Squatting on the three-foot by eighteen-inch window sill, she coiled the rope beside her.

Amami gazed at the royal library. Thirty-foot high, dark cherry bookcases lined the walls, with a half-dozen wheeled ladders about. "Skylights... I haven't seen those in a while." Amami marveled at the high-ceiling. "There are so many of them. What a most respectful feat of engineering wasted on so few."

The heart of the enormous library was a labyrinth of smaller bookcases. From Amami's perch, she could see two sitting areas, one with a fireplace. In the middle of everything was a sealed off room. "That must be the office I need."

A thought popped into her head, and she froze. Carefully, she studied the window frame for traps. Finding nothing, she slowly ran her fingers around the edge until she felt something. Swallowing hard, she wiggled it free and brought it into the light. "A rusted razor? Someone's been here before, and no one's fixed the trap?"

She stared down at the library. "St. Malo's said to be the highly paranoid type; he must have known something happened. So what happened to him?"

Bracing the grapnel, Amami scaled down the wall to the top of one of the bookcases. Walking along the tops, she found a ladder and made it to the floor, and then to the office.

The door was suspiciously ajar; an odd noise emanated from the room. Amami reached into her cloak with one hand as she gently pushed the door open with the other.

There was a young man, about sixteen, asleep at a huge, mahogany desk covered in paper and disassembled devices. His mop of blond hair looked greasy, which contrasted with his expensive silk shirt. The room was a sea of crumpled up papers. The walls were decorated with schematics and maps of all sorts.

"You are definitely not Simon St. Malo," whispered Amami as she carefully made her way into the room and studied the papers on the wall. "Sketch of one of their bloated, flying pigs." She glanced at the hand-scrawled note—*Skyfallers should have lower as well as mid-level wind-catchers to allow them to rotate properly, allow them to point their cannons upwards (somewhat)— idiots.*

Another picture caught her attention, and she removed the schematic from the wall. "A steam train boiler. This is interesting." She folded it up and hid it away.

She crept up behind the young man and delicately

examined the papers around him. "Given how you have signed everything, you must be Franklin Watt. And judging by all of these bitter notes, I will gather that you have problems with the train boiler."

Crouching down, she looked at the scratch marks the chair had made on the floor. "This is new. St. Malo's reputation says he would never allow such a thing to happen. So, the question is, what happened to St. Malo and is he on the castle grounds somewhere?"

Amami pulled out her pocket watch and glanced at the time. "Hmm. I believe some retribution is worth the risk for the man who betrayed Tee and Elly." She then gingerly removed a dozen sheets from Franklin's desk, even carefully lifting his arm to get a few.

Franklin stirred. Amami held her breath, a hand automatically going to the back of her belt. Her fingers wrapped around a slapjack. After repositioning his arms, Franklin drifted back to sleep. With a sigh of relief, she swept the room with her eyes and noticed a brass tube in the corner.

After making her way to it, she opened it up and with her eyes focused on Franklin, removed the papers from inside. A name and signature on one of the papers brought a smile to her face. "Tee will be pleased to get these back." She then returned the papers to the tube and put the ones she'd collected from the office into her cloak.

"I will not wish that a painful justice finds you, Franklin Watt. I will bring it to you."

CHAPTER TWELVE
TUNED FOR DISCORD

Tee put the makeshift screwdriver in a belt-pouch as she heard someone approaching. She looked past the crackling campfire and over at Sam, who was sifting through a pile of coded letters just outside his tent. A half-dozen crank lanterns surrounded him, as if they were warding off evil as they kept the early evening at bay.

Not far behind him were Alex and Richy with another set of lanterns at their makeshift worktable.

"I didn't expect that you'd take another two days before returning," said Sam, not bothering to look up. "It would have been nice to know."

"There were matters to attend to," replied Eleanor, walking out of the forest and into the camp's clearing, Elly right behind her.

Tee tightened the strap on her armband grapnel and slipped the backpack full of cable over her shoulders. With a nod to Elly, she started walking into the forest, her yellow hooded cloak left neatly folded by the fire.

Richy and Alex glanced over from their work table.

Elly waved, motioned for them to stay, and went into the forest.

"Eleanor, there are some disturbing reports we must discuss," said Sam, waving one of the letters in the air. "My biggest concern is it feels like there are reports that are being intercepted. Some of these seem like the second part of reports, and sometimes they're referring to things that I have no clue about."

"I don't see why there's any confusion, Sam. You got what you always wanted. There is no more Tub. Why is it any surprise if messages aren't being delivered, or if people have stopped making sense?"

Sam glared at her. "That is not right nor fair."

"And yet here we are," she said, sitting down by the fire and planting her cane in the ground. "I'm not in the mood to discuss this right now, Sam. Let's leave it for tomorrow."

He grumbled in reply.

"There's word that the younger Piemans are up to something. I'm expecting things are going to boil over in Relna sooner rather than later. I need to think about our next move."

Sam put the papers down and looked at her. "I'm a dwarf, not a child. Our next step is simple: When Amami's back, we finish our plans to get Nikolas Klaus out. Then we leave the rest of this madness behind."

"Ah. Because the affairs of the world don't concern us?

It's not that simple, Sam. We can't be spymasters for decades and then just walk away. Mind you, you've always been good at leaving at the key moments, haven't you?" she said, shaking her head.

Forcing herself up, she plucked her cane from the ground. "I'm tired." She left the fire and entered her tent.

Richy made his way over to Sam. "What was that about?"

Sam gave him a knowing smile. "It's not personal. When Eleanor's highly focused on something, when she's stressed, she gets a very sharp tongue. She always has. She doesn't mean anything by it."

"Really? I'd hate to hear her when she means it," said Richy.

"Don't worry about me. There's a lot of things going on and always have been. The only problem is that we're not in the position we're used to being in, and it makes all of this... more challenging." Sam glanced over at Alex who was still focused on their pet project. "Now, I suggest you return and double-check all the changes you've made since your sister left because otherwise, she's going to take that winged thing all apart again when you're asleep."

"She keeps doing that," said Richy.

"I know, and trust me, as a light sleeper, I don't appreciate it any more than you do," said Sam, giving him a pat on the arm. "She'll be here soon. I'm sure of it."

Richy's face filled with worry. "Amami shouldn't be this late."

"No, but she's going to be okay. She's one of the best at what she does."

Richy raised an eyebrow.

"Go invent something," said Sam, waving him off.

Eleanor stepped out of her tent. "Where's Elly?"

"She said she'd be back in a moment. Anyway, there are some Skyfaller movements that I want to talk to you about."

"Sam, please. Not now," said Eleanor, rolling her eyes.

"Well," said Sam, rubbing his chin, "I would have thought that a dozen Skyfallers heading directly for Relna would have been of concern."

"How many?"

"Over a dozen," he said turning to look at her. "Feeling better all of a sudden?"

"Just show me the reports you received."

CHAPTER THIRTEEN

WATT IS DONE, IS DONE

Simon's ears perked up, and he turned, unsure if he'd heard something at the door of his prison villa. He squinted at the shadows in the small prison home. The lantern light was never enough, particularly in the dead of night. Putting his pen down on the blotting cloth, he quietly stood, picking up his chair and placing it silently a few feet away.

He turned his head, and his eyes moved about the small, two-room living quarters. The door to the bedroom was open, and the lantern inside was throwing no unexpected shadows.

"Hmm."

He rushed the four steps to the front door and opened it.

A grey-hooded figure slipped out of the rain and passed him, entering the room.

Simon scanned about and then closed the door. "Where are the guards that are always posted outside?"

The figure stood there silently.

"I don't get a lot of visitors, being under house-arrest, but I never expected a northeastern Moufan-Man." He waited, his head slightly tilted. "Not surprised that I know you're from the north and not a pretender? I can see a hint of the obligatory red sash. And that embroidery. A skilled eye like mine doesn't need to understand the language to recognize the distinct characters."

"Was your position as High Conventioneer taken from you by Franklin Watt?"

"A woman? I didn't expect that. I don't know if I've encountered a female Moufan-Man before. Heard of them, yes, met one, no." He raised his chin and scowled at her. "Clearly, you're not here to kill me, or you'd have done so."

He shook his head. "Do you have a name?"

"The Fox."

"I find that hard to believe," said Simon.

"Why?"

"I've heard of the Fox, and you... you don't strike me as the Fox. She has a reputation, small, but known."

"Huh."

He smiled and pointed at her. "You are her. That pitch, that deliberate pitch you made. One of surprise and recognition. Knocked you off that mental perch you Moufan-Men stay on so that you can focus on whatever your mission is." He folded his arms and leaned back. "Is it true that you repaired a mechanical horse?"

"I'm not here to answer your questions."

"Ah, scrambling back onto the perch." Simon gazed about. "You've seen the insides of my cage. You're welcome to leave now."

"I can help you reclaim your position."

Simon lay his hands on the back of the chair and drummed his fingers on it. He narrowed his eyes at her. "Such an offer, from a Moufan-Man, would usually come with the expectation of something expensive. I heard saving Kar'm cost the Tub their lands and rights. Such a pity." He wagged a finger at her. "But making a deal with the Fox? That's a level of warning that parents in the countryside tell their children about."

"Would you like to embarrass Franklin Watt and have a chance at being High Conventioneer again?"

Simon laughed. "I'd like a great many things. However, I've been put on the shelf, in case the Regent's new favorite displeases her, and then I'll be taken back down. It's all a matter of time."

"And if that toy proves worthy? Then won't the Regent simply clear the shelf of clutter?"

Simon tried to force a grin, but immediately his expression soured.

"Right now, he is vulnerable."

"Why should I believe you?" asked Simon, his scowl returned. "And more importantly, what will it cost me?" He stared at the grey figure, studying its every movement.

"I want the number of Skyfallers and their locations."

Simon waved off the request. "Trivial. Next?"

"Detailed plans for the city of Relna."

"It's a busy place to choose as a holiday destination this time of year but, again, trivial. What are you really after?" asked Simon, leaning forward. "I'm assuming there isn't a fool beneath that hood. I also believe that you weren't expecting to come here and have this conversation. You found something and figured you'd take advantage of the opportunity."

He drummed his fingers on the back of the chair again. "You're smart and apparently capable. If you are indeed the Fox, then answer me this: What's the fundamental thing that everyone gets wrong about the MCM engines?"

"I want an unconditional favor when the time comes."

Simon laughed and snapped his fingers. "There it is. The real cost of everything."

"And I won't be answering your question."

"Then how do I know I will owe the real Fox anything?"

She pulled up her sleeve and pointed at an array of tattoos on her arm. At the centre was one of a fox.

"You're so young to have such a reputation," said Simon in suppressed astonishment. "What's your name?"

She hesitated, fixing her sleeve. "Amami."

"Amami... you can't be more than twenty-two years old, can you? And yet you have a reputation that puts you on par with few others." Simon grumbled, his fingers curling and uncurling. "I'm forty-five and have genuinely earned mine."

She straightened, the edge of her mouth curling up. "The answer to your question about the MCM engine is that everyone believes it's the magnesium that is the key, but it is not. It's the magnetic balance and initiating the spin correctly."

Simon's mouth hung open. "Ha ha ha, ah… beautiful. Truly the answer of someone who knows what she's talking about. And yet," he wagged his finger at her, "and yet you've given nothing away. Well done." He grinned, a rare respect woven into his expression. "You are indeed the Fox." He extended a hand.

She looked at it then at him.

"I assure you that if I had any trick or weapon, I would have had to be paranoid or masterful to have it tucked under my sleeve," said Simon.

"You are famously paranoid."

"I am," he replied, his grin turning devilish.

Amami shook his hand.

"And we have trust." Simon licked his lips. "So, what do you believe could warrant a favor from Simon St. Malo?"

Amami pulled out a bundle of papers from under her cloak. They were tied together with leather straps, and the outer layer was wet. She placed the package on the table, pushing the package's edge to make sure it aligned properly with the table.

Simon stepped in front of the table and dove into the package. "Let me see what you've brought me." He glanced up. "Sifted through these outside, did you? Did you take the brass tube that was in the office as well, or did you miss that?"

She stared at him unflinchingly.

Simon shrugged and went methodically through the papers. "All three steam trains had their boilers explode? With weeks between each one? Astounding." He burst into laughter. "This was his proposed set of solutions? Even this latest one is flailing nonsense. He might as well have said for them to wear a fish as a hat and see if that fixed the problem."

He stared at Amami, his eyes intense and thoughtful. "You've brought me quite a gift. I... accept your offer. Though, there's one thing I don't understand."

She tilted her head, her eyes and face giving nothing away.

"I thought the Moufan-Men were always aligned with the Tub. Granted the Tub is apparently in ruins because of my Regent, but I read history. That won't be for long, or it could simply be a ruse. So why would the Moufan-Men allow me to help Caterina, leader of the One True Fare, with her steam train and thus her plans? She'll be able to rain down destruction wherever she pleases if you do."

Amami took a breath and stared right into Simon's eyes.

"Deliver what I've asked for at the edge of the forest facing the south wall of the Royal Library no later than ten tomorrow morning."

She then opened the door and disappeared into the rainy night.

* * *

Franklin awoke to his head hitting the floor of the office. He scrambled, blurry eyed, over to the wall, his hands up in a feeble attempt to defend himself.

"Ah, ever ready for the world, Mister Watt. How nice to see."

"Simon? What are you doing here? Why are you dressed like that?"

Simon glanced down at his robes and smiled. "Ah, you mean like a proper High Conventioneer? You mean, dressed the way I used to be?"

Nodding, Franklin pushed himself up against the wall, papers crumpled behind him.

"I'm reclaiming my office and title if you must know, Mister Watt." A fiendish smile spread on Simon's face.

Franklin was about say something when he noticed Alfrida standing behind Simon.

"Ah, you've noticed. Well, the good news is that Alfrida has offered to escort you and your two... associates to the other side of the portcullis personally. Once there, you may roam among the other back-biting beasts and animals."

Simon then brought his face within an inch of Franklin's. "Of course, if I were to have my way, you'd be living out the rest of your years in complete torment. But,"—he straightened Franklin's collar and shirt—"a man can't always have what he wants."

"What are you talking about?" Franklin stared at Alfrida. "What's he talking about? I'm High Conventioneer!"

Simon turned to Alfrida.

She held a rolled piece of paper.

Franklin noticed the open Neumatic Tube cylinder sitting on the edge of the desk.

"Regent Caterina, also known as the Lady in Red and officially by the mistaken title of Regent Catherine, hereby declares the reinstatement of Simon St. Malo to the position of High Conventioneer for the kingdoms of Staaten and Elizabetina."

"Oh, I've had a promotion," said Simon with fake surprise and excitement on his face.

"How's that possible?" said Franklin, his hands outstretched and looking like claws.

"Well, I don't mean to burst your boiler. I'm sorry,"— Simon waved away a pretend laugh—"I meant bubble. It's all about having genius versus riding the coat-tails of others." He slapped a piece of paper on to Franklin chest.

"What's this?"

"Look at it. Take a moment. It might be a while before you see anything remotely like it," said Simon.

"The boilers... you proposed a fix? I was going to do

that this morning." He examined the paper. "This is identical to my solution!"

Simon came up beside Franklin and pointed at a part of the diagram. "It's nothing like yours. It's the correct one. Yours differed here, which would have created a cascading problem through here, here, and here." He tapped his chin. "Come to think of it, I believe you owe me a good deal of thanks."

"What for?" exclaimed Franklin.

"For helping you avoid enraging Her Majesty and losing your head. Have you heard what she's done lately with her generals who have failed her? It's been 'off with their heads.'"

Simon stepped away and opened the balcony doors, taking in a big breath of the refreshing outdoors. He stared at the forest's edge and nodded to himself. "Now, if you wouldn't mind leaving, I have some obligations to attend to."

"You're making a big mistake, Simon!" yelled Franklin as he fought pointlessly against Alfrida. "I'll come for you, one day! I'll come for—"

Alfrida banged Franklin's head into the door, rendering him momentarily quiet.

"Are you going to need anything, Simon?" she asked.

He twitched at her first-ever use of his given name. He could see in her eyes that life was going to be different and that he would be reminded of how thin a thread he clung to every day. Simon forced a smile.

"No, thank you, Alfrida. I'd like to be left to my own affairs for the remainder of the day. I need to bring some order to this mess of Mister Watt's, and then maybe I'll go for a walk. It's been so long, I'd like to see some nature. Maybe I'll even see a fox."

CHAPTER FOURTEEN

RECONNECTED

Elly crept through the forest, the modest early evening light barely an aid. Finally, at the edge of a small clearing, she saw Tee leaning against a dead pine tree.

"I don't think they'll find us," whispered Elly.

Tee put her finger on her lips and pointed upwards.

"Really?" whispered Elly.

Glaring at Elly, Tee waved her over.

Elly nodded and grabbed Tee firmly around the waist.

Tee fired her grapnel upwards and pulled them up onto the canopy bridge.

"I didn't realize there were any around here," said Elly, holding on to the railing.

"Alex and I ran into one a few days ago. After that, I started exploring and found this one. It's not connected to anything anymore, for whatever reasons. Anyway, I thought it'd be a good place for us to be able to chat finally, away from your grandmother."

"I know. Every other time she's just stepped out of the shadows," said Elly, sitting down. She covered her face with her hands. "You have no idea how hard it's been."

"Then tell me." Tee sat down and casually started recoiling the cable.

"Well," said Elly, putting her hands. "Let's see... when she wasn't telling me how I'm going to be the next great big thing, she tried to make me think my parents were dead."

"What?"

"I know, right?" Elly looked away from Tee; her eyes tried to find the end of the canopy bridge that was melting into the darkness. "And apparently there was some major thing between her and my mom."

"Your mom's awesome," said Tee.

"Yeah, she is..." Elly swallowed hard and looked up, her eyes shiny with fledgling tears. "You have no idea how much I miss my parents. If I didn't have you, I don't know what I'd do. I'd have no piece of home."

Tee reached over and squeezed Elly's hand. She squeezed back.

Elly laughed. "I have no idea how my mom could ever have been around that woman."

"Maybe your mom was hit in the head with a log, and poof, completely different person. Thus we have your super nice, though firm, mom."

"Hmm, I don't know if I like that. It means that she was evil." Elly tilted her head.

"Possessed by a friendly ghost?" offered Tee.

Elly shook her head.

"I'm all out of ideas. All out! Empty! Devoid! Ah…" Tee glanced around, her hands outstretched. "I don't even have words. No words!"

Elly laughed again.

They sat for a while, giggles escaping here and there.

"I can't believe she tried to make you think your parents were dead. Maybe she butchers feelings. But if that's the case, my grandpapa should be called the Baker. He makes all those cookies."

"I miss those cookies," said Elly.

"Why would your grandmother say that?"

Elly raised a finger. "Oh, you'll like this. It was so that I'd somehow feel good about reading that Bakon and Egelina-Marie might be dead."

"What?"

"Yeah."

Tee shook her head, a bemused expression on her face. "No. No, you missed that part. That seems—oh I don't know—a bit odd."

"Yes, a tad."

"Indeed."

Elly sat up. "And there was something weird about that letter she showed me, the one that said they were probably dead. The paper was weirdly untouched. I mean, I've caught a glimpse or two at all those letters that your granddad has, and I feel sorry for him. I mean, Monsieur Baker's papers look like they've been handled by a dozen people at least. But this one, Eleanor just pulled it out and it looked like new. It was like the only hands to touch the letter were the person who wrote it and hers."

"Huh. You aren't saying that you think your grandmother was trying to have Bakon and Egelina-Marie killed, are you? Because that would be crazy talk."

Elly stared at Tee, horrified. "You don't think—?"

"That would be crazy talk," repeated Tee, glaring at Elly.

"But what if that's what she did? Maybe she had Mounira killed too?"

"Okay, stop. Firstly, she's a former leader of the Tub," said Tee.

"She thinks we should make the Tub again."

"What?"

"Never mind, keep going," said Elly.

Tee raised an eyebrow.

"Keep going. You were on a roll." Elly waved at her.

"Secondly, no one can kill Mounira, unless they stuff a sock in her mouth first. At worst, it'd be a draw. The person would kill Mounira, and Mounira's questions would make the person's head explode. But your grandmother's still around, so I'm assuming that Mounira's safe." Tee looked up at the moon. "I can't imagine why she'd try to kill Bakon and Egelina-Marie."

Elly shrugged. "I don't know. She hates the Piemans though."

"They took my grandpapa, so... I kind of hate them. Actually, no. If they hurt him, I will absolutely hate them to my dying day and will not rest until I have their beating hearts in my hands." Tee looked at Elly, who was captivated by Tee's dramatic performance. "But right now I believe I'm simply, genuinely annoyed at them."

Elly laughed and sighed. "I needed this."

"Me too."

"I miss being up in the treehouse. I miss my old house and the new house and the sail-carts and... life was so simple."

"Then LeLoup showed up." Tee poked at the bridge.

"Hey, I heard that tone change," said Elly, staring at Tee. "Don't throw away all this happiness. I know it's my fault, but—"

"Alex thinks he heard some Red Hoods say his name," said Tee, stabbing a finger at the canopy bridge floor.

"What?"

"Well," said Tee, wincing, "he thought they said Lou. I thought it might have been LeLoup."

"Tee, he's not coming for you. He's a crazed nut job who is going to walk into the ocean and forget to swim."

"Yeah, I hope so."

In the distance, they heard someone yell. They both stood up.

"Was that Richy?" asked Tee.

Elly leaned over the edge of the bridge as the person

yelled again. "Did he just say Amami's back?"

"Let's go find out."

As Tee and Elly approached the campsite, they noticed everyone was huddled around the makeshift table. On the ground, off to the side, were all the pieces and tools Alex, Richy, and Amami had been working on so diligently. Six crank lanterns were sitting on the edge of the table.

At the centre of the huddle was Amami, with Eleanor and Sam beside her and Alex and Richy on the edges.

"Elly, I expect better of you than to go wandering off at a critical time," said Eleanor, her eyes glaring at Tee.

Tee was about to say something when Elly grabbed her arm.

"We were scouting," said Elly. "Tee'd mentioned she and Alex had run into some Red Hoods the other day, and I could have sworn I heard a rifle shot. We didn't find anything."

"Good job," said Sam, beating Eleanor to the punch.

She glared at him.

"So, you were saying—" Sam stopped, his face scrunched up.

"Are you okay?" asked Richy.

"Yeah." He put a finger in his ear and wiggled it. A moment later, he did it again. "I need to tend to something."

Elly looked at Tee.

"Did you hear that?" she whispered.

Tee nodded.

"Sam!" said Eleanor as he started to walk off.

"Ah. The dinner's bothering me, good thing you missed it," he said, waving. "Whoo, it's getting bad. Good thing you're all upwind."

Eleanor glared as he disappeared into the night. "Always with an excuse to miss the critical moments," she grumbled.

Alex and Richy looked away, shifting from side to side uncomfortably.

"Tee, I have something for you," said Amami pulling away from the table.

"Hi Amami," said Tee with a friendly smile. "We were worried about you."

"Why?" she asked, her eyebrows furrowed. "I said I would return."

Tee laughed uncomfortably. "Ah... well, you were gone longer than expected."

"Did Sam not say I would return?"

"He did."

Amami shrugged.

"Never mind," said Tee. "I'm glad you're back."

"Oh... okay, I appreciate that," replied Amami. She handed Tee the brass tube.

"Wait, what is that?" said Eleanor, pointing. "You should have given that to me."

"It has the signature of Nikolas Klaus, her grandfather. It is rightfully hers," said Amami matter-of-factly.

Eleanor glared at Amami. "You have an obligation."

"There is no disservice done here," said Amami.

Richy shivered. "Well, it's getting cold here. What is it, Tee?"

"I… don't know." She opened it and sat down beside the fire. "I can't believe it Amami… you found his plans for the horseless cart."

Eleanor straightened up. "The what?"

Tee caught the look in her eye and froze. "It's what he called our sail-carts before we came up with the name."

"Well, if we have a need for children's toys, I'll be sure to let you know, then," said Eleanor, shaking her head.

Elly looked at Tee, to which Tee just shook her head.

"Thanks, Amami," said Tee, putting the plans back. "This means a lot."

"I have a debt to you for taking care of my brother, a debt I can never repay. I am happy to have found this token."

"Where did you get these?" asked Tee.

"Franklin Watt had them, shortly before he lost his position as High Conventioneer."

"He was the High Conventioneer?" said Elly, her face twitching.

Eleanor gave Amami a sideways glance. "This is unexpected news. How come I haven't heard of it?"

"It happened as I left," said Amami, her gaze low.

"Who's the High Conventioneer now?" asked Eleanor.

"Simon St. Malo."

"What happened to Franklin?" asked Elly, her hands shaking.

"I heard," said Amami, glancing up at Eleanor who was no longer paying attention, "that he was thrown out, along with his two thugs. They are shamed, outcasts."

Elly smiled. "A bit of justice after all."

CHAPTER FIFTEEN

A Sticking Point

"You know, I can't believe I'm going to say it before him for once, but I'm dead tired."

Emery laughed, drying a dish and setting it down on the tavern's counter. His belly brushed the water basin as he turned. "It's a good deal better than the dead dead you're supposed to be, Egelina-Marie." He scratched his grey, grizzled face and smiled.

She put down her mop and gazed about the empty tavern that had been their secret home for weeks. Eg looked over at Bakon, who was wiping one of the last tables. Soon they'd be able to get some sleep before starting everything all over again.

"You know, I'd heard about this place from my father for years. Never thought I'd visit it like this."

"Who's your father?" asked Emery, tossing a wet towel aside and taking a new one from the stack at his side.

"Captain Archambault," said Bakon. "He heads the Minette Guards."

"Oh, I've met him. Mustache, big fellow."

Egelina-Marie smiled sadly. "He always said people treated this place as neutral ground."

"That they do, more or less," said Emery. "This place has been home to many, for whatever time they need. It didn't take me more than a few seconds to know when you showed up, bleeding and everything, that you needed help and that you were honest people."

Bakon looked up. "Kind of scary not to realize that someone was trying to kill you until they almost do."

Egelina-Marie pointed at him and nodded. "Good thing we found this place."

"The previous owner used to say everyone finds their way to the Pointy Stick Inn at some point. Over the past two years, it feels like this is where you can get hints of trouble brewing," said Emery.

He tossed another wet towel aside and grabbed the next in line. "That Mister Jenny's come through here a few times over the years. Nice enough, but those eyes... always haunted. This time was worse somehow. He gave me a chill just looking at him, like he'd been asked to hunt down his own kid."

Emery put a plate down and stared at the far corner. "He sat over there, the world on his shoulders and a beer in his hand. I kept him company for an hour, and he just talked. He told me about the Council of the Fare and them being all dead and how happy the Lady in Red had been. Then he leaned forward" —Emery raised two fingers and pointed them at his own eyes— "and asked me, staring into my soul, if you two were dead. Even though he'd done that when he first came in. After I told him, he was relieved and left. Weirdest thing." He wiped his forehead and bald head.

"What's the Council of the Fare?" asked Egelina-Marie.

He stared at Eg and then Bakon, his eyes full of regret. "Pretend you never heard any of that. It's probably all wrong, anyway. Just the babbling of an old man. Let's just be thankful Mister Jenny was eager to get back to Relna, whatever his reasons."

The door of the Pointy Stick Inn opened.

Emery glanced at the clock that hung on the wall above the kitchen. "Sorry, we aren't open yet. Only doing breakfasts on the first Sundays of the month."

"That's good to know, however, I'm not here to eat. I'm here for them." She pulled back her hood. "I'm Richelle Pieman."

"I know you," said Bakon, his face twisting in anger. "You're—"

"Trying to save the lives of a lot of people right now," interrupted Richelle.

"What?" Bakon stared at her, confused.

Egelina-Marie glanced at him and then at Richelle. "Wait," she said, narrowing her eyes. "Who are you?"

"This is Richelle Pieman," said Bakon, drawing in a sharp breath. "She's responsible for the death of Pierre DeMontagne. She's part of the Fare."

"Ah ha, well, not really. We thought we were, but

betrayal is a twisted tale," said Richelle. She pushed her cloak over her shoulders. "Your friend's death was because of my overly eager associate, the Hound. He brought some unqualified help who lost control."

She glanced about the room. "You'll remember that I had the opportunity to kill that girl with the yellow hood, but I didn't. The plan was to remove Anna Kundle Maucher off the board of the Grand Game, and so I did."

"And you kidnapped Nikolas Klaus," said Bakon, gripping a rag with both hands and preparing himself.

"While there are two of you, allow me to warn you that I am more than capable of killing you both. That said, I'm not here for that purpose. And yes, Nikolas was taken. He wasn't kidnapped or imprisoned. My grandfather, Marcus, knew that others would come for him. He's safe, for now."

Egelina-Marie stepped forward. "Is that a threat?"

"No, it's an opportunity and the reason I'm here."

Bakon and Egelina-Marie looked at each other.

Richelle shook her head. "You know my uncle, Abeland, correct?"

"He's your uncle too?" Egelina-Marie stared at Bakon.

"We're cousins?" asked Bakon.

Richelle cracked her neck from side to side. "This isn't the time to walk through the family history." She stared at Emery. "Do you have other things that need attending to?"

"I... I do. I'll bring some wine up from the cellar for this evening." Emery walked away.

Once he was out of sight, Richelle stepped forward. "You were sent westward to die." She pulled out a small note that had seen better days.

Eg opened and read it. Her eyes were filled with rage when she finished. "Whose stamp is that?"

"The Butcher of the Tub," said Richelle, her voice calm and detached. "She's the one who sent Mister Jenny after you."

"There's blood on it," said Bakon, glancing at it.

Richelle took the note back. "It came off Mister Jenny himself, so I know it's genuine."

"Did he say it was Eleanor DeBoeuf?"

She stared away. "He wasn't in any condition to answer any questions. But I can assure you, he's no longer a threat."

Bakon shook his head and paced. "Why would she do that? She said she wanted to know what was happening in Minette."

Richelle stared at him in disbelief. "Do you think the head of the Tub needs someone who is untrained to venture off to gather intelligence? Let me ask you, did she give you a means of sending back anything you discovered?"

Both Egelina-Marie and Bakon had a sheepish look.

Bakon rubbed the back of his neck. "I never really thought about it."

"I can't believe I didn't think about that," said Egelina-Marie, her hands over her eyes.

"You need to understand, Eleanor DeBoeuf has a very long standing feud with my grandfather, Marcus Pieman. It runs deep, and it runs cold. Somehow she knew you were related to us."

"What did he ever do to her?" asked Egelina-Marie.

Richelle's grimaced. "Her little sister fell in love with him and supported his ambitions. Eleanor took it as a betrayal of the Tub and of her personally. Now, with much of the continental leadership in Relna for the Trial by Royals, I fear my grandfather is facing not just the Lady in Red, but also Eleanor. And if he dies, then all the protections offered to Nikolas Klaus are gone."

Bakon's face went red. "I knew we shouldn't have abandoned Nikolas."

Egelina-Marie took his hand. "How do we help?"

Richelle raised her hand. "If you come, you come as part of my team. I will give you a crash course, and you'll need to be in charge of small teams."

"We're in," said Bakon.

Richelle smiled. "You aren't afraid of heights, are you?"

CHAPTER SIXTEEN

A Moment, Ms. Vunderlan

The moonlight silhouetted Sam as he arrived at the edge of a clearing.

"You can stop with the whistle, Alice," said Sam, wiggling a finger in his ear. "But if you wouldn't mind coming down from the tree, I'd appreciate it. I'm too old to climb unless a bear is chasing me, and even then it depends on the bear."

"I didn't hear your reply whistle," said Alice, making her way down, only the slightest creak of branches giving her away.

"I lost my... whistling thing at Kar'm." He breathed into his cold, clasped hands. "I haven't had an opportunity to get another one. Our friend, the Butcher, has been doing her best to keep things off balance and busy for weeks. Speaking of whom, we better make this quick. One of these days she's going to realize that I'm not some flake, and then everything will fall apart."

Alice landed and brushed herself off, her hooded cloak

nearly identical to his. "I thought you'd want to know about this at all costs."

Sam lifted his head. "You've most definitely got my attention."

"I have someone who witnessed what I believe was a Hotaru attacking and destroying a SkyFaller."

"Where was this?" asked Sam, a hand under his chin.

"In the northern Teuton Mountains."

Sam stroked his chin. "That would mean that the Piemans are nearly ready for whatever they're planning. My best guess is that they were planning on challenging Caterina directly, but with the trial, they'll need to be more careful. You can't just fly an airship into sovereign territory without starting a war—not without a good reason." He paced. "Do you have any idea how many Hotarus they might have?"

Alice shook her head.

"And what of this witness?"

"The witness is a shepherd. He's believable and articulate, though his manner of describing the incident is a touch on the colorful side."

Sam raised an eyebrow. "Meaning?"

"He's under the belief that a piece of the sky fell and destroyed the Skyfaller as a sign of justice for the destruction of his village."

Sam laughed. "Oh, I needed that. In all seriousness, he believes that the sky just…"

"He says that the sky fell."

"But just a piece of it?"

Alice put her hands up. "To him, he witnessed a religious miracle. I thought with the Trial by Royals you could make use of him. Maybe disrupt things, and allow you and the others to get Nikolas Klaus out of Relna, and stop whatever Caterina's planning."

"You and I both know what she's after: to be recognized as the queen instead of the regent and to break the influence of the Piemans. And if people die along the way, oh well. She's not the Lady in Red for nothing." Sam gazed up at the half moon. "You already know what I'm going to say. I'm surprised you didn't just inform me of what you were planning."

A mischievous smile appeared on Alice's face. "If I've learned anything as one of the Baker's Dozen, it's to think twice and act once when it comes to powder kegs of history. Best to risk the Butcher discovering the Dozen exist than send the continent to war."

"Silskin?"

She nodded.

"Smart woman. But we can't be seen to be anywhere near it. He wouldn't trust us, no matter what, and for good reason." He stopped his pacing and looked at Alice. "We need someone that will be both the rock and the hard place."

"I have someone in mind. It will also put them in our debt. We might need that."

He studied her face. "Don't tell me any more, best that I not know. If there are any problems, let me know. After you've taken care of this, stay nearby but unseen."

"I have the perfect place, and it'll allow me to clear a personal debt," said Alice, pulling her hood down and vanishing into the night.

CHAPTER SEVENTEEN

LIDDEL HANDOFF

The fruit merchant took a breath and called out to the crowd. "Nectarines and apples, the best of Belnia!" She waved for the young boy helping her to hand out the sample slices he had on a wooden plate. "I've never seen so many people."

"With the royals come the ambassadors and dignitaries, and then you have the wanters, the scoundrels, and the miscreants," said Ron-Paul Silskin. He was bald and sweaty, his once fine garb replaced with fraying, drab robes. "Good for your business, as everyone needs to eat."

The fruit merchant brushed her long hair out of her face and smiled. "The nectarines are particularly good this morning. We picked them fresh."

"I'm sure you did, though you never said when—which is a good move. There are no farms with nectarines for quite a few miles," he said. "No matter, they're still good."

"I can make you a good deal."

"Wonderful," said Silskin glancing over his shoulder. "How much for the boy?"

She laughed nervously. "He's not for sale."

He grinned menacingly. "All things have at a price. Fruit, a home, one's dignity. It all has a price. But, my apologies. Old habits die hard." The menace fell away, and he simply looked awkward and out of place.

The fruit merchant picked up a nectarine and handed it to him. "Try it. If you like it, pay for it."

"Ah, creating the sense of obligation. I like that," he wagged the nectarine at her. "But, you see, I know what you're doing, so I actually could just eat this and leave."

"I'll make sure he pays," said the voice of a woman from behind him. "But I'm sure Mister Silskin will pay. Only lords have people following them, paying for their misdeeds. Isn't that right, Ron-Paul?"

Silskin held on to the nectarine and glanced up at the fruit merchant. Her face told him nothing about who was behind him. With a measured sigh, he slowly turned.

"Lady Pieman, this is… rather unexpected." He took a bite out of the nectarine. "I appreciate the lack of knife in the back, though I almost feel you've come to mock my… humble station. Gone are the good old days, as some would say. Or are you here to kick me further down the hill? I did try to kill you, after all."

"You tried your best," she said with a twisted grin. Her red hood was down, and the cloak was draped over her shoulders. She was wearing her trademark dark-brown jacket and pants.

"I did."

"It wasn't good enough."

"Piemans are hard to kill," he said with a shrug.

"You look tired, Ron-Paul."

He let his political face relax and gave her an honest look. "I am. I truly am. This existence is intolerable." He stepped away from the vendor's cart.

Richelle cleared her throat, getting Silskin's attention. She nodded at the fruit merchant.

Glaring at first, and then offering a practiced smile, Silskin reached into his robes and found a copper coin and handed it to the woman. "Content?" he asked Richelle.

She reached over and handed the woman two silver coins. "We were never here," she whispered, and the fruit merchant nodded.

"So, to what do I owe the almost unnatural pleasure of your company?" asked Silskin as they started to stroll. He took another bite of the nectarine.

"Strange times make stranger bedfellows."

"They do," said Silskin, nodding. "And these are rather strange times."

Richelle glanced about, her eyes drawn to all the people sporting fashionable red hoods and cloaks. She shook her head, annoyed. "They are. I heard you left Caterina's inner circle. Anything to do with the rumor that the Council of the Fare's gone?"

Silskin shrugged. "Rumors are funny things, but the truth? It's expensive. But tell me, Richelle. Are we now old friends catching up?"

"Let's say that we are, and let's say that I am here because, as a caring friend, I have an opportunity for you to elevate yourself back into reasonably good standing."

"Huh." Silskin scrutinized Richelle's expression; it gave him nothing. "Well, let's say if that were the case, it would create a certain level of debt."

"One would expect that, yes," she replied.

Silskin stopped and gazed about at the old section of the market where they had ended up. "I would be open to listening to such opportunities and concerns. I should have gone far away, but here I am, a moth to the flame of all this royal pageantry and of the intrigue that will naturally sprout from it." He narrowed his eyes at her. "What would make you come seek me out?"

"I have a gift. The sort that rarely, if ever, comes by." She motioned at a door that sat poorly on its rusted hinges.

Silskin licked his lips and looked up. The building had boarded-up windows and was in desperate need of repair. It was one of several on the edges of the market.

Richelle opened the door. "As a friend of mine would say, down the rabbit hole we go."

"I suspect that you picked this dim and dank location because it reminds you of home?" asked Silskin as they made their way down a slippery set of stairs.

Richelle scoffed. "A man in your position should remember that I have no issues with throwing my plans to the wind and leaving you here to bleed to death." She flashed a devilish smile.

Silskin swallowed and squinted ahead at the dozen lanterns that lay about on the floor in the chamber ahead. "My apologies. My manners, like my attire, are lacking these days."

There were paste marks on the walls from where the wallpaper had peeled off, showing the aging wood behind them, and filthy windows. At the far end of the room was a long-haired and bearded man, reading.

"I'm astonished he can read in this light." Silskin came closer, his eyes darting about every detail of the man that he could get. He frowned disapprovingly. "I'd say he's more used to robes like mine rather than the silk ones you've given him."

Richelle didn't say a word.

Silskin noticed a wooden box on the floor near the man. "And that?"

"You can't very well do what you need to in that attire, so I've acquired some appropriate garments for you," said Richelle.

"Hmm. So, who is he?"

"He is the end of the Lady in Red."

A flurry of laughs escaped Silskin. "And I will fly like a Skyfaller. You can dress a pig as a royal, but that doesn't make it divine."

"This is Chikahn Liddel. From what I understand, the

Lady had a Skyfaller do a weapons test on his village... in Teuton."

"And was it successful?" asked Silskin. "Because if he's alive, I'm assuming it wasn't."

The man looked up. "It destroyed my village."

"Huh," said Silskin, his hands folded in front of him. "You can speak Frelish. Accented, but still clearly. Where are you from?"

Chikahn stood up. "From northern Teuton, at the foot of the border mountains with Myke and Belnia."

Silskin watched Richelle out the corner of his eye. "And so why are you here?"

"Because after that airship destroyed my village, I screamed at the sky and... and then a piece of the sky came and brought justice for me."

Shaking his head, Silskin leaned in. "Sorry, I didn't understand. What did you say?"

"The sky, it gave me justice; with the sound of thunder, it destroyed the airship. As it left, so did the hum of a hundred windmills. Now I am here to warn and share."

"Windmills?" Silskin stared at Richelle, his eyebrows up.

She raised her chin and looked at him sideways, a smirk hidden behind steely calm.

"The Hotarus? They're real?"

Richelle scratched her face, her eyes revealing waning patience. "The point of this is that you have proof that

Regent Caterina has committed a clear act of war, and that will undermine all of her credibility."

"Indeed." He licked his lips and rubbed his forehead. "Chikahn, is it? If I showed you a drawing of such an airship, would you recognize it?"

He nodded. "I cannot forget the two balloons and the ship's body. It will haunt my dreams forever."

Silskin's head bobbed up and down in excitement. "And you said you are from the Teuton Mountains? The border mountains?"

"Yes."

"Okay," said Silskin, pacing, rubbing his hands together. "Would you be willing to bear witness to this? To tell a room of royals what you saw?"

Chikahn straightened up. "This is why I am here. To speak of the miracle that came when the sky felled our enemy, and gave us justice."

Silskin waved his hands at Chikahn. "Ah, we'll need to avoid words like miracle." He looked at Richelle. "You're hoping to derail the entire trial, aren't you? You do realize that if that happens, Caterina won't stand for it."

"Make good use of this gift, Ron-Paul, and remember who gave it to you. Let me worry about the rest." Richelle walked away.

CHAPTER EIGHTEEN

DISTRACTED

Tee spun around, her fists clenched tight and sweat dripping off her face. Elly stood at the ready beside her. They were both in blouses and baggy brown pants, their cloaks and weapons in backpacks on the ground a dozen yards away.

"Are you okay?" asked Tee, relaxing. Her breath steamed in the crisp morning air. "Every time we start to spar, you seem to freeze."

Elly averted Tee's gaze. "It's... I'm just out of practice. I'm sure my grandmother's going to appear any second and whisk me away for one reason or another."

A shot crackled nearby.

Tee and Elly dropped to the ground, their eyes darting about the small clearing.

"Where did that come from?" whispered Tee.

"I don't know, but it was close," said Elly. "Want to make a break for our stuff?"

"Oh, the question: Do you or don't you? And if you do, what is the consequence?" said a familiar male voice.

Tee's face went white. "LeLoup?"

"No," said Elly, grabbing Tee's forearm, her own hands shaking at the idea of his return. "No, I don't think so. It doesn't sound right."

"Ah, it has been a while," came the voice, having moved.

Tee curled her hands into tight fists. "It's him. I'd know that voice anywhere. Where is he?" She cleared her throat. "You're a bad shot, what happened?"

"Ah, but you see, it went precisely where I wanted it to go. It brought me your attention."

"Whoever it is keeps moving," said Elly. "Tee, what's the plan?"

Elly waited.

"Tee? Teelandria Baker, what's the plan?" she asked, shaking Tee.

Tee frowned at her. "That's not my name."

"Good, you can hear me. How about you dash southeast, I'll go northeast, then once we're in the forest, we can double-back for our stuff. Nothing beats a bullet-proof cloak."

"Unless—"

Elly shoved Tee. "Go! No more thinking!"

Tee and Elly bolted.

"Oh, the game's begun!" said the voice. Immediately two shots fired, nipping at Tee's ankles. "Almost, almost. Oh, and here I was worried we weren't going to play."

"He's in a tree," said Tee, pointing.

Elly slid into the pile of backpacks and cloaks. The fear on Tee's face told her everything she needed to know. Elly pulled a shock-stick from her pack and twisted it back and forth. She held it up as Tee cut in front of her and snatched it.

"Where are you, you pargo?" muttered Tee as she rounded the edge of the clearing, glancing about.

A shot hit a tree in front of Tee, showering her in bark.

"Ah, now I've got your attention. I'd like my wolf back if you don't mind."

Tee froze, her body covered in sweat. "LeLoup?" she said with a gulp.

"Did you miss me?"

"I didn't," yelled Elly charging at a tree and throwing a shock-stick blindly into it.

A shadow dropped out of the tree and ran off. "We'll be playing again soon! I was only here for a rendezvous anyway."

Elly slowly went over and picked up the unspent shock-stick, her hands shaking. She deactivated the shock-stick and put her hands behind her back. "Why did he just leave? I didn't get him."

"Tee! Elly!" yelled Richy and Amami as they appeared through the forest.

"We're okay," said Tee, waving them over.

"I'll be okay... I just... I was hoping that Alex had heard

wrong." She took a big breath and nodded at Elly, who nodded in return. "You're never going to let me forget that I made you think my name was Teelandria for a day when we were five, are you?"

"Not a chance, Ms. Baker. Not a chance," said Elly with a warm smile.

Tee narrowed her eyes at Elly. "Are you okay?"

"I'm fine! That was just a bit of unexpected excitement."

"I'm glad to hear it," said Sam, appearing out of nowhere. He coughed and hit his chest, clearly out of breath.

"It was LeLoup," said Tee.

"Well, we... ah... we think it was." Elly stared at Tee, her head at a tilt.

"How could he have known where to find us?" asked Tee, scratching her head.

Elly raised a finger. "Where are Alex and Eleanor?"

As Sam studied where a shot had hit a tree, he said, "She left about half an hour ago for something. Alex... Alex left camp when the rest of us did." He scanned about. "That's odd."

Amami shook her head. "He is not lost. We must return to camp."

As they entered their camp's clearing, everyone fell silent.

"Where's half our stuff?" asked Richy.

Elly shook her head. "Alex is missing too."

Richy rushed forward to the tent he shared with Alex. "All of his stuff is gone."

"She took all of it," said Sam, pinching the bridge of his nose. "Her tent, half the food—never mind my secure, metal boxes of letters, notes, and maps."

"I never noticed those," said Richy.

"I always put a camouflage tarp on them and place them at the edge of the clearing when we camp. They were over there." Sam pointed.

"Why would she do this?" asked Tee. "And where's Alex?"

"He went with her," said Elly, pushing each word out painfully. "She must have been talking with him like she was talking with me."

Sam turned to her. "Excuse me?"

"She kept talking about doing things to bring back the Tub..." Elly stared at the ground, her face twisted and red. "I thought she was just trying to convince me that it was important, not that she was going to abandon us."

"She didn't just abandon us. She took everything that we needed to get Nikolas out of Relna." Sam ran his hands through his hair. "I can feel it in my bones that she's going to make the situation here worse. She took a huge gamble when she allowed herself to be captured by Marcus. I have no idea what transpired, but I know that she had a hand in literally bringing Marcus' world crashing down around him."

He scratched the back of his neck. "The question is, what do we do now?"

"We rescue my grandpapa, that's it," said Tee, sharply.

"The news from my latest shopping trip is that things are about to get a lot more complicated in the city."

"We're not abandoning him."

"No," said Sam, putting a hand on the side of Tee's face. "No, we aren't."

He pointed at Amami. "Can you start getting whatever supplies we'll need to the horse and cart? Assuming it's even there. I didn't tell her where it was, but you never know."

"Certainly," said Amami, rushing off.

"And what about us?" asked Tee.

He waved a finger upwards. "Would you mind? I should have asked Amami before sending her off."

"Mind what?" said Elly, frowning.

Tee gave Elly a look. "He keeps a stash of things, always has. Mom calls him the paranoid squirrel."

"I guess it pays to be paranoid," said Elly.

CHAPTER NINETEEN

CAT AND MOUSE

Morning sunlight streamed in through the two large, open windows of Marcus Pieman's guest room. It wasn't presidential in size or decor, but he didn't care. It was functional, with ample room for his double bed, a desk, and a small seating area. The third-floor view of the gardens and inner-keep market were particularly appreciated.

The most important element of the room, from Marcus' perspective, was that it was on the same floor as the Belnian royal family. After Mister Jenny's failed assassination attempt, it had been child's play for Marcus to convince the King and Prime Minister that he needed proper protection if the trial was to be legitimate. They agreed, and in doing so, Marcus ensured that Caterina took up residence in the keep as well.

There was a knock at the door.

Marcus' eagle eyes peered over the edge of his book at the reinforced wooden door. He was lying on his bed, a notebook and stack of novels on the side table beside him.

He put a strip of leather in the book, took another from the stack, and put the first on top.

"You may enter."

The door creaked open, and a page stepped into the room. He was older than the others Marcus had seen. His face had signs of morning scruff which seemed out of place. The royal banner draped over him seemed a size too small. He'd never seen a royal page, or messenger, looking so odd.

The page frowned at Marcus, who was fully dressed, his black boots on.

"Never seen a man lying on top of his bed and reading before? It's my standard practice after my morning exercises." Marcus lay the book closed on his chest.

The young man stared at him, then glanced around the room, before focusing back on Marcus.

"And?" said Marcus, sitting up slowly, the book firmly in hand.

The page took a quick step forward then retreated.

"Your hands please," said Marcus, his voice was deep and commanding. He stood up.

"What?"

"You mean pardon or more appropriately, pardon me, my Lord."

The young man lunged at Marcus, who stepped out of the way and whacked the page hard on the head with his book. The failed assailant dropped to the floor, his knife clattering to the ground. Marcus kicked it under the bed.

"What the yig is that book made of?" The page reached up and rubbed his head. "I'm going to have a welt from that."

He studied the man for a moment. "Inexperienced, uneducated, and unprepared... someone's trying to send a message or trying to tilt the board in the Grand Game."

The young man attempted to stand, and Marcus whacked him again with the book.

"Gah! That really stings."

Marcus turned the book over. "Hmm. I admit that it's a bit heavy on the character development... the plot doesn't find its footing until halfway."

He noted the fear and anger in the young man's eyes. "One of the things about being my age is that I don't have much in the way of patience. It ran out in my fifties... and that was twenty years ago." He tossed the book onto the bed.

The young man stood up, straightening his fake page uniform.

With surprising speed and strength, Marcus grabbed the young man by his shoulders and dragged him to the nearest window. "Do you like the smell of that fresh air?" Marcus pushed him halfway out.

"How can you do that? My grandfather can't even get out of bed!"

"A daily exercise regime does one wonders. I recognize your inexperience, but this is the part where you plead for your life and tell me everything."

"You're insane!" The page pushed back with everything

he had. He twisted and punched Marcus in the ribs. He screamed like a child and shook out his hand furiously.

"One wears light armor at all times in my line of work." Marcus shoved him out the window a bit further. "You see all those people in the garden and market down below? They won't say a word about you plunging to your death, because you're on the royal floor."

"You're insane."

"And you're repetitive."

"Okay! Okay!" screamed the young man. "I live in the slums. Some red-hooded guy offered me some money if I stabbed you a few times."

"They didn't ask you to kill me?" said Marcus, slipping forward. "Hurry up. You're getting slick with panic."

"There was a bonus if I killed you, okay? They got me inside the keep, all the way to your door. Pull me in?"

The door opened. "Lord Pieman!" A guardsman raced over to Marcus' side. "May I be of... service?"

Marcus glanced over his shoulder, his face red and sweaty. "Yes, if you don't mind. I'm losing feeling in my hands."

"You're what?" yelled the young man.

The guard pulled the page back into the room.

"My apologies for this, Lord Pieman. How did this happen?" asked the guardsman.

The page stared, terrified, at Marcus.

"He probably tried to steal something from the kitchen

and panicked. Every now and then I have unexpected visitors, a consequence of being so close to the stairs... and of poor security."

"Shall I get your room changed?"

"No need. Just remove him from the keep's grounds, and put in a word for more security if you can." Marcus reached into his vest and took out a small purse of coins. He thrust them into the chest of the page and glared at him menacingly. "I am feeling uncharacteristically generous. Start a new life, quickly."

The young man nodded and tried to run, but the guard grabbed him by the collar. "I will escort you out."

"Thank you, Guardsman."

"Certainly, Lord Pieman."

Closing the door, Marcus retrieved the knife. Sitting on his bed, he turned over the crude weapon, shaking his head. "And a pawn is played, but for what purpose?"

"I must say, Regent Catherine, that you seem to forget that you are a guest and not a member of the parliamentary council," said the King of Belnia. He had a thin black beard with patches of grey. His long black hair was in the traditional braid of Belnia and went down to the middle of his back. His hands were perched on the sides of his black-and-silver, collarless, long coat, and his expression was one of irritation. "This is the last time I'm going to permit such an interruption. What is it?"

His voice echoed around the marble floor and walls of

the chamber. The King was sitting on one of several ornate couches arranged around a large wooden platform where, ordinarily, musicians would play or actors would give private performances. Instead, there were only the Prime Minister and one of her ministers.

"Seeing as how you are the neighboring kingdom, and host, I would ask you once again to please address me properly as Regent Caterina," she said, her voice stern, her chin high.

"And once again," said the Prime Minister, with sharp emphasis while glaring at Caterina, "as you are serving as a regent, you will be addressed how your name is in the Book of Royals. Since you are marked there as Catherine, so we will call you. Now, if you were an elected official such as myself, we could simply choose to call you whatever you wish." She was a broad-shouldered woman, her hair in a blond braid.

The Prime Minister turned to her minister. "I'll call for you when we are done here."

The minister left.

Caterina cracked her neck, her face twitching with anger. "I will be free of this last remnant of my father's hold over my life," she muttered. "I have learned that this can be changed. It's simply a petition to be signed by five recognized royals: queens... kings." She stared at him.

"We're aware of such things," said the King, shaking his head.

"And yet, you've never said a thing," replied Caterina.

The King rubbed his face in frustration. "I recognize that you have not been Regent for long—"

The Prime Minister stepped forward. "To say nothing of the fact that you don't have support from the peoples and elites of Staaten and Elizabetina, but it's not our concern, issue, or even item of interest."

The King gave the Prime Minister a look.

"Best the Regent hears that despite the support she's given us over the years, there's a limit." The Prime Minister turned to Caterina. "You should be grateful that we never contested your regency and be content with that."

Caterina moved towards a seat.

"No, you won't be staying." The King raised his hand.

She bowed her head a moment, thinking. "May I at least advise Your Majesty that there's been a second attempt on Marcus Pieman's life?"

The King scowled. "What's this?" He glared at the Prime Minister.

"It's nothing," said the Prime Minister. "I learned of it on the way here. The report I received said it was a case of a buffoonish page who stumbled into Lord Pieman's chambers."

Caterina folded her hands. "I have reason to suspect that he organized it."

The Prime Minister scoffed. "For what purpose?"

"Attention? Maybe to curry further favor with those who are running the Trial by Royals? There are a hundred reasons," said Caterina, sitting down.

"He has curried no favor at all, nor will he," said the King. "There are no favors to be had. We've extended him less courtesy than we have you, Catherine."

She winced at the wrong name.

The Prime Minister smiled.

"But your continued impositions make me believe that extending anything to you was a mistake," said the King.

Caterina shrugged. "Perhaps it was just a distraction."

"Again, for what purpose? And why do you think that was sufficient to allow you to waltz in here?"

"Because, my dear Prime Minister," said Caterina, her voice laced with malice, "you may say I am many things, but remember, I have the Fare at my disposal."

The Prime Minister scoffed again. "Oh please. What precious little of it that remains. I've heard that it's fallen through your fingers like sand."

Caterina tried to smile and failed. "There are forces at play here. Given all the ambassadors, dignitaries, and royals, it's no surprise. So many old scores to settle with each other, never mind with Marcus Pieman."

"And just as many wanting to put a knife in your back as his," said the Prime Minister, a hint of delight in her otherwise stern expression.

"Ah, so you're seeking further protections for yourself. Is that it?" asked the King, running a finger along the edge of his thin beard.

Caterina walked over to an open window. "I want to make sure that you are aware and are taking the proper measures to protect everyone. I'd hate to have to take steps myself."

"And what can you do?" The Prime Minister folded her arms.

"It's hard to see the enemy when they're standing beside you," said Caterina. "But from the sky, you can see everything."

"We have our own air balloons." The Prime Minister waved in exasperation to the King. "I've had enough of this, Your Majesty. If you want us to put our balloons in the sky, let me know and I'll tell the cartographers we're commandeering their two. Otherwise, I would like to leave."

He nodded and waved.

After the door closed, he covered his face with his hands and groaned. "Catherine, you need to—"

"Caterina."

"Whatever!" yelled the King.

She sighed, her eyes slowly making their way around the room, ensuring it was just the two of them. "You have balloons, Your Majesty. They are little more than rafts that sway in the wind. I have the war galleons of the sky. Think about that for a moment."

Caterina ran a finger along the edge of her jawline, her gaze piercing the King. "Abeland Pieman will come for his

father, and when he does, do you think it will be a polite
knock on the door and a formal request? Or do you think it
will be to level Relna the same way that they did Myke,
sending a message to any and all who oppose them? I'm
the only one who can protect you."

The King stood up, shaking with anger. "This is why we
are having a trial. These manipulative accusations of yours.
The Piemans destroyed Myke, did they? I wonder. And
your claims of airships? I don't care if it's yours or theirs,
it's all fantastical nonsense."

"I only want to help. Our kingdoms are neighbors." She
pulled out a roll of papers from beneath her red cloak.

"What are these?"

"Plans for airships like mine," said Caterina, her head
tilted.

The King stared at them then at her. "Is this a joke?"

"No. Look. See for yourself, airships are very, very
real." She offered the papers to him again.

He reluctantly took them.

"I have some built, tested, and ready to protect your
kingdom and legacy. But the Piemans? My spies tell me
they have hundreds."

"How could you possibly know that? My spies have
heard nothing of the sort."

"I'm the Lady in Red. I have spies everywhere."

The King unrolled the plans and stared at them quietly
for a moment. "They seem like genuine schematics." He

rolled the plans back up. "I'll have to have my High Conventioneer confirm they are legitimate."

"Go ahead. They are my gift to you. I am very serious when I say that I'm concerned about the security of this whole affair. I am doubly concerned about justice for those who have wronged the greater good."

"Marcus Pieman," answered the King.

Caterina nodded. "You may have a far greater army than any of your neighbors, never mind considerably more resources. But does any of it matter if war rains down from the sky?"

He stared at her, his eyes betraying his nervous thoughts.

"Think about it, Your Majesty." Caterina walked towards the door. "Let me know if you'd like my Skyfallers up there, protecting you and everyone else."

The King glanced out the window. "How long would it take you to have them here, should they be needed?"

She shrugged and smiled. "A half day or so?" She left, closing the door behind her.

"A half day? What other magic does she wield?"

CHAPTER TWENTY

FALLING APART

"Sir?" asked Abeland's chief engineer.

He looked up from the note he'd just been passed and at the heads of his various teams seated in front of him.

"Sir, we're waiting for you to continue your thought. Or should we all go back to work?"

"Sorry..." Abeland scratched his head. "Lady Pieman needs us to move at least two more Hotarus to her position. She feels that her recruits are doing well." He tapped the rocky table, thinking. "Can you hand me the Neumatic cylinder this came in, please?"

One of the six soldiers in the room stepped forward and handed it to him.

Abeland checked it thoroughly and then put it down in front of him. "It's definitely from Richelle." He looked at the chief engineer. "Paranoid days indeed."

The chief engineer nodded.

Staring at the people in front of him, Abeland brought his fingertips together. "Where was I? Ah, I was being given excuses as to why we still only have three Hotarus operational, other than Richelle's. Every day I'm told we need another day, then another, then... then it becomes two more. What's happening?"

The four engineers in the room all looked at their chief, who sighed heavily.

Abeland turned, his jaw tight and eyes narrowed. "What haven't you been telling me?"

"I was waiting to get confirmation, which we now have," said the chief engineer, restlessly rubbing his hands together. "We've been having some trouble with the MCM engines we've been making. The first few were fine, but then something changed. We aren't sure what or why."

Abeland drummed his fingers on the table. Everyone squirmed in their chairs. As his gaze passed over each one of them, they could feel the fury of the demon that lurked below the charming layer Abeland had. They'd seen him lose his legendary temper a handful of times, and everyone worked their utmost to keep him happy. "And?"

"We believe the only way to resolve this is to decommission the fourth Hotaru and take apart its MCM engine to see how come it's working," said the chief engineer with a gulp.

Abeland stroked his temples. "When did we start suspecting a problem with the engines?"

"Three weeks ago," piped up an engineer.

The chief glared at him.

The man cowered.

"Do you all think that this is the best course of action? Will that get the Hotarus in the air?" asked Abeland, glaring at his team. He watched as modest nods appeared here and there.

"Then get it done. I want a report in the morning."

The three engineers and chief froze as they heard the distinct sounds of Abeland's boots hitting the metal walkway. They were huddled over a large mess of dissembled machinery.

One of the two female engineers turned to the others. "What do we tell him?"

"We tell him the truth. That's the only thing we can," said the chief.

"Anything to report? You all look like it's been a long night." Abeland gazed at the exhausted and grease-covered faces.

The chief engineer stood up. "We've taken apart all four of the MCM engines on this Hotaru, and even have taken apart how they connect to the steam engine... but no answers yet, my Lord."

Abeland softened his expression. "You know sir is fine here." He put a hand on the chief's shoulder. "There's no reason to be afraid. You've done well by me, and while I might be angry at us running into roadblocks, I have no reason to believe it's the fault of any one person."

"Thank you, sir," said the chief.

The engineers all nodded and smiled.

"Are the other Hotarus being readied for transport? I didn't see them in their docks," said Abeland.

"Yes sir, they're all ready to go. The steam trains should be ready to take them wherever you need."

"Good. I'll see you all in say, an hour? I'm sure you'll have an answer for me by then," said Abeland walking away.

After he was out of earshot, one of the engineers turned to the chief. "We know why they're not working. Someone's been sabotaging all of the engines."

"Shh! I can't tell him that, what do you—"

Suddenly the entire cave shook.

"What's that?"

A siren started from high above.

Shouting started.

A piece of the ceiling fell, smashing into a Hotaru.

Abeland ran back. "Get out! Now!"

"What's going on?"

"We've been betrayed! Get out while you can!"

⸻

Abeland walked through the burning wreckage of the downed Skyfaller. "Where's the captain?"

"Dead sir. He's over here," said one of the soldiers.

"All of them are dead... well, I can't blame you soldiers for your efficiency. The modified ballista did what it was supposed to."

"It was like a giant crossbow shooting a balloon," said

another.

Covering his eyes with a hand for a moment, Abeland muttered to himself and took a deep breath. "Chief, get on the train. You're coming with me. As for everyone else, I have nothing to say. Until we have our position restored in Teuton, I don't have the funds to rebuild this. When I do, I will come for you."

The chief watched as Abeland kept shaking off the despair of the moment.

"Are you going to go with him?" asked one of the engineers.

Shrugging, the chief stared out at the cave-in. Smoke was streaming out. "Decades of work…"

"Well, there are still three Hotarus. They didn't get them all."

"No, they didn't," said the chief, wandering off.

The two women engineers came over.

"He's taking it better than I expected," said one of the women.

The man nodded.

"He's a lap dog to the Piemans. They could do and say anything, and he'd ask for more," said the other woman.

"Do you feel it was worth it?" asked the man.

"I don't know where the Butcher got the money for that size of reward, but I wasn't going to refuse it," said the first woman.

The second woman reached into small pack slung over

her shoulder. "I had to look up the seal on that offer letter to make sure it was even real."

"I can't believe we lost track of the date. Pulling an all-nighter almost got us killed. There would have been no reward," said the man.

They all nodded.

"I still can't believe the Tub and the Butcher are real," said the second woman. "Best we go and collect our reward. It's a long way to that Staaten border town."

The whistle of the steam train sounded.

CHAPTER TWENTY-ONE
CHALK ONE UP TO SUSPICION

"The crowd's too thick. Let's pull over for a moment," said Sam, tugging on the reins and shushing the horse to a stop. "Relna's crazier than I expected."

He swung his legs over the bench and faced Tee and Elly who were in the back of the otherwise empty cart.

"I didn't know if those soldiers were going to buy our story about picking up garbage and hauling it away," said Elly. "Do you think my song about loving trash was a bit much?"

Tee made her eyes as big as possible and nodded.

Elly tried and failed to give her a smack.

"I think my original idea to have the horse and cart at a point further in the city as our rendezvous point isn't going to work," said Sam, turning about and scratching the back of his neck. "I'll find a place to station it, and then I'll do my shopping."

He twiddled his fingers. "Something feels off. This

many royals and aristocrats… there's a thousand coins in clothing just in the next twenty yards. Something's going to happen. I just need to find out what, first." Turning to Tee, he pulled out his pocket watch. She did the same.

"Elly?" asked Tee.

"My grandmother took mine," she said, her lips pulled in.

"Okay, I've got eleven fifteen," said Sam.

Tee adjusted her pocket watch. "Match. We'll see you in three hours."

He looked at both of them. "When did you girls get so big?"

"A week last Thursday," said Elly with a smirk. "Remember the quick rainfall followed by the bright sunlight? Boom. We're weeds."

Sam smiled. "Alright, just stick to the plan and out of trouble. If things go badly, hide, and I'll find you. There's nowhere in this city that I won't be able to get to you." He paused. "One more thing. If you run into Eleanor, please be careful. I'm hoping that she's only up to something that I wouldn't agree with and not some scheme that will bring us harm. The last thing we need is a war amongst ourselves."

"Hey! What are you doing out here hiding in the bushes?" said a guard running over to Nikolas. "How did you get into the courtyard gardens?"

"Burbles?" said Nikolas, looking about, his eyes wide

and confused.

"You could have accidentally walked over to the gate. It's not safe for an old man," said the guard putting a hand on Nikolas' shoulder.

Nikolas offered a huge smile and tapped the guard's face with one hand. "Good birdy bingo. Good bingo. So sweet." He put his other hand behind his back.

"Let's get you back to your villa before anyone sees you. They'll blame me somehow. I know they will," said the guard. He gently pushed Nikolas forward.

Several yards later, Nikolas stopped and pointed at the flowers. "The gardener. Today?"

"The gardener? Ah… it's Wednesday so… no. Anyway, I heard they fired that guy. There should be a new one in a few days."

"Oh, but there is the birdy nom noms!" said Nikolas, his finger up and his face like that of an excited five-year-old. He did a little dance.

"Get moving."

The guard opened the door to Nikolas' villa and ushered him inside. "I think I'll need to talk to the captain about having a lock put on the outside of your door like most of the other villas. I don't know why they haven't."

"The poops," said Nikolas, his eyebrows wiggling.

"Oh, geez, you're the poops guy. Right, I can only imagine what you'd do if you couldn't get outside now and then. Just… don't come out unless there's a guard in sight.

We're stretched thin these days, with all the royal security and stuff. We've even got soldiers on the edges of this little villa area too, and they're not as friendly as guys like me. You could get hurt."

Nikolas winked and saluted.

"Don't do that. That's not even the Belnian salute. Just... don't get hurt," said the guard as he closed the door.

Nikolas leaned against the door, staring at the prize he'd retrieved before the guard's arrival, a piece of chalk. He turned it over and smiled at a set of particular hash markings. "Hello, Sam. It's good to know you are out there."

He tapped the chalk against his hand. "Hmm, what to do next? What is your plan, Sam?"

Leaning his head back, he muttered to himself until his eyes lit up. "The old story we used to tell Tee when you visited..." His fingers twiddled back and forth. "The Tale of Twin Rabbits." Staring at the piece of chalk, he shook his head back and forth. "It would have to be five inches precisely."

Scanning about, he found the pile he wanted and reached into it, pulling out a ruler. "Five exactly. What a brilliant man you are, Sam, yes?"

Nikolas smiled at the door. "You, my friend, need some color."

CHAPTER TWENTY-TWO
DANGEROUS GAMES

Caterina stared at her wall of maps, leaning against the opposite wall, a delicate smile on her face. On the marble table beside the fruit bowl was an opened cylinder, and a note that had earned a rare yelp of triumph from her.

There was a knock at the hidden side door.

"Come in Zelda," she said, straightening up and taking a breath.

"You look… remarkably relaxed?" Zelda gazed about the room.

Caterina picked up the note and handed it to her. "Good news has a way of washing everything away, at least for a moment."

"This is astounding. Are you certain it's true? In one fell swoop, we've destroyed all of the Hotarus? I have to say, I didn't believe the Butcher would come through for us."

"Honestly? Neither did I. But here we are. I don't know how she found their lair, but she did."

Zelda walked over, filed the paper away in the appropriate basket, and removed the cylinder from the table. "I have another piece of good news for you, Your Majesty. Simon St. Malo has found a way to fix the boiler issues in the field. One of the trains that was stranded is already fully operational."

Caterina looked at the ornate crown molding, her eyes running along to the corner. "I can't let all of this good news go to my head. I'm sure the Piemans will find some ways to cause me distress shortly."

She tugged on her cuffs. "But... but this changes the Grand Game quite a bit. Without their airships, the Piemans are finished. Even if Marcus somehow walks out of here a free man, he'll have lost his grip over Teuton. No more power, no more money, just ash and regret."

Caterina smiled. "Do we need to worry about Mister Watt?"

Zelda shook her head. "I gave his... handlers some financial motivation to keep him out of trouble. They're supposed to take him to Farkees."

"Farkees? Good riddance. I'm sure his sensibilities will have a rude awakening in that lawless nation of barbarians and criminals. It's just the place for the backstabbing and arrogant Mister Watt."

Caterina stood up and went over to the wall map. She tapped at several of the metal pins. "With the trains working, how quickly can we get more Skyfallers within striking distance of Relna?"

"We have the two that were brought on rail-raft and are hidden within a few hours of here. As for more..." Zelda rocked on her heels, thinking. "We could probably have eight more here in just over a day, assuming that the field repairs for the other trains are nearly complete. Those would be the ones we currently have stored here, here, and here," she said, pointing at places on the map.

"And those are all near Neumatic Tube lines, good. Send the word. I want those ships here. Also, I want the rest of the Skyfallers in and around our capital cities in Elizabetina and Staaton and highly visible. I want it very clear that we might be small in size, but we are mighty."

Zelda nodded. "I fear we've been a bit too efficient in finding and eliminating spies over the past two years. I think the best course of action in getting the news out, is for us to free the few we have locked up."

"Feed them, clothe them, send them on their way." Caterina laughed. "Tell them that it's a sign of good faith regarding the Trial by Royals. They'll eat that up."

"Very well. Is that everything?"

Caterina nodded.

Zelda opened the secret door and left. As the door closed, a hand appeared and opened it back up.

"Eleanor, how unexpected," said Caterina, removing all signs of her good mood from her face. She glanced at the mahogany grandmother clock sitting on a shelf. "You're surprisingly on time."

Eleanor glared at Caterina with narrow, beady eyes as she stepped into the room. "You do not summon me. Our arrangement was simple and clear."

"Yes, and I regret to inform you that the information you provided about the location of the Hotaru facility was wrong. I'm rather disappointed," said Caterina taking an apple out of the fruit bowl.

"That's impossible." Eleanor shook her head.

"And yet here we are. Who would have thought after so many successful, clandestine campaigns—even with the Candlestick Maker causing problems for you at every turn! —that you'd come up empty? I guess the Tub truly is gone. It's a shame. I had so much fun playing you and Marcus against each other."

Eleanor's nostrils flared. She pushed her shoulders back and composed herself. "The ruse you wanted with Marcus is done. Surprisingly, he gave the boy a purse of silver."

"Odd. Maybe he's losing his mind. He is the oldest man I've ever known. On to more important matters: I need you to act this afternoon. Things are changing quickly."

"I do not work for you," said Eleanor.

Shrugging, Caterina pointed at the attached room. "Let's sit in the parlor." She walked through an archway into the larger, more open room.

As Eleanor followed, her cane clicked as it struck the marble floor.

Caterina opened the balcony doors. "Some fresh air always does good in moments like this."

"I hear rumors that the trial might get disrupted. Is that why you're willing to risk everything?"

"We have an agreement, and if you're to fulfill your part of the deal, then you'll act. I don't owe you anything," said Caterina. "I gave you the information you needed, when you were held prisoner by Marcus, to prove he murdered your sister. You still owe me."

Eleanor's face twitched, and she tightened her grip on her cane. "I heard the King's avoiding you."

"I see him every day. As with the Hotarus' location, you are simply wrong," said Caterina. "You sound paranoid."

The Butcher leaned forward. "You're playing with fire."

"I'm willing to get a bit burned if it means setting the world ablaze and owning my own destiny." She took a bite of the apple.

Eleanor stood up. "You've done nothing but make a mess. I handed you Marcus on a silver platter."

"Says the woman whose entire organization was destroyed by him."

"No, you did that with your attack on Kar'm," said Eleanor bitterly.

Caterina forced a tight-lipped smile. "You knew what you were getting into when you made this bargain."

Eleanor stood up and pulled at her dress and cloak.

"How's that hired hand working out for you? I heard he used to have quite the reputation."

Eleanor let her eyes wander around the room. "LeLoup's serving his purpose."

"Good, now serve yours."

CHAPTER TWENTY-THREE
AND THIS LITTLE PIGGY

"I think we should have taken the horse and cart. I haven't learned to drive, yet," said Elly. "I keep thinking of the stories you told me about visiting your Aunt Gwen."

Tee laughed. "Which part of losing control and flipping the cart over, nearly killing myself, sounded fun?"

Elly pondered for a moment. "Most of it? The speed in particular. I bet Richy would have loved all of it."

Tee nodded. "That he would have. I think my grandpapa's horseless cart will be more your thing. Nice, slow."

"For now. I bet I can get that thing going like a rocket-cart given half the chance."

"Well, someone's embraced her abominator side," said Tee.

"I believe the socially correct phrase is..." Elly tapped her chin. "Let me think, let me think. Ah yes. I believe the phrase is: Shut up Tee before I punch you in the face."

"Oh, I didn't know that was an official phrase," said Tee.

Elly nodded. "It is. I read it in a book."

"Really?"

"I'm pretty sure. It was in the endnotes. The print is always so small. Perhaps it said something else entirely."

They laughed.

There was a sudden explosion.

The girls turned to see sparks of green, yellow and red dancing in the air.

A boy their age was laughing until guards grabbed him.

"Who sets off fireworks in a crowded place like this?" asked Tee.

"They're going to spook the horses," said Elly shaking her head.

"Boys," said Tee.

"I know!"

"At least you don't have to worry about them," said Tee, shaking her head. "I keep trying to think if I'll ever find a reasonable one. Maybe I can become a spinster."

Elly smiled. "There's always hope of becoming a spinster. Maybe a pirate captain spinster. Oh, that'd be cool."

"Airship pirate captain spinster!" said Tee. "I like the sound of that."

They strolled through the streets, peeking in at the occasional shop or merchant stand.

"I'm surprised your granddad thought it was okay for us to wear our yellow hoods," said Elly.

"The Baker, they say, has mystery ways... and apparently there's some old law about hooded agents of color. He didn't get into it."

"Weird."

"Hey, do you ever wonder if our dads were like that boy?"

Elly stopped and put her hands out in protest. "We do not think about my parents as people. Did you get hit in the head? The idea that they dated or... anything, that just violates the Not Going Crazy Rule," said Elly.

"True. Right up there with the No Dying Rule."

"Elly's three rules of life."

Tee tilted her head. "And the third being?"

"Elly can make up more rules. What, you're surprised?"

Shaking her head, Tee pulled out her pocket watch. She ran a finger along its silver-and-brass edge. "We've got about an hour until rendezvous."

Elly looked at the crude map they'd been making to keep track of where they were going. She put her elbows up to keep the dense crowd at bay.

"Hey, look over there. That guy's dressed like Amami. The dark pants, the light shirt and the red sash. No hood, though."

"Maybe he's undercover," said Elly with a silly face, wiggling her eyebrows.

Tee chuckled. "I'm noticing the weird people. I bet you're also noting the dresses."

"Seventeen pretty ones, twelve notables, and four with smart little jackets."

"I like those too," said Tee with a smirk.

"I'm going to have one some day. Did I mention the twenty-seven adults with red hoods?"

"Hmm, I counted twenty-four. Six had some form of shiny embroidery on the edges," said Tee.

A woman in a red dress caught Elly's attention for a second. She turned to say something to Tee, who to her surprise, was several yards away. "Tee?"

Tee dove into the crowd.

"Tee!"

CHAPTER TWENTY-FOUR

LIDDEL DEAL

"Good morning, Your Majesty. I hope that you are well," said the Prime Minister, closing the door to the courtroom. The sound echoed throughout the chamber.

The floor was white marble with silver and black streaks in it. The throne was relatively modest, and before it was still the ornately carved old table and three chairs used for official discussions between the King, the Prime Minister, and her aids. While she had most of the power, he had most of the people on his side. It was a delicate balance that had worked for decades.

The King was standing on the stone balcony, gazing down at the royal garden. "I am, Madame Prime Minister."

"Sorry I wasn't available the rest of the day yesterday. There's only so much of Regent Catherine that I can take."

"Indeed." The King turned and smiled as she joined him. "I never get tired of this view."

"With good reason," she said.

"That conversation was... unexpectedly entertaining."

"Was it?"

He nodded, stroking his beard. "She provided us with plans for an airship. She claims to have them."

"Did she?" asked the Prime Minister, a curious smile on her face.

"I have the High Conventioneer going through the plans in detail. He gave me his thoughts an hour ago. He believes that the plans are legitimate." The King glanced at the Prime Minister. "You look surprised."

"To be honest, Your Majesty, I am. Now, it's my turn. I had a most interesting conversation as well. Funnily enough, it confirmed that she has an airship. It also confirmed that she has committed at least one act of war. We have an eyewitness."

The King raised an eyebrow. "That's a most serious accusation."

"The witness has an advocate, someone who wants to ensure the man's safety and... a bit of something for himself. He's had a rough go of it lately."

"You sound as if I know him."

The Prime Minister nodded. "You do indeed, and I say that, as a long-time friend of yours."

There was a muffled knock behind one of the tapestries that hung on a court wall.

The King raised his other eyebrow.

"Right on time," said the Prime Minister walking over and opening the secret door.

"It's been a while, Lord Silskin," said the King, reaching

out and shaking his hand. "Your attire looks a bit... common for you."

Silskin looked down at his clothes. "No one thinks twice of servants walking about."

"I'd heard that you are no longer in favor with the Lady in Red."

"I am a man with... opportunities," said Silskin.

The Prime Minister looked at Silskin and then the King. "I will leave you two."

"Thank you." The King smiled.

Silskin pointed at a painting on the wall. "I saw the princess on the way in. I can't believe how much she's grown and how much she looks like her mother, yet with your eyes."

The King offered a sorrowful smile. "She would have been proud."

"You know," continued Silskin, "some would think it's random, picking a child to look like the parents, but it isn't. To be able to look at something so innocent and to see what it will become—I truly believe it's a gift. But without the ability to keep secrets, it's worthless. Wouldn't you agree, Your Majesty?"

He glared at Silskin. "Are you here with a noble purpose or are you going to try and blackmail me, Silskin?"

Silskin put up a gentle hand. "The noblest of purposes, I promise you. I have never spoken of our deal for the baby princess, and I can assure you that Regent Caterina has less than innocent intentions. I have a man named Chikahn Liddel under my protection, and I believe he has something that your panel of judgment needs to hear."

The King glanced about the empty courtroom. "Where is this Liddel?"

"Waiting in the passage behind the secret door. I have taken every precaution with him, for I am certain if Caterina heard of him before he had a chance to speak, he'd be dead."

"It's unlike you to care for the welfare of another if there was no profit in it," said the King, folding his arms.

Silskin looked at the King blankly.

"You didn't find this man. Someone gave him to you... okay, I'll listen to what he has to say and then decide if he gets to speak to the panel. Is your hope to cancel the trial?"

"Your Majesty, I believe the charges are valid. However, I believe they have been laid against the wrong person."

The King smiled and nodded. "I see. And am I to assume that you have a fee for this opportunity to swat that annoying fly, Caterina?"

"Just a small stipend, something modest each month to allow me to live a reasonable life to the end of my days."

The King nodded. "Very well. Let me hear this Liddel fellow, and if I believe he is convincing, then we have a deal."

CHAPTER TWENTY-FIVE

LeLooking For Something

"Where did you go?" yelled Tee, planting her hands on the shoulders of a man facing the other way and pushing herself up to see over the crowd.

"Excuse me! What are you doing? Get off me!"

"There he is," she said, dropping down.

Tee fought through the busy street to the mouth of a narrow alley.

The sound of a bucket getting kicked over up ahead tugged at her.

"Tee!" she heard Elly yell in the background.

"I'll be back in a second," she replied over her shoulder. She curled her shaking hands into fists and turned the corner.

A dark figure dashed off, filling the alley with ominous laughter.

Tee reached into her yellow cloak and pulled out a shock-stick. "I'm going to end this, LeLoup. No more haunting my dreams or Elly's."

At the end of the alley was a small, abandoned courtyard. Empty flower pots and chunks of broken stone finishings were scattered around. The three-story buildings surrounding the courtyard were derelict. Their windows were missing or smashed, their paint was peeling, and all signs of life were gone.

Tee cranked the shock-stick and then took out another.

"Ah, your crutches. A symbol of your weakness," said a voice from higher up.

She turned about, trying to figure out which building it had come from. "I'm glad you remember them because they've shocked you twice, or is it three times now? I beat you every time."

"Well, every time save one. How is Elly doing?"

Tee's face twitched. "Why don't you come out here? The real LeLoup lost his mind."

There was a suppressed laugh, followed by the tapping of something metal on stone. "You have no idea how badly I want to come down there and end this. To beat you down and then stare at you right in the eyes as I take back what's mine. But... but that wasn't the deal I made."

Tee moved about the courtyard, her eyes sweeping the area. "All of these buildings probably have stone or stone tiles as part of the walls," she muttered to herself. "What deal, faker?"

The sound of metal scraping across stone came to a

stop. "Faker? Such a crude attempt to get under my skin. Tee, I thought you were more professional than that by now."

"I don't believe you're LeLoup. He wouldn't cower in some building. Sure, he'd have some minions to try and wear me down, but he'd be standing right here." Tee said, crouched and ready.

There was a loud grumble, followed by metal hitting stone again and again.

Tee tugged her hood a bit further over her face. She shifted her weight back and forth; her hands clasped tightly around her shock-sticks.

Dark laughter filled the courtyard. "Maybe I can break the rules a little. Where's the harm?" A shot fired, hitting the wall directly behind Tee, right by her head. "Oh, did I miss?"

Sweat dripped off the end of Tee's nose.

"Let's see, how about a second shot? A little more to the left maybe?"

A shot fired on the other side of Tee.

"Where are the witty remarks? The goading? I do so love the goading."

"Tee?" yelled Elly approaching.

"Elly?" Tee's eyes went wide, and her hands started to shake.

"Let's bend the rules a wee bit more, shall we?" The courtyard filled with laughter again.

"There you are!" Elly started running for Tee.

"No! Elly! It's LeLoup!" Tee screamed as she bolted toward Elly, her voice echoing off the abandoned buildings.

"So you do believe it's me! How wonderful. Here's a present."

A shot fired, hitting part of the wall between Tee and Elly.

"Drop down!" said Tee, tears streaming down her face. She was a dozen yards away.

Elly slid to the ground and pulled her cloak around her.

"And this little piggy fell down. Oh, my, time to reload. Oh, I lie, there's always one more."

Another shot fired, hitting Tee on the side of her hood. She tripped, hit the wall, and fell to the ground.

"Tee!" yelled Elly, scurrying over and pulling her cloak over Tee.

"It stings like a… but I'm okay." She tried to sit up. "Woo. Dizzy."

Elly ran her hand around the inside of Tee's hood. "Oh, thank goodness, no blood." She stared at Tee. "Why that look?"

"He's reloading. He'll shoot again," she said, her eyes darting about the courtyard. She reached to pull off Elly's cloak. "We've got to go."

"Don't. Maybe that's what he's expecting," said Elly. "He could have a rifle or something else ready to go."

Tee stared into Elly's eyes, confused by the deep fear in

them.

They waited until Tee shook her head. "He's gone." She stood up, looking around.

Elly picked one of Tee's shock-sticks off the ground.

"Why didn't he shoot again? He had us," said Tee.

CHAPTER TWENTY-SIX

LIDDEL WORDS

Marcus stood, arms folded, his head leaning against the cool, dark marble column. He'd been waiting outside of the banquet-hall-turned-courtroom for an hour.

He listened eagerly to the raised voices. Clearly something exciting had transpired in the past fifteen minutes. Opening his eyes, he looked at the beautifully carved double doors and wondered how many of the royals, ambassadors and dignitaries were close to each other's throats.

"Lord Pieman, this is unexpected."

He turned and smiled, offering his hand. "Madame Prime Minister, it's always a pleasure to see you."

She shook his hand and glanced about at the empty foyer. "No entourage of guardsmen? We cannot guarantee your safety."

"With all due respect," he said, stopping and coughing. "Sorry, I fear that my age might finally be catching up with me. Anyway, within the confines of the keep, I feel better with a minimal entourage. Less betrayal to worry about."

She smiled.

The double doors opened, and the captain of the guard stepped out.

Marcus noted that it seemed to be unexpectedly peaceful inside.

"Captain?"

"Madame Prime Minister, the witness is ready to be brought into the courtroom."

"Thank you." She looked at Marcus curiously. "I was not aware that you were going to be attending this. Has there been a change?"

"I'm to speak afterward."

She thought for a moment. "Yes, I recall that change to the agenda. At some point, we should sit and have tea. I need to hear how you swim through the shark-infested political seas and yet come out dry and with a basket of fish, none the less."

He nodded and leaned back against the column as the doors closed.

The Prime Minister of Belnia stepped into the makeshift courtroom. Dozens of tables had been put together in a u-shape, with the head seat left empty, awaiting her. Most countries and kingdoms had sent an entire delegation, but only one representative for each was allowed a seat at the table.

The representatives drifted about the room, eyeing each other and making meaningless conversation. In the far corner was the King of Belnia with a cloud of people around him, all trying to get something out of him.

Along the wall were guards in ceremonial dress with pikes.

Taking her seat, she picked up the pair of ornately carved wooden spoons and smacked them together. A hush fell over the room, and everyone went to their seats.

"It has taken some time for us to determine how best to proceed, as modern times have no precedent for a Trial by Royals," said the Prime Minister, her eyes sweeping over the faces in the room. "If you are ready for the first order of business, I ask that you put a fist forward, as is Belnian tradition."

One by one, fists came forward.

"Excellent," said the Prime Minister. "Captain, would you please bring in our witness and his counsel?"

The captain of the guard nodded and issued the order. He picked up a chair and placed it in the middle of the U of tables.

Looking to her right, the Prime Minister saw the King resting his head on his hand and glancing about nervously.

"We have to do this in the open," she whispered.

"I agree. I just don't like the feeling that this could all blow up in our faces. Caterina will get wind of this in minutes."

The Prime Minister stood. "Captain, I would like to ask that the doors are sealed until we have completed our affairs with Misters Liddel and Pieman. We wouldn't want any sensitive information to be leaked, creating a problem."

The captain was surprised. "Madame Prime Minister?"

"Do you have an objection to security, Captain?" Her commanding tone silencing the room.

There were no raised fists.

"Very good. You have been so instructed, Captain," she said, sitting.

"I... will lock up and be on my way."

"No," she said raising a finger. "You will remain, Captain—until the end."

A glare momentarily escaped from the captain before he bowed and turned away.

Two guards opened the back door of the banquet hall. A guard came in, followed by a bald man in a distinctive brown coat and high-collared shirt and a similarly dressed, taller man with shoulder-length hair. The taller man kept touching his clean-shaven face.

"Some of you know me; I am Ron-Paul Silskin. I was the right hand of the Lady in Red, known to most as Regent Catherine or Caterina." He turned and gestured to the taller man beside him. "This is Chikahn Liddel of Teuton. He is the reason we are here today, and he has born witness to an act of war by Regent Cater... Catherine on the Teutons."

"Nonsense," heckled one of the Royals.

"Order!" said the Prime Minister. "Please continue."

Silskin nodded. "He has witnessed one of her airships,

called Skyfallers, bombing a small village. He is the sole survivor."

The King leaned forward, his hands together. "Mister Liddel, would you please tell this judgment panel what you said to me in private."

CHAPTER TWENTY-SEVEN

I'm Pooped

Elly emerged from the market crowd with two large, round, red-and-orange fruit in hand.

"What are those?" asked Tee, her face lighting up. She was sitting at the western edge of the market on an abandoned crate. "They're enormous."

"She said they're called peaches. She let me try a slice. It's like honey and apples had a baby, but better."

They eyed them in anticipation.

"Three, two, one…" they said in unison.

They bit into their peaches.

"Holy Mother of Mercy this is good," said Tee, the pieces almost falling out of her mouth and the juices running down the edges of mouth.

Elly waved a hand at her. "Shh, eating." She took another bite. "Oh wow. Remind me to thank Sam for the coins he gave you."

"You finally called him Sam."

"Shh, eating!"

After they had finished, Elly tossed her peach pit. "I

didn't think I would need to remind you about the No Dying Rule so soon. But just in case, no dying."

"Got it," said Tee with a failed chuckle. "That was extraordinarily stupid of me."

"Yup."

"This isn't a game, is it?"

"Nope," said Elly.

They sat in silence, watching the vibrant market. Merchant kids were running from table to table and shop to shop, making their own fun and getting yelled at or swatted at by their parents and older siblings.

Too many had thin faces and ragged brown-and-grey clothes. Their faces transformed in an instant at the hope of receiving a coin. When the moment passed, the weight of their world would return to their expressions.

Tee looked at her peach pit, a guilty twist in her stomach. "One day, I want to make life better for these people."

"You won't get to if you're stupid and get killed."

Tee nodded.

"How are we doing on time?"

Tee checked her pocket watch. "About twenty minutes until we're supposed to rendezvous. Let's head back."

She stared walking and then realized Elly wasn't following. "Are you okay?"

Elly was looking at the ground, her eyes tearful. She winced and fought to clear her throat. "I just... I can't imagine what you went through after I was shot and until I woke up at the Abbey." Her hands shook. "I don't know if I have what you have inside to do all of this."

Tee put her hands on Elly's shoulders. "You're joking, right? Do you remember when those horsemen were chasing me? You switched cloaks with me. You took down a Skyfaller at Kar'm, by yourself! You are a hero."

Elly slowly shook her head back and forth. "When I was fighting those two Red Hoods, it hit me deep down that I might die. Now this pretend LeLoup... I realized that I don't know what I would do if you died."

Biting her lip, Tee didn't say anything for a moment.

After letting out a deep breath, Elly nodded. "Sorry, I'm good."

"You're one of the strongest people I know, Elly. I'd— wait is that your grandmother?" asked Tee, pointing with her chin.

"What's she doing here?"

"Want to follow a spymaster? My granddad did say he'd find us wherever we were."

Elly nodded. "What's the worst that could happen?"

As Tee and Elly turned the corner, they came upon the main boulevard leading to the keep. An eight-foot-high fence, made of iron rods with spear tops, ran the perimeter of its grounds. Within the confines of the fence were trees and bushes and flowers, along with tents where colorfully dressed people were enjoying the warm, autumn day.

The boulevard ended at a classic stone archway with ancient script chiseled along its face and a huge flag of Belnia flying high overhead. Four guards were standing together, talking. They wore bright ceremonial dress, with large feathers from their helmets, and had gold-colored pikes in hand.

Tee and Elly turned around, shaking their heads.

"Where did she go?" asked Tee.

Elly scratched her head. "It's like she just disappeared." She gazed over at the five-floor grey keep. It was structured like a layer cake, with colored flags as its only decoration. "I can't believe that people live in a place like that. It's right out of a story."

"And yet there were those other people in the market, who don't have anything," said Tee, frowning. "Anyway, the Butcher's gone." She paused, thinking. "If she'd seen us, then I figure she'd try to contact you. If she didn't, then I can only think that she went into the keep."

"Huh."

"What are you thinking?" asked Tee.

"What if she just walked right in? What if they know her?" asked Elly.

"I never thought of that." Tee stretched. "I'm guessing we can't do that."

Elly shook her head. "We need to go in there. I'm certain of it."

Tee raised an eyebrow. "Whatever it is, we need it now

because those four guards at the archway are staring at us."

Suddenly someone came out of a side road on the other side of the boulevard, screaming and yelling.

"Is that a guard?" asked Tee.

Elly squinted. "What's his armor covered in? It looks brown."

"I think… I think it's poop," said Tee as they cracked up and crossed the road.

The archway guards burst into laughter as the other one approached.

"He got you! Hahaha!" said the first guard.

"Oh, I've got to tell the guys. He got another one," said the second, doubled over.

"You knew this would happen!" yelled the mess-covered guard.

"Stop there! Just stop. That smell's all the wake-up we needed. Any closer and I swear I'll pike you," said a third guard, waving his weapon.

"You guys are a bunch of pargos. You knew about this? Why the yig didn't someone warn me about that old freak?"

Tee touched Elly's arm. "Slow down. I have a funny feeling."

The first guard motioned for his colleague to calm down. "I'm going to give you the same answer I told all the other guys," said the first guard. "You didn't ask."

The archway guards broke into laughter again.

"Shut up!" The poop-covered guard stomped around in a circle. "Why's that guy in with political prisoners? He should be in the dungeon. Geez, he's bat-sheep crazy and allowed to do this? To someone like me?"

"That Klaus guy's connected to Pieman. Touch him or complain about him, and you might just not wake up in the morning. That's what my buddy said," said the first guard.

"They said Klaus," whispered Elly.

Tee scanned the exits from the area. "He came from that direction, didn't he?"

"I think so," said Elly.

"On the positive side," said another guard. "That means the old man's safe for a couple of days. He's only got so much ammunition."

His buddies laughed.

"Let's go before they notice us," said Tee.

CHAPTER TWENTY-EIGHT

LIDDEL SPEECHES

The banquet hall doors were flung open. Caterina stormed into the room, Zelda and three guards at her side.

Marcus stopped talking and slowly stood up from the witness chair. "There you have it. That is my offer," he said and bowed.

"Why was I not notified of him talking to the panel? Protocol states—" said Caterina.

"You no longer have privileged standing with the panel," said the Prime Minister, rising from her chair.

"I represent Staaten and Elizabetina. I have a right to be on the panel." Caterina glared at everyone in the room. Most turned away; a few nodded at her in quiet support.

"You have committed an act of war," said the Prime Minister. "The vote was unanimous to have you removed."

"War on whom?"

"On Teuton," said Marcus with a smile. "Where you left an eyewitness, an apparently convincing one at that."

"One person convinced you?"

"No, but that's not a matter to be discussed with you.

Now, Your Majesty, I believe we need to investigate who alerted Regent *Catherine*," said the Prime Minister.

Caterina growled.

"I would agree," said the King, rising from his seat.

Marcus raised a hand. "Madame Prime Minister, if I could have an answer to my offer after your scheduled break, it would be appreciated."

"It's the next order of business," she said. "The panel is dismissed for an hour."

Caterina marched right up to Marcus. "What offer? How are you bribing the panel?" Her eyes burned with fury.

Marcus offered a wry smile. "I should have seen you coming, but I didn't. I'm not foolish enough to think that I can win the Grand Game the way I'd once hoped, but I can prevent a loss. I've revealed the existence of the railroads and the Neumatic Tubes. Their locations and the designs for all of it will be given to them in the morning if they agree."

She glared at him.

"Why should we have all the fun?" He left.

"You have no idea the fun I will bring upon all of you."

CHAPTER TWENTY-NINE
HUNTING FOR A GOOD KLAUS

"Let's try down here," said Elly as they explored another road. She glanced down at her map. "I think I screwed up. We might be just going in circles."

"Well, there are people on this road, so it's got to go somewhere. And I don't recognize any of this," said Tee. "I haven't seen a shop in a little bit. That's probably a good thing."

Tee jumped as a black cat screeched and ran past them.

"Age erodes subtly, let me tell you," said Sam.

Elly turned around. "How could you find us? We can't find us."

"It's what I do, Elly," he replied with a laugh.

"Have you been following us the entire time?" asked Tee.

"No. I had a bit of shopping to do and a few other things to attend to first. I've been with you for about ten minutes. I will point out that you did walk right past me twice."

"We saw a guard covered in poop. We think grandpapa did it. He's not in a dungeon, but he's a prisoner."

Sam snapped his fingers. "The political prison." He frowned. "But I've had someone check all the names there."

"They said something about him having no name."

Closing his eyes, Sam shook his head. "I should have thought of that. I just figured that Nikolas wasn't important enough for them to do that." He sighed. "I need to retire."

"Do you think we should get Richy and Amami?" asked Elly.

"I have a way to get Amami's attention if needed. She's a smart woman. She'll know what to do if we're not back in time," said Sam. "But for now, the fewer, the better. Now, follow me."

───────

Tee and Elly peered out of the alley at the fenced courtyard and the locked metal gate. Two female guards were sitting at a table on the inside.

Suddenly there was an explosion in the distance.

Elly whipped her head around. "What was that?"

"I think that was Sam. He did say we'd know when to move." Tee shook her head. "My dad says he has the soul of an imp. He's always full of surprises."

"Just so you know, I think your family's crazy," said Elly. "Come on. That distracted the guards.

They glanced about as they crossed the road to the iron

rod gate.

"All the buildings around here are abandoned," noted Tee.

"Hmm," said Elly, leaning in and examining the lock.

"Maybe up and over?" said Tee. "I think I can boost you high enough."

Elly smiled and pushed the gate open. "Best to try the obvious, right?"

They ran into the compound and along a cobblestone walking path. They stopped when confronted with a confounding sight.

"Look at the rows of identical villas," said Elly. "There's got to be what, a dozen rows?"

Tee rubbed her face. "And over a dozen villas per row. How are we going to find him? Think, Tee. Think."

There was another explosion.

"Woo, I think Sam might be having too much fun," said Elly.

Tee snapped her fingers. "Fun. He was pranking those guards."

"Right, so?" said Elly.

"He wouldn't do that just to mess with them. He would do it to get them out of the way." She paced, twiddling her fingers. "He's probably tried to escape. But if he had succeeded, Sam would have known. So, he's still here."

Tee turned around, looking at the surrounding area. "Maybe he was trying to send a message. We found where he is, so how do we find which one is his?"

Elly stared at one of the little prison homes. "Maybe he did something subtle. But what?"

CHAPTER THIRTY

OATH WALKER

Richy dropped his tools on the makeshift workbench and stared at Amami. "I'm positive that one was an explosion. Something's got to be wrong."

Amami gestured at the forest around them with her wrench, her focus still on the contraption in front of them. "We're surrounded by a forest. It would have to be a significant explosion and on the far enough of town. The chances are slim."

There was another boom in the distance.

Richy started running, then stopped and turned around to face his sister. "Come on. You have to admit that was an explosion. Look at the plume of smoke!"

She carefully put her tools down and took off her goggles. Squinting at the afternoon light, she looked up. "There is no sign that we are needed."

"What are you talking about? My friends need help."

Amami studied the sky. "No. I have learned over the years that to rush into a situation when you are not needed, and not requested, can make things far worse than they need to be."

"And I've learned that sometimes you have to trust you gut and feel the moment," said Richy. "This feels wrong." He walked towards her. "What don't I know?"

She narrowed her eyes and put her fingertips on the table. Her black hair covered part of her face. "I have had a complicated life, Riichi. Eleanor DeBoeuf supported me in my search for you, at least I thought she did. Now, in understanding her better, I wonder if she always knew where you were and just waited to see if I would find you."

Richy shook his head. "I don't think that."

Amami smiled at him. "That is the spirit of the Dragon in you, always fiery and honest, always trusting and certain." Her smile fell away. "Though I never joined the Tubmen, I did swear an oath to Eleanor. My pledge was to never act against the Butcher unless she proved unworthy of the title."

He frowned at her. "Which she's done."

"No," said Amami, her voice soft and thoughtful. "All she has done is gone away without leaving word." She pulled her sleeve. "I want to show you something.

Richy came over.

"This is called the Mark of the Guardian. It is an oath I took early on in my search for you."

"What's this one? It looks puffy, like it's new." He went to touch it; Amami pulled away.

"That is the Mark of the Dozen. I took an oath at Kar'm

to the Baker."

Richy stared at his sister.

She waited silently.

"Are you stuck between two vows?"

She nodded.

He rubbed his face. "Okay, I get it."

"You do?"

"Yeah. You can't go because you don't know who's doing what," said Richy.

"And until the Butcher has proven herself unworthy of the role, I cannot take any action against her... save one."

Richy straightened up. "What do you mean?"

Her eyes swept over the camp and stopped.

He followed her gaze. "What's that way?"

"My King's-horse." She picked up her goggles and put them on.

Richy was about to ask a question then stopped. He was about to ask another then stopped himself again. He paced about, muttering the wording to himself and finally snapped his fingers. "Did the Butcher use your King's-horse?"

"Yes, on several occasions."

"Is there anything there that could belong to her?" he asked, running his hand through his black hair.

She nodded.

Richy ran off.

Ten minutes later he returned, a bundle of tied-together letters in his hand.

He waved a hand at his sister, working through the wording again. "Did you place these letters in the hidden compartment you showed me of the King's-Horse?"

"Yes."

"Were you asked to?"

She shook her head.

"Wait, ah… I got it. Were you asked to get rid of the letters?"

Amami smiled, a tear in her eyes.

"Okay, so… does that mean I have these legally? Or legitimately or something?"

She nodded. "Yes."

Richy sat down, pulling off the twine. He was about to read the first one when he looked up at her. "Did you have to live like this? I mean, on a tightrope between different loyalties?"

"Sometimes, but it allowed me to find you, and that is all that mattered. And know, Riichi, that I will gladly face the penalty of breaking any of those oaths over hurting you."

He got up and gave her a hug.

"What was that for?" she asked, perplexed.

"Just… ah," he wiped his eyes. "I don't know. I had an extra hug that I needed to use up."

CHAPTER THIRTY-ONE

KLAUS IT'S THE ONLY PLAN

Tee doubled over, out of breath. "I don't know, Elly. That's the fourth lane we've been down. Maybe this is a bad idea."

Elly's face was flush, and sweat dripped down her face. "I never really thought about how hot these cloaks get. We should put some vents or something in them."

"Yeah, like dragon scales or something," said Tee.

"Oh, I like that." Elly shook her head. "I think we lost those two guards. That was a bit scary though."

"Nothing like turning a corner and running right up behind someone and yelling 'oh crap'. Nicely done, by the way."

Elly bowed. "Thank you. I tried my most theatrical exclamation. Followed by my most athletic hauling of butt."

Tee laughed. "Thank goodness for the bush-covered parks at the ends of these lanes. Otherwise, they'd have found us. Speaking of which, we need to keep going. Mind you, I'm not sure I'm right. I mean, there are eight more rows to go."

"And half that last row looked like empty villas."

Nodding, Tee turned around. "Are we missing something? I figure he would have left us a sign. Something." She bowed her head. "Something to say that he believed we were coming for him."

Elly's eyes lit up and hands raised in the air. "Oh!"

"What?" asked Tee.

She started bouncing.

Tee took Elly's hands and leaned towards her with a piercing gaze. "More talking, less bouncing."

"Tee, I think there was something faint marked on a door back there."

"Which row?"

"I'm not sure... maybe the third?" said Elly.

———————

Tee and Elly raced past the end of the lane and turned the corner to head for the second row when they slid to a stop.

"Oh crap," said Elly, again.

The two women guards pulled out their pistols and fired, their bullets bouncing off Tee's and Elly's cloaks.

"Through!" yelled Tee, running up and knocking over one of the guards.

Elly knocked over the other.

They raced up the lane, heads turning to look at the

villa doors.

"Stop!" yelled one of the guards shooting.

"No thanks, we're a little busy," said Tee.

Elly shook her head. "Not that one. Not that one. Come on, where's that door? I'm sure I saw it."

"Tee?" said a voice.

They skidded to a stop.

"Who said that?" asked Tee.

"Up here," said Sam, crouched down on the roof of a villa.

"Tee, that's the door!" said Elly, pointing at the same villa.

Its door opened.

"Tee?"

"Grandpapa!" Tee ran at Nikolas, nearly tackling him with a hug. Papers scattered everywhere.

"Inside, Elly. Quickly. I'll lead the guards away and then will double back. Give me a couple of minutes," said Sam.

Elly ran to the villa. Seeing the papers all over the floor, she leaped, landing on the chair and nearly knocking it over. "Ah! Yesh."

Nikolas closed the door.

"I can't believe it's you. My Tee!" he said, squeezing her upper arms. "And you, Elly! How did you girls get so big?"

"I think it was last Thursday. Lots of rain," she said with a nervous undertone to her voice.

Nikolas took off his spectacles and rubbed his eyes. "I

cannot believe this. It is like a miracle."

"I have to ask," said Tee.

There was a firm knock at the door.

They all froze.

Nikolas waved at the girls to go up the stairs, and walked over to the door.

"Has anyone come in here, Herr Klaus?" asked one of the guards in clear Brunne.

"You want to come on?" he replied, touching his lips. "No cookies for the baskets, though."

The other guard snapped her fingers in front of Nikolas' face. "Did you see two Yellow Hoods?"

He frowned and shook his head.

"Thank you."

He closed the door.

"They know you speak Brunne?" asked Tee, coming down the stairs.

"She's a smart one, that one. I overheard her telling her colleague about her own grandfather, how he responded better when spoken to in Brunne. So, I figured I would do the same, yes?"

Tee smiled. "So, you've pretended to be an old man who's lost his mind?"

Nikolas nodded. "It wasn't the fun that I expected."

"I'm not sure about that," said Elly. "Did you cover a guard in... ah, poop?"

Nikolas started laughing. "Did you see him?"

"That's how we found you," said Tee.

"Yes!" said Nikolas, his hands in triumphant fists.

There was another knock at the door, followed by a second knock.

Nikolas opened the door, and Sam rushed in.

"They'll double-back soon, I'm sure," said Sam, huffing and puffing. "I'm too old for this."

"You're doing great," said Tee.

He smiled at her. "Your lying's getting better. You almost believe that, don't you?"

Tee smiled. "You're doing great."

Sam stood up and peeked out the window. "I'll keep an eye out while you get caught up. After they pass by here again, then we'll make our move." He checked his pocket watch. "Or after five minutes, whichever is first."

Nikolas gave Sam a pat on the shoulder.

"You're welcome," said Sam over his shoulder.

"Oh, I have something for you," said Tee sliding off her backpack. She reached into a side pouch.

Nikolas stopped her. "What marvel is this?" he asked, pointing at her grapnel armband.

"I made it in Kar'm. Before it was destroyed."

"Kar'm has been destroyed? What is this?" Nikolas covered his mouth, his face dropping.

"You've missed a lot of fun," said Sam.

"Anyway, this is nothing," said Tee.

"Nothing?" interrupted Elly. "She's made several

editions, all of it from memory of what you'd made for Franklin."

Nikolas brightened up. "Oh? Where is that boy?"

"Hopefully dying in the bottom of a ditch being eaten by spiders," said Elly, forcing a smile.

Sam raised a hand, his eyes still focused on the lane outside. "Ah, remember when I said you missed a lot? That's part of the lot."

"Ah." Nikolas scratched his head.

"Anyway, I saved this from your home in Minette," said Tee, presenting him with the framed picture of her grandmother. Her eyes welled up. "I remembered how you always said that home was anywhere with you, me, and Grandmama."

Nikolas held it, tears rolling down his face and disappearing into his white beard. "You…" He grabbed her, squeezed, and planted a kiss on her forehead.

"I don't know what you're saying, I don't speak Brunne," said Tee. "And you're choking me."

"Sorry," said Nikolas, letting her go.

Sam knocked on the door. "Time's up."

"Oh, I have keys!" Nikolas tossed papers off his table until he found what he was looking for. "I don't know what they are for, but I took them off a helpful guard. They'll help us, yes?"

"Maybe," said Sam. "Okay, here's the—wait." He went back to the window. "Ah, things just got a bit more complicated. Soldiers just walked by."

"What does that mean?" asked Elly.

"That means that things are going yigging wrong, bit by bit." He looked at Tee and made a guilty face.

"I say worse," said Tee.

"I can vouch for that," added Elly.

Tee took a swipe at Elly, who blocked it.

Sam lowered his head and gently scratched his forehead. "With all the royals and people of import around, tension is high. Security is paramount. One of those explosions wasn't mine."

"Where did you get the explosives?" asked Tee.

He shrugged. "I went shopping." Opening his eyes, he pointed at Nikolas. "The best I can figure is I'll take Nikolas. We'll go to the south of the villas, cut across the parks and run up the western fence wall to the gate."

Tee wiped her lips.

"Wait, what's the other part of the plan?" asked Elly. "I'm missing something."

With a sigh, Tee turned to her. "You and I need to get out of here and make our way back to camp, or at least stay out of trouble until Sam can come back for us."

He nodded. "Sorry, but if anyone realizes that the person they have here is *the* Nikolas Klaus, things are going to get a thousand times worse. Trust me when I say that my gut is turning inside out at the thought of anything happening to you girls, but Eleanor's left us in a real tight spot."

Tee stared at him.

Sam looked at her then away. A few seconds later, he looked at her again. "What?"

"We're going to be okay. We're Yellow Hoods."

"You need to leave those here."

Elly recoiled. "What? Why? They're bulletproof."

"Yes, but I'm sure the word is already out to look for any Yellow Hoods, and frankly, there aren't any others."

Tee and Elly took them off.

"Oh, I have some red ones," said Nikolas, heading up the stairs.

"Do we want to ask where he got them from?" asked Elly.

Tee and Sam shook their heads.

Sam pulled at his beard. "I don't like this plan, but I don't have a better one."

"I do not like this plan. They are just little girls," said Nikolas.

"We'll be okay," said Tee. "What about contacting Amami?"

Sam shook his head. "That only works when it's dark. I have a flare hidden under the cart. This is the plan we've got. We all run south; then you girls break east, and we'll break west." He peeked out the window. "Ready?"

Tee and Elly finished attaching their red hoods. They both gave him two fingers up.

"Good luck."

Passing the last villa, Sam, Nikolas and Elly arrived at the park.

"Good luck," said Sam as he and Nikolas turned westward.

"Where's Tee?" said Elly, spinning around.

Tee was standing, her shock-sticks out, fighting a soldier.

"That girl will take on the world by herself, given half a chance." Elly headed to join the fight.

"Sam, we can't leave the girls to fight," said Nikolas.

"Go!" yelled Elly over her shoulder.

Sam grabbed his fellow grandfather's arm. "They are warriors now. You'll laugh when I tell you what they did at Kar'm, but for now, we have to go."

Nikolas nodded, and they left.

As the soldier dropped to the ground, twitching as electricity arced over his body, Elly arrived.

An explosion went off in the distance to the east.

"What was that?" asked Elly.

"More trouble. Do you hear those?"

Elly scrunched her face and listened. "It sounds like gongs. Why do they have gongs sounding?"

"Maybe it's a way of warning everyone in the city." Tee looked around.

"Soldiers are going to be everywhere," said Elly. "So

where won't they be?"

She and Tee looked at each other.

Tee pointed a shock-stick at Elly. "The keep."

Elly tilted her head. "Excuse me?"

"That place was already guarded as much as possible. So if the city's going to pieces, they'll probably lose guards and soldiers to help protect the city. At the very least, to fetch important people and bring them back. So, as they're going out—"

"We go in," finished Elly.

They started to run.

"You know that's crazy."

"Absolutely," said Tee.

CHAPTER THIRTY-TWO

LIDDEL VALUE

Silskin picked a peach out from one of the many baskets on the cart. He glanced about the mostly deserted market, where only the bravest or most stubborn seemed to be out. The gongs were banging away in the distance in every direction. Despite having checked several times, his eyes were drawn up to the sky and its few clouds.

"This is too much," said the woman, holding out his gold coin. She had brown cloth wrapped around her head, and her skin was darker than most of the merchants around. Her face had a gentle beauty to it.

"You kept me fed when I was hiding in the alleyways and abandon buildings."

She stared at him.

"You don't recognize me?"

She shook her head. "My memory is not very good."

"Hmm. Well, you treated me like a person, you treated me with respect, and I didn't do anything to deserve it," he said, squinting at her.

"I help everyone. Everyone I can." She waved the coin

at him. "This is too much."

He stared at her. "It is the wrong amount, isn't it?" He reached into his pocket and took several more. He put them in her hand and gently closed it. "I rarely do the right thing, but let this be one of them."

She frowned at him.

"Allow me to buy some forgiveness for my past deeds."

Taking her handful of money, she shook her head at him. "You are very weird."

Silskin walked away, pulling his new beige-and-brown robes up so as not to scrape along the dirt road. Several blocks away, he stopped at an abandoned building.

"Hello Ron-Paul," said a voice from behind him.

With a heavy sigh, he nodded to himself and turned around. "I was wondering if we would run into each other again, Eleanor."

She was standing in the middle of the side street, the Candlestick Maker's cane in one hand. The embroidery on her black cloak was catching the afternoon light. "You shouldn't have gotten involved, Ron-Paul. You've created a problem for me."

"I'm sorry to hear that," he said, licking his lips and glancing about the market. "I was going to enjoy my peach and the rest of the afternoon."

He stepped to the side, but she stepped in front of him again. He looked up at the sky. "Why are you here, Eleanor? I won't even ask why you're doing Caterina's bidding now. I guess your involvement was one more secret she was keeping from me."

"My plans are my own. You were always an irritant, but I could accept it in the background. However right now, you've caused some much-unappreciated upheaval."

He nodded. "Are you to kill me? Is that it?"

"Marcus' trial is collapsing, and they are considering holding one against Caterina."

"Are they? Well, I can't say that I'd feel bad about that," said Silskin. "Now may I go?"

She came within a yard of him.

Silskin shook his head. "I always thought you wanted to take down Caterina, not help her. I guess with Anna Maucher working unconsciously for Marcus, and you for Caterina, that makes Sam the only one who was working for the Tub. Poor fellow."

Eleanor pointed her cane at him. "I need your witness to disappear."

"What, now? The city will be locked down tighter than a miser's last coin."

"I heard that you already had a merchant smuggle Liddel to a nearby village." Her stare was icy cold. "Clever move, keeping him close but unable to run into accidentally."

"With him gone, he can't be called to give his testimony against Caterina. But without him, I could lose my stipend."

Eleanor hit the cane on the ground, bringing out the two sharp spikes and making it crackle with electricity. "A fair trade for your life, wouldn't you say?"

He looked down at his clothes. "I was starting to enjoy a new station, but I guess it wasn't meant to be."

Hitting the cane again, Eleanor turned to go. "Oh, tell me, how did you find Liddel?"

A politician's smirk crossed Silskin's lips. "A man of my experience and connections has a way of finding his way back into the world."

Eleanor nodded and left.

After she was out of sight, he leaned his head against a wall, swallowing hard. Nodding to himself, he pushed off and headed back to a shop beside the peach merchant.

"I need to send a message," said Silskin, picking up a nectarine.

The man frowned at him. "But you're holding a peach in the other hand. How can I trust a man who holds two opposing fruit? Do you even know where your loyalties lie?"

Silskin took a coin out and hit the man in the forehead with it. He glanced about to make sure no one was paying attention.

The man bent down and picked it up. "That's no way to treat a friend."

"I want you to send a message. I need to clear the board so that I can play whatever pieces I'm dealt. You know the man I had you smuggle out?"

The merchant pretended to think about it and then nodded. "Yeah, the chicken guy."

"Chikahn, yes. Tell him to go spread his word if he wishes. His work is done here."

"And this?" asked the merchant showing the coin.

"Payment for my conscience."

CHAPTER THIRTY-THREE

Looks Like

"Up ahead!" yelled Elly as she and Tee ran towards the northern gate. "What are those two soldiers trying to do?"

"They're trying to lock it," said Tee. "If they do, we'll be trapped in here."

"Hey!" yelled Elly, waving her arms at the soldiers who were fifty yards away. "I wish we'd found where my grandmother had hidden my shock-sticks."

Tee offered her one of the two she had in hand.

Elly shook her head and tapped her belt-pouch. "I still have a few throwing weights."

The soldiers turned and faced the girls. They were wearing shiny breastplates with the Belnian emblem stamped on them. At their sides, they each had a pistol and a short sword.

"Ah... we don't have cloaks, and they have guns," said Tee. "I'll flank them. You distract them. Don't get shot." Tee poured on the speed as she broke away from Elly.

Elly nodded and slowed down. She waved at the soldiers again, who stared at her and then at each other.

"That's it, be all confused," she whispered.

"How did you get in here?" one of the soldiers demanded of Elly.

"Stop!" the other one shouted at Tee who was now running right at them. He drew his pistol and pointed right at her. His colleague immediately did the same thing, pointing his pistol at Elly.

"Halt!" they yelled.

Staring at the barrel of the classic flintlock, Elly felt her heart stop. She tripped and fell to the ground. Her pouch of throwing weights emptied out everywhere.

"Get up, Elly!" Tee pointed her armband at one of the soldiers and pulled its smaller lever.

The soldiers ducked as the grapnel shot passed them and hit the gate. Their eyes followed the long, black cable all the way back to Tee.

As one soldier turned his pistol on Tee, the other let out a loud grunt as Elly's weights hit him in the stomach. He fell on all fours.

Tee tossed a shock-stick over to Elly, who was on one knee. Her face was scratched up, and she had a nasty scowl. Throwing her other shock-stick at one of the guards as a distraction, Tee jumped in the air and activated her armband. She raced through the air and knocked a guard clear off his feet and into the gate.

Elly nailed the other guard with the shock-stick. "I didn't realize you could use your armband thing that way."

"Neither did I," said Tee, unhooking the grapnel. "Help me gather this up properly. You never know when we'll need it again."

Elly surveyed the two guards. "Yeah, we probably have a few minutes."

"Are you okay?" asked Tee. "You've got this weird angry, scared thing going on."

"I'm fine," said Elly. "I just tripped, made me mad."

"Elly?"

She looked at Tee. "What?

"Why are you holding the guard's pistol?"

Elly furrowed her brow and then looked where Tee was pointing. Her head slowly shook from side to side. "I don't know."

"You should drop it," said Tee, coiling the cable properly into her backpack.

Elly flexed her hand around the pistol's grip.

"You kicked butt. You did a great job, but we don't need that," said Tee.

She stared at it and then nodded. "Yes, you're right."

Tee closed her backpack and watched as Elly hesitantly put the pistol on the ground. "Everything okay?"

Elly's face was a mix of emotions, but then she brought it all together and nodded.

"Good, because we better get moving," said Tee. "I'm going to guess that this northern route ends up at the keep, because it's in that direction."

As they passed the gate, Elly glanced back at the pistol.

"That's all of my coins," said Tee as they snuck out of the laundry area and into an empty corridor. The walls were a plain white plaster and the floor tiles an uninspired grey.

"I'm surprised how easily those servants were convinced to help us." Elly looked at the plain clothes they'd been given. "Feels weird to be wearing stuff on top of my clothes, though."

"The more I see of the world, the more I feel that a lot of people aren't treated very fairly."

Elly shook her head. "Why can't the world be more like Minette?"

"Maybe that's why they burned it to the ground?" Tee pointed at some stairs.

With a confirming nod from Elly, they carefully went up the spiral staircase.

"Look at the paintings on the wall and the shiny floor tiles," said Elly. She leaned forward. "I hear people."

Tee climbed another set of stairs.

After several minutes of walking down corridors, ignored by every guard and person they passed, they stopped at a large receiving area. There was an open set of double doors, with light and excited voices coming from the room beyond them.

"I wonder what's going on in there," said Tee.

"Looks like important people. They're all dressed

colorfully. I've never seen so many shades of skin color before; it's amazing. Do you see that woman who looks like plaster? And that man who looks like midnight? Wow. Is that what the world's like?" wondered Elly.

"There are a lot of guards in there."

"I only see a few people in armor," said Elly.

Tee pointed. "Look at their eyes."

"Ah, got it. Wow, there's quite a few unarmored guards in there."

"What are you two doing here?" boomed a female voice from behind them.

Tee and Elly spun around and stared up at a very annoyed, very stern-looking woman. "We don't have need of any laundry maids here, particularly not juniors. Get back to the washing room, or I'll have you fired—or worse."

"Yes ma'am," said Tee and Elly in unison.

They watched as the women left.

"Let's watch from the corridor there," said Tee.

Elly followed, and they lurked in the shadows for a while.

"We should find an empty room or something, a place to hide until we can sneak back into the city," said Tee.

"I thought the whole point was to hide in here."

Tee shook her head at Elly. "We come in here when they're all out there looking for whoever set off the other explosions; then we leave here when it's dark so that Sam can find us."

"Right, that makes sense," said Elly. "I don't know why I just keep feeling weird. Like Eleanor's in my head, distracting me."

"Come on, let's go before someone else comes along," said Tee.

Elly grabbed her arm. "Look, that guy's dressed like Alex."

"That's because he's my uncle."

CHAPTER THIRTY-FOUR

THE ROYAL SOON

Zelda stepped into the room from the hidden side door and closed it immediately behind her.

Caterina was in the process of pinning something on her map. She glared at Zelda, pins in her mouth.

"The King is coming. He'll be here in a few minutes. There have been explosions going on around the city."

Completing her task, Caterina put the rest of the pins down. "And he's coming straight here?"

She nodded. "I'll start straightening up the parlor?"

"Yes," said Caterina, tapping her forehead with her fingers. "I misjudged how high I've pushed their level of suspicion. I need to come up with a plan." She looked down at her common and comfortable clothes. "I need to change as well."

A few minutes later, she walked out of the bedroom, pulling at the edges of the short jacket and blouse she'd put on.

"The dark red skirt with that beige-and-red jacket was a good choice," said Zelda.

There was a strong pounding on the main door.

"How's my hair?"

"Regal enough."

"Good." She closed her eyes and thought. "I'm not giving these idiots any opportunity to pull apart my arguments and threats because of it."

Zelda closed the door to the map room.

Caterina fingers twiddled in the air, her eyes still closed.

"Shall I receive them?" asked Zelda.

She shook her head and raised a finger. "Where are the Skyfallers?"

"Four are at the end of the rail line—two hours' flight given typical wind. A fifth is en route, about four hours away," replied Zelda as another pounding came at the door.

"Good. Let them in." Caterina tugged on her white sleeves and then the edge of her red-and-cream jacket.

Zelda opened the door, offering the king and his two armed guards a polite smile. "My apologies for the delay, Your Majesty. We were in the far chamber."

He glared at Zelda and stepped into the room.

"Your Majesty, what a delightful surprise," said Caterina. She gestured to the balcony. "I've seen plumes of smoke rising. I hope that everything's okay."

"We must speak," said the King. He pointed at Zelda. "Leave."

Zelda turned to Caterina.

"Would you mind fetching me something to eat, Zelda?

I've been working so intensely that it slipped my mind."

"Yes, Regent Caterina," Zelda replied, her eyes fixed on the King's. "Your Majesty." She left, closing the doors behind her.

Caterina motioned to the round table and set of high-backed chairs with a view of the open balcony. "I do have to say once again, thank you for such excellent accommodations."

The King brushed off her remarks. "I am certain these explosions are your doing, are they not? Retribution for the panel considering to acquit Marcus? You realize that you're only making things worse for yourself, don't you?"

She flashed a fake smile and then sat down, her eyes sweeping about the room. "It would be crude, don't you think, for me to do such a thing? Could I? Yes, absolutely. But, you see, this is exactly the problem that I warned you about."

"Do you think me an idiot?" asked the king.

"Idiot? No." She tapped her lips with a finger. "Incapable of making a decision related to power or control over your country? Almost."

"Excuse me?"

"Your Prime Minister. I've been saying this for a decade, and while it's okay to have philosophical differences, here's where practicality matters. You can be here and bluster all you want, but you are simply the figurehead, Your Majesty," she said, her eyes forcing him to take a step back.

Pointing out the window, Caterina shook her head. "You can yell and threaten, but in the end, you can't do anything without your Prime Minister. And she, in turn, is limited by what she can do without a vote in parliament. And, if I'm correct, parliament has been suspended during the trial. Hmm, that's problematic."

The King scratched his face, his gaze shifting from her to the floor and back.

"I have something for you," she said, getting up and opening the door to the map room. A moment later she returned with a piece of paper, closing the door behind her. She walked over and handed it to him.

"What's this?"

"It's an official amendment for the Book of Royals," she said, touching the cuffs of her blouse. "To both correct my name and grant me official status as rightful Queen."

"For Staaten and Elizabetina? You annexed Elizabetina!"

"Did I? I could have sworn that I saved them from a ruthless rebellion. Huh, funny how facts change."

The King glanced at the agreement. "How... how did you get four signatures? How on Eorth did you get the Frelish to sign? You pushed them into a civil war that's left them nearly bankrupt!"

Caterina shook her head. "Again, how facts change— but there's the signature. Four of the five that I need. I believe that a pact protecting Relna, in exchange for your signature, would be mutually beneficial. Don't you think?"

She smiled at him.

"Ha." The King threw the paper on the table. "Didn't you just finish lecturing me about my lack of legal power?" He walked away, his back to her. "And for what? So that you can have an idle reign? You have no children. What good is a kingdom without legacy?" He turned and glared at her. "Is your ego truly that large?"

Caterina walked over to one of the paintings on the far wall. "Just like the reason why I brought this from my home, my reasons are important only to me. And looking outside at the plumes of smoke rising above your city and thinking of the number of powerful guests under your protection, I worry. I'm worried, Your Majesty, that everything is about to unravel and you'll have a siege on your keep, on your reign, and on your legacy."

The King did his best to hide the chill that ran down his spine.

"When I took over Staaten, we had an uprising that was ugly and brutal, but I put it down. You don't have to like my methods, but if I may offer some advice from your smaller neighbor, never underestimate your opponent."

Bursting into laughter, the King shook his head. "Ah, Caterina, you speak a good game, I will grant you that. And I believe wholeheartedly that you are behind this, or at best,"—he shook a finger at her—"at best, you know who's behind this. Never forget that Belnia is the military dragon of the continent. Everyone quickly forgets what we are like, because we have been peaceful for a long time, but there's a reason why the trial was to be held here. It wasn't convenience; It wasn't tradition, it was fear, pure and simple. If the dragon awakens, then there will be a wrath unleashed that will burn the neighboring countries to the ground."

He picked up her paper and threw it on the floor, laughing. "Do you think it genuinely wise to threaten me? We have tolerated your little pretend reign on our edge. But never think for a moment that you have anything to offer."

She forced a grimace.

The King opened the door.

"You know," said Caterina, her tone forcing him to turn around. "I have half a mind to leave that paper right there so that I can savor the moment when you have to bend down to pick it up. Have a good day, Your Majesty. I'm sure we'll be talking soon."

CHAPTER THIRTY-FIVE

GREATER GOOD

"Alex? What are you doing here?" asked Tee, walking over to him.

His hair was cut short, and he was wearing a new, blue, long coat with silver buttons and a crisp, high-collar, white shirt. The buckles on his black boots sparkled in the light. Tucked under his arm was the well-worn, brown book he'd had since Kar'm.

Alex frowned at Tee. "I was reunited with my uncle. But you knew that; why didn't you come?"

"What are you talking about?" said Tee and Elly together.

"Eleanor DeBoeuf said that when the signal came for all of us to head here, she'd have us under the protection of my uncle." He stared at the girls. "She said she'd briefed both of you."

"Ah, not even close," said Tee, shaking her head.

Elly put her hand up. "I thought you said your uncle was dead?"

"That's what I was led to believe, but Eleanor showed

me a letter that proved otherwise. I didn't want to trust her, but I knew I had to see for myself."

"Since when did you start calling her Eleanor?" asked Tee.

"Since my station was restored and I have the right," said Alex, irritated.

"What are you talking about?" Tee looked at Elly, who shrugged. "We thought you'd abandoned us. Eleanor stole nearly everything from camp, except some food and the prototype you guys were working on."

"I'd like to have that back, actually," said Alex. "My uncle is quite interested in my work." He tapped the book at his side.

Alex stroked his chin. "Now, the matter that more concerns me is what you two are doing here dressed as maids. It doesn't surprise me that the Butcher was playing games. My uncle has always said that the Tub cannot be trusted."

The girls stared at him.

"You're doing something for the Baker, aren't you? Can't see what they're doing to you?" Alex took in a deep breath. "You need to come with me, to my uncle. Turn yourselves in, and we can get this sorted out. Most likely we can get you returned home, in time."

Elly leaped forward and grabbed Alex by his collar. "Why are you talking like that? What's wrong with you? We're your friends."

Alex slapped her hands off. "Who do you think you are? You don't touch a prince."

"Prince?" said Tee, throwing up her hands. "Come on Elly, let's go."

"No," said Alex, his voice firm and deeper than usual.

Elly looked at him over her shoulder. "Excuse me?"

"I couldn't save you when I came aboard that airship, Tee, but I am going to do so now. Those explosions throughout the city, the assassination attempt on Marcus—all of this has to stop."

"We had nothing to do with that," said Tee, her face going red.

Alex gripped his notebook tightly. "I honestly believe you're a good person deep down, Tee. You're just misguided. I'm doing this for your own good," he said. "Guards! We have intruders!"

Elly grabbed Tee by the arm, and they bolted across the open area, through a short corridor, and up a set of stairs.

———

Elly leaned against the wall in the dimly lit hallway. "Who has marble floors and walls?"

"There aren't many doors, and guessing how all these lanterns on the wall are turned down to half, maybe they're bedrooms. Important-people bedrooms. Let's try that door over there," said Tee, looking at the dark forms of the mahogany doors and their shiny silver knobs.

"Shh, I hear someone coming." Elly moved her head about. "Is that coming from in front of us or from behind?"

Tee shook her head. "I've still got half a mind to double back and knock some sense into Alex."

"It's from in front. Let's head back to that other stairwell we saw. I think there was a door there we didn't try."

They carefully crept through the corridor and arrived at the door.

Elly bounced nervously as Tee took her time in turning the knob.

Taking a breath, Tee gently pushed the door open. She motioned for Elly to take a peek.

Shrugging, they looked at each other.

"What's that over there?" said a guard.

Tee and Elly rushed into the dark room, only the moon gleaming through the open balcony offering any light. There was a silhouette standing by the shining glass doors of the balcony.

Elly banged into something. "What the—?"

There was a crash of dishes and the sound of something metallic hitting the floor and sliding.

"Who's there?" said a silhouette, cranking up a lantern beside him.

Tee and Elly shielded their eyes.

Holding the lantern was a tall, white-haired, old man in a white shirt and black vest. He was wearing an eyepatch over one eye. "Eleanor!"

Tee and Elly turned to see Eleanor DeBoeuf in a black cloak, broken dishes all around her.

Just then the door burst open. Three guards rushed into the room, all in ceremonial armor. One was more elaborately decorated than the rest.

Tee glanced about and then froze. At Elly's feet was a black-and-silver pistol with a long barrel.

Elly followed her gaze and burst into a sweat. "Get out of here!" she yelled at Tee.

"Stop her!" shouted Marcus, pointing at Eleanor as she slipped right past the captain of the guards and out of the room.

"Grab the blond girl!" said the Captain, not noticing Tee.

Elly held Tee's gaze and motioned to the balcony with her head.

Her eyes welling up, Tee darted past everyone and fired the grapnel of her armband. A moment later, she was gone out the balcony.

"Are you hurt, Lord Pieman?" asked the Captain.

"Why didn't you go after Eleanor DeBoeuf?" he asked, his face red.

"Who?" replied the Captain.

"The woman who was here trying to assassinate me!"

The guards hauled Elly away. "We have the woman. You say her name's Eleanor DeBoeuf? Thank you. Have a good night."

CHAPTER THIRTY-SIX

PLANS MADE AND UNFOLDING

Richy slowly folded the last of the dozen letters and put it on top of the pile beside him. He stared at the ground, shaking his head. His face was slack; his eyes, distant.

Amami put her tools down carefully one by one, making sure to line them all up correctly. She turned down the crank lanterns on the work table and silently walked over to the inviting campfire to join Richy.

She warmed her hands and looked about at the late darkening sky. "I had not noticed how quickly the temperature lowers each afternoon."

Richy gestured to the letters. "I read most of them. Did you read these?"

She shook her head.

"Right, of course not," said Richy. "Did you know the Butcher sent this Mister Jenny guy to hunt down Bakon and Egelina-Marie? That Tee's father was sending requests for help to fight the slavers from Kabaan?"

Amami ran a hand through her long, black hair. "Some of it I knew, but I could do nothing about it for I was not supposed to know."

"Did you ever act on anything that you weren't supposed to know?" asked Richy in frustration.

She looked at him and then the fire.

"Oh, for me..."

She nodded. Amami pulled her hair into a ponytail. "My life hasn't been simple, but it is getting better." She smiled at him. "I have been given opportunities that few can dream and have lived through moments..." She fell silent. Hesitantly, she reached out and held his hand. "All that is important is that we are family."

There was a rustling in the bushes.

Amami drew a sword off her back and squinted at the darkness.

"Where did that come from?" yelled Richy, staring at the sword. "Is that why you've got that bulky blouse?"

"Richy! It is good to see you," said Nikolas stepping into the clearing.

He turned around. "Monsieur Klaus? Your beard is huge."

Nikolas laughed as Richy came over and gave him a firm handshake. "You have no idea how good it is to see you, Monsieur Klaus."

"Hello Amami," said Sam, warming his hands at the fire. He frowned at the pile of letters. "What are these?"

She looked at Richy.

"Ah… I found them in the King's-Horse," said Richy. "I think Madame DeBoeuf may have forgotten them after she went on a ride. I read them."

Staring at Amami, Sam picked them up. "Did you?"

Richy walked over. "I believe they were all meant for you, and they're all recent. Some seemed like people have tried several times to contact you."

Sam grumbled. He slapped the letters. "Thanks for finding them," he said, giving Amami a sideways glance. "Have Tee and Elly returned yet?"

Amami shook her head.

"That's troubling. Richy, would you be so kind as to make a bed for Nikolas? I have some supplies just at the edge of the clearing over there. I need to read these letters."

"I can tell you what a bunch of them say," offered Richy.

He smiled and shook his head. "Most of the letters will be written in code, allowing for hidden messages. Sometimes people will write one thing, but mean the opposite. I need to read them myself."

"Oh, okay," replied Richy.

Amami looked up to see Nikolas standing beside her.

"I am Tee's grandfather. My name is Nikolas Klaus, yes? And you are?"

"That's my sister," said Richy, a huge smile on his face.

"Excuse me?"

"My sister, Amami," repeated Richy.

"A sister? Hmm, this is something I knew nothing of."

Amami stood up, studying the old man's face. "You are from Brunne, are you not?"

He nodded, cleaning his glasses on his shirt. "Yes, a long time ago." Putting his glasses back on, he smiled at her. "I did not know Richy had a sister, hmm?"

"When he was three, Marcus Pieman took him from us. My mother and I created the airship they wanted, but they never returned him. I found him in a jail in Wosa."

"Wosa?" said Nikolas turning to Richy.

"I told you, you missed a lot, Nikolas," said Sam, crumpling up another letter and tossing it into the fire. "I can't believe this."

Richy pointed at the makeshift worktable. "You should see what she's helped us make. We started trying to remake the rocket-packs, but we didn't have the stuff for the propulsion so now they're more like glider wings."

"Oh, may I see?" asked Nikolas, his face lighting up.

"And you have to see her King's-Horse. It's unbelievable."

Nikolas froze, his gaze shifting to Amami.

Richy continued. "Yeah, it's a mechanical horse and it goes faster than anything I've ever seen. Well, except for the rocket-cart. Monsieur Klaus?"

Nikolas closed his eyes and pinched the bridge of his nose. "This King's-Horse, it is Christina Creangle's, yes?"

Amami shook her head. "I have heard of the Creangles,

but I have never met them."

"Are you okay?" asked Richy. "You look kind of upset."

"No, I am fine. Thank you," replied Nikolas, waving him off. He folded his arms, his chin leaning on a fist. "The King's-Horse, where did you get it?"

Amami bowed her head. "I made it."

Nikolas wagged a finger. "No. This is not an explanation, no. They were all destroyed. All save the one that Christina has and the one I took apart for its engine long ago."

"Actually, Nikolas, she built it from spare parts and ruined King's-Horses the Tub collected long ago. She has a gift for it, like you and Christophe did," said Sam, looking up, his jaw clenched.

Amami narrowed her eyes and stood up. "How do you know so much about them?"

"Because Christophe and I made them, long again. The height of our genius, yes?" Nikolas' hands shook. "So long ago."

She took a breath and stepped back. "You… you are the Brunne-Man."

Both Sam and Nikolas looked at her.

"Where did you hear this name?" asked Nikolas.

"I read it on the inside of one of the MCM engines. There were two signatures."

"And it still works?"

Amami lowered her gaze. "I am honored to meet you.

And yes, it does, though I had to fix it."

Nikolas walked away. "If you were able to, then maybe Marcus' statue was real," he muttered to himself.

After a sigh, he looked over at Amami. "I apologize, my child," he said coming over and taking her hand. "I am a rude old man. You have done a marvelous thing, and I am the one who is honored. Would you show it to me?"

Amami face broke into a huge smile.

"She can smile like that?" said Richy.

"Yig!" yelled Sam, throwing the rest of the letters into the fire.

Everyone turned to look at him.

"You are worried," said Amami.

"I am." Sam's face twitched. "Abeland Pieman sent a coded message that was intercepted and copied for me. He's coming with three airships; the rest have been destroyed. And it appears Caterina has more than a dozen Skyfallers around the city or on the way." He shook his head. "This situation is going to get very nasty, very quickly."

Amami clenched her fists. "The Piemans have lost all of their Hotarus?"

"Apparently all but three, yes." Sam watched the fire.

A dark, satisfied smile crossed her lips.

"Are you planning on getting revenge for Marcus Pieman killing Dad? Because revenge doesn't solve anything," said Richy.

She stared at him, her eye twitching. "I made peace with our father's death. But the Hotarus are our responsibility, and I will not have pain and suffering be our family's legacy."

"It looks like our problems have already arrived." Sam pointed at the city down below.

Nikolas squinted. "Against the moon, what is this?"

"That's a Skyfaller," said Sam.

"Do you think the Butcher knew about all of this?" asked Richy.

Sam turned to him. "Eleanor is many things, but I doubt there's any way she'd support this. This is a problem because now the city will be more heavily locked down. No hoods or anyone else are going to be able to get in or out."

"What about Tee and Elly?" asked Nikolas.

In a blink, Sam vanished.

"What do we do?" asked Richy. "We need to help them."

Amami nodded. "We do, but how do we get in?"

"You're stealthy. Can't you just find a way in?"

She offered Richy a half-smile. "We need a better way."

Nikolas walked over to the table. "Hmm. If one cannot walk into the city, how about flying in?"

Amami joined him.

"Dropping from one of those, yes?" Nikolas pointed at the Skyfaller.

"There's another one," said Richy.

"Yes. I presume there will be many? And do these things land for fuel or some change?"

Amami nodded. "We will need to make changes to the wings. They will need to glide better."

Nikolas laughed and rubbed his hands together. "It has been a long time since I had to do such a thing away from my workshop. This shall be fun, yes?"

Amami smiled.

"Get out of the way," yelled the King of Belnia at Zelda who was blocking the doors to Caterina's quarters.

Zelda was standing with her legs shoulder-width apart, her hands behind her back, and her head bowed and eyes closed. Her elegant white, leather armor looked brand new. Metal plates protected strategic areas and were free of scratches and dents. A white hilt peeked out from behind one thigh, while the grip of some form of pistol hinted itself out from behind the other.

Opening her eyes, she gazed at the King, the Prime Minister, and the small delegation behind them. "What brings such a prestigious lot to the Regent?" she asked coldly.

"We demand to see Regent Catherine this instant," said the Prime Minister, her face distorted in rage. "How dare she make such a declaration of war upon our country? Upon the entire continent? Does she not realize that this act is against every one of the families and nations under our protection?"

Zelda's eyes darted through the crowd, noting which ones were cheering in support and which ones stood in uncomfortable silence. "There is no Regent Catherine here. However, if you would like to speak with Regent Caterina, I'm sure I can arrange for her to see you."

"Get her out of the way," said the King to one of the guards.

As the guard went to lay a hand on Zelda, she tilted to one side and kicked the side of his knee. The man crumpled to the ground, screaming.

"Now," said Zelda, scratching the side of her mouth. "Would you like an audience with Regent Caterina? Because, if you would, she's in the royal meeting room downstairs. She's been there for some time."

"Just waiting out in the open?" asked the Prime Minister.

"She has nothing to hide, and I believe you'll find that she's acting to protect all of your guests. A task that you seem to be failing to do." Zelda avoided the Prime Minister's gaze.

There was a confused muttering as people started heading out.

"Downstairs everyone," said the King, making his way to the front of the crowd.

"You and your false Regent won't survive the year," said the Prime Minister, her finger in Zelda's face.

Zelda smiled, her expression devoid of malice or anger. "And I believe your career won't survive the night."

CHAPTER THIRTY-SEVEN

RECIPE FOR A PIEMAN

The prison door groaned as it opened, light cutting away the darkness.

Elly lifted her head from knees. She'd been a tight ball in the corner of her cell for the past two hours. Her nose wrinkled at the pungent damp of the dungeon.

A beam of light swung as two forms came to stand before the rusted bars of her cell.

She shielded her eyes.

"Put the stool there," said a deep, commanding voice. "And that will be all."

After a moment of hesitation, a set of footfalls return to the prison door, and closed it.

"My name is Marcus Pieman." He turned up the crank lantern. "I must say that we are fortunate. They deemed you such a threat that they put you here by yourself. Never mind that no one would believe that a man would want to speak with his assassin."

Elly squinted at him, her arms tightly around her legs.

"I saw you tell your friend to leave, and I saw the look on Eleanor's face. She recognized both of you." He wagged a finger at her. "But you in particular."

She turned her head away.

Marcus kicked a small box at his feet. "I've brought you a change of clothes and some food, in exchange for a few answers."

"Don't you think that this was part of my plan? I could stab you in the throat or something."

He smirked and shook his head. "Those that intend to do such things don't use phrases like 'or something.' Nor do their eyes hold fear and confusion, like yours do."

Marcus leaned back, his hands on his knees.

Elly lowered her head back onto the tops of her knees. Her hidden fists clenched tightly. "I know who you are. You're responsible for the death of my friend, Pierre DeMontagne."

"I've been responsible for a lot of things over the years. At my age, names are harder to hold on to, but that name doesn't ring a bell."

"It happened when Richelle Pieman kidnapped Anna Kundle Maucher, and you took Monsieur Klaus." She glared at him.

"Ah. You're one of the Yellow Hoods Richelle mentioned." He looked up at the ceiling. "So that means you're from Minette. You aren't Nikolas' granddaughter, as he told me her name." He smiled. "Thus, you must be Eleanor's granddaughter. How peculiar that you were the one to foil her plot to kill me."

Elly stared at him.

He reached into the box and pulled out a book. "Coming from such a small village, you don't know how the world works, I assume. With all the royals and ambassadors here, they are going to execute you."

"I didn't do anything wrong. I'll tell them, and they'll let me go."

Marcus frowned, touching his lips as he thought. "There is no justice, not at times like these and not for people like you. I will freely admit to having done things for which I should have received more retribution than I did. However, for a poor girl like yourself there is only ever the semblance of justice. The powerful will feel good about executing you. It will make them feel like they have done what needed to be done; despite the fact that they will all know it really did nothing."

Elly let go of her legs, extending then tucking them under her. "But that's not fair."

"No. In the grand scheme of things, it isn't. Yet if you look at the Grand Game, this is simply how it's played," said Marcus.

"My friend's going to come and get me. There's nothing she wouldn't do for me or me for her."

Waving his book at her, he smiled. "I feel the same way about my family. For them, I'm trying to salvage what I can of the game." He tapped the box with his foot again, drawing Elly's attention back to it. "I felt it was only right to give you a chance to redeem your life. Steer clear of your grandmother and her dealings, otherwise you'll end up dead like many who came before you."

Elly frowned. "Is that why they call her the Butcher?"

"One of the reasons," said Marcus. He held out his book.

She took it, running her fingers along the soft leather cover. "What's this?"

"You strike me as a smart young woman. It's a collection of thoughts about how the world works and how it should work. I wondered if I'd find someone who could understand." He placed the lantern right up against the bars and cranked it up. "About a half hour after I've left, the guards at the door will leave, and the door will be open. Read until then, if you like."

"I'd heard you were an evil man," said Elly as he stood up and walked away.

"Evil? No. I do nothing out of a simple desire to destroy or to improve my self-worth at the expense of others. No, I'm driven. Driven to give a better life to my family and my people. Driven to allow those who have been held under the thumbs of brutal kings and tyrants the chance to rule their own lives." He paused, the sounds of his boots grinding the pebbles as he turned. "But you understand that, don't you? It's that feeling you had when you told your friend to jump. You believed in her, and you wanted her to escape the fate that was about to befall you. You would have done anything to protect her."

The door moaned.

"You and I, we're very much the same. Make good use of this chance. I would."

The door thumped closed.

Elly reached between the bars and rifled through the wooden box. In it was a red-hooded cloak, a map, and Eleanor's pistol.

CHAPTER THIRTY-EIGHT

HOTARU DOING

Richy jumped up, shedding his blankets. "What was that?" he yelled, wiping his face in a panic, his breath making clouds of fog in the crisp morning air.

"Sorry, that was louder than I expected, hmm," said Nikolas, a piece of metal in his hands. "The idea of these wings, it is splendid."

Richy rubbed his eyes and reached out for his yellow-hooded cloak. "Where's Amami?"

"After you fell asleep, she covered you. We worked for a while until we noticed those," said Nikolas pointing to the sky. "There are more of them now."

"That's a lot of Skyfallers," said Richy, gulping. "This is starting to feel like Kar'm all over again."

"Weapons of war are for one purpose, are they not?" Nikolas didn't divert his gaze from the contraption before him.

"So, where's my sister?"

Nikolas pointed at the campfire. "There is some water in the kettle, and breakfast is in the pan, yes? Eat quickly. I suspect she shall be back soon."

Richy scratched his head. "But where did she go?"

"Ah," said Nikolas, finally looking up. "She has gone to find the rails. She stated that the Skyfallers go over land, on long metal lines. I need to see these things later, very curious. So many marvelous things that I have missed."

Richy joined Nikolas. "What happened to the second set of wings?"

"I had to make some changes. I needed the parts. The wings must be collapsible, like a fan." He stopped, raising his head. "What is this sound?"

The King's-Horse roared into the clearing, skidding to a stop. Amami slid off, her grey cloak snapping in the wind.

Nikolas stood up and caressed the head of the King's-Horse, his eyes those of a delighted child. "This is remarkable," he said running his hand along it. He put his ear against its body. "Truly remarkable. The sound is so smooth."

Placing a hand on the mechanical horse's heart door, he turned to the two of them, smiling. "The engine is running warm and evenly. Amami, this is remarkable. Is there even an off switch now?"

"Yes, to conserve the battery." Amami bowed and stepped forward, opening the mouth. She reached into it and transformed the vibrant King's-Horse into a still statue.

Nikolas laughed, stroking his beard. "We must find the time to discuss this. You have taken what we did and—" He made a grand gesture with his hands. "And you are so young. Remarkable."

She straightened her shirt and smiled briefly. She pulled out a piece of paper and unfolded it. "This is the map that I made. There is a rail line that splits to the north. I believe both have been used to transport Skyfallers."

Glancing about for the sun, she turned and pointed. "It seems that some Skyfallers are landing about ten miles that way. I was able to get close enough to see that there are rail carts and teams of soldiers."

"Interesting, yes." Nikolas stroked his chin.

"As I was returning," continued Amami, "I saw a different train head that way."

"Why would they go somewhere else?" asked Richy. "Unless… unless it's someone else."

"Maybe this is the Piemans, yes?" Nikolas breathed into his hands. "If Abeland or Richelle are there, they will speak to me. They could get us over and into the city."

Amami dropped her gaze.

"It'd be less dangerous than trying to get on board a Skyfaller… probably," said Richy.

Nikolas nodded.

Amami reluctantly looked up. "Then let us hurry."

Richy crawled out onto the forested bluff and peered down at the rail line below. Two dozen people were busily working away.

"I can't get a good look at what's on those rail-carts," he said over his shoulder to Nikolas and Amami.

"Oh yig," said Richy, noticing someone look up then straight at him.

A shot fired.

"Someone saw me!" He scrambled backward.

Amami reached into her cloak.

"No," said Nikolas, his hands out. "No, we are going to walk over there and talk to them. No killing."

She glared at him.

"He's right," said Richy.

Amami shook her head. "They will most likely shoot us."

"Then... then I will go first." Nikolas took a deep breath and started walking. "Follow behind, but no weapons. We do not want to frighten them, yes?"

"Hello there? Yes, hello," said Nikolas, waving his hands and smiling. "Please do not shoot. There is no need to shoot an old man." He ducked under a branch and stepping out.

There were four people with weapons out awaiting him to exit the forest.

As he looked up, he barely caught sight of a man rushing him. Immediately he was grabbed around the chest and turned about in the air.

Out of the corner of his eye, Nikolas saw Amami draw a

weapon.

Richy pushed down his sister's arm. "Bakon?"

"Richy!" yelled the man, dropping Nikolas. "Ha! Ha! Ha! Oh, this is a good day!"

"You have no idea how good it is to see you," said Richy, sniffing as they stood there, staring at each other.

Bakon turned back to Nikolas. "It's so g..." his throat closed. His face was pained, and tears started running.

"Come here my boy." Nikolas smiled at him and waved him in for a proper hug. "Whatever that guilt is you have, it should go away. You have survived in strange times and I am fine, yes? All fine."

"I wanted to come free you," said Bakon, his voice cracking.

"Shh, it's okay. Like when you were little at home, and there was thunder. Everything is okay now." Nikolas smiled. "Oh my..." He released Bakon. "My dear, how are you?"

Egelina-Marie had a tearful grin. "Um, I'm good."

"Now you come here," said Nikolas, waving her over.

"It's great to see you." She gave him a hug. Stepping back, she waved off the two soldiers. "What are you guys doing here?"

"Are those airships Hotarus? Are you with the Piemans?" asked Amami, her tone sharp and fast.

Egelina-Marie stared at her. "Amami, right? How do you know they're called Hotarus?"

Amami bolted passed them.

A soldier tapped Abeland on the shoulder. "Sir, someone's racing down the hill."

Abeland handed his notebook over to the chief engineer and looked up.

"Sir, should we fire? She appears armed with a sword and a pistol of some kind."

"That's the hill where Bakon and Egelina-Marie went, is it not?"

"Yes," said the soldier nervously.

Abeland looked over at the dozen soldiers nearby, all with their repeating rifles ready. He then looked over at the dozen personnel getting the Hotarus ready for flight or servicing the steam engine.

"If she goes for the Hotarus, shoot her," said Abeland. "But if she comes to me, let's see if she'll talk." He pulled his brown long coat aside and removed an elegant pistol from its holster.

"Amami, wait!"

Abeland glanced at the hill. "That's Egelina-Marie. She knows the woman." He frowned as he attached a tube from under his sleeve to his pistol's handle, his eyes all the while on the rapidly approaching woman. "I think they mentioned her. She was at the Battle of Kar'm."

"What does that mean?" asked the soldier. "Do we shoot her?"

Amami finished getting to the bottom of the cliff and

ran directly towards Abeland.

"I'm not sure yet," said Abeland, shifting his grip on his pistol. "Let's hope we can have some reason, shall we?"

He pointed the pistol at Amami as a whirling sound started up from beneath his coat. "My name is Abeland Pieman, and I'd advise you to stop!"

"She's not slowing down sir."

"I can see that." With an ear-piercing screech, the pistol went off and kicked Abeland's hand back.

Amami skidded to a stop, staring at the smoking hole ahead of her. She glared at him with a fiery gaze that gave Abeland pause.

"Who are you?" he asked, pointing his pistol aside. "Clearly you know Bakon and Egelina-Marie. I'd rather not kill you, as we need all the allies we can muster."

"Marcus Pieman killed my father and stole my brother!" She pointed a katana at the Hotaru. "I made the first of those!"

"Sir?"

"Shh, I'm thinking. She said a lot all at once," he said, his eyes locked on Amami's. He walked forward several paces, leaving about ten yards between them. "Does your brother have blue eyes?"

"Yes."

"You're Tsuruko's daughter," he said, grimacing.

"Yes." Amami pointed her sword tip at the ground.

Abeland sighed. "If you want revenge for your brother

or your father, the man you want is Silskin—Ron-Paul Silskin. He instructed the hired hands that accompanied my father to shoot someone, and he was the one who stole your brother and tried to ransom him, to no avail." He looked past Amami at Bakon and the others as they came racing down the hill.

"Leave my sister alone!" yelled Richy.

"She's fine," Abeland replied, with a chuckle. "Family…" He put his pistol in its holster. "I am not your enemy here."

Amami put her sword away, hidden beneath her loose blouse and pants. She cinched her red sash.

"I've never met a young woman Northern Moufan-Man before. My niece passed the rites of being declared a man in Hattar; I suspect you two have a lot in common." He ran his finger along the top of his pistol. "I'm profoundly sorry for your loss, truly. That whole situation in getting the first Hotaru was a mess, from what I hear. My father involved me in almost everything after that."

"Hello Abeland," said Nikolas with a smile. "It has been a long time."

"It has." Abeland scratched his chin. "Well, I see you don't need rescuing anymore."

"No, but my granddaughter and her friend do. So, carry on," he said, waving.

Richy came up beside Amami and frowned at her. "I thought you said that you let go of everything."

She stared at the ground, her shoulders slumping. "Sometimes I feel like I need to do something to honor what happened to us. But... killing this man will solve nothing."

"You aren't alone, you know," said Richy, taking her hand and giving it a squeeze.

She smiled and then freed her hand.

"Will you help us? We have an enemy who wants to watch the world burn," said Abeland.

"Only if you show me your Hotaru," said Amami.

Abeland faked an embarrassed look. "Well, that's a bit forward... but fine, this once. We could use your expertise."

CHAPTER THIRTY-NINE

CATERINA'S GAMBIT

Caterina turned and watched the door as the thunderous sound of feet in the hallway approached the meeting room. She smiled as the guards realized the double doors were already open. The King and Prime Minister were visibly irritated at being denied bursting the doors open.

She tapped on the table playfully as the guards went from lantern to lantern, increasing the illumination in the room.

The King and Prime Minister muttered to themselves, occasionally throwing a glare over at Caterina.

"If all of you would please sit," she boomed, standing up.

Everyone went silent, caught off guard by her tone and steely expression.

"We do not have much time. There might very well be more assassins about. As we all know, none of us can get in or out of Relna because the Prime Minister has locked us in. It's almost like she wanted it that way."

"What?" muttered several delegates as they sat. "Is that

true? Is this a plot by Belnia?"

Caterina hid her smile as her supporters embraced their fear-promoting roles.

"Do you deny that you have an airship above Relna at this very moment?" asked the Prime Minister. "Do you deny that this is an act of war?"

Caterina glanced at all the faces around the table. "Actually, by now I likely have three of my Skyfallers in the air. But they are not here to declare war. They are here for protection, mine and yours. Clearly you cannot see what's transpiring from the ground, so I propose to assist from the sky."

She turned her sharp gaze on the Prime Minister. "I offered you assistance when things seemed problematic, but you declined. I told the King to take matters seriously, but that was brushed aside. Now, where are we?"

"Indeed," said one of Caterina's agents, banging on the table.

"This is a plot by Regent Catherine to undermine—"

"Undermine, what? The trial? The trial from which you've now managed to let the most dangerous man in recent history go free and allowed him to turn on me?"

The room grumbled and whispered.

Caterina stood up and pointed at the wall. "Are you going to tell me that you have everything under control? You have explosions in the city, an escaped political prisoner, and an agent of the Tub attempting to assassinate

Marcus Pieman."

"How did you know?" asked the Prime Minister.

"Because it is my business to know! I have been working with almost all of you for more than a decade, warning you. But would you listen? No, you preferred your pomp and circumstance, your ceremony and self-aggrandizing gestures. None of you were wise enough to recognize that a Trial by Royals would be an easy way for Marcus Pieman, or some other lunatic, to wreak havoc on the entire continent by picking us off one at a time."

She sat down, eating up the nervous expressions of everyone in the room. "Go on, what do you have to say?" She gestured at the Prime Minister. "Nothing?"

"I suggest we all sit down," said the King.

The Prime Minister glared at him.

"Now," said Caterina, her tone soft and velvety. "I understand how my taking this unilateral action to put Skyfallers above Relna causes concern. But I had to act in our collective self-interest. I knew if you wouldn't accept my help to start with, you might after it was in place. And for that discomfort, I apologize." She bowed her head. "And if you tell me that it is positively unneeded, that you want me to remove them, say so here before everyone, and I'll do just that. I'll place my trust in your ability to stop a calamity on a scale we haven't seen in generations."

The room turned to the Prime Minister and the King who were seated at the far end.

"I, for one, believe we should leave them," said an

ambassador, tugging on her robes anxiously. "The more strength, the better we can stand against this menace."

"We have the matter well under control," said the Prime Minister, her tone firm. She leaned over to the King, and they whispered back and forth.

"Maybe put it to a vote?" offered Caterina.

The room pounced on the idea, everyone adding their support for the notion.

"ENOUGH!" yelled the Prime Minister. She glared at the King.

"Please," he said, nodding at her.

The Prime Minister shook her head.

"I am asking you, as my Prime Minister, to please speak for the nation," said the King.

"I cannot do this. This is wrong. Every instinct, every shred of my being, and every scrap of information we've received for months—"

"What information? Have you been hiding information from us?" barked out a delegate.

Caterina ran a finger along the table, watching her supporters make another spectacle.

The Prime Minister slammed her hand on the table. "I hereby tender my resignation."

Caterina looked up. "Pardon?"

"You can't," said the King, his face in shock.

The Prime Minister stood up. "I will not take this action you're asking of me. We should get her airships out of the air. We should put her in prison. You won't support that, so enjoy the road to ruin. I formally resign."

With a loud, tired exhale, she turned and headed out the door.

"What does this mean?" asked one of the delegates.

"Their parliament's shut down. It means the King must now serve as the head of their government," said another.

An awkward silence fell upon the room.

"So, Your Majesty, what would you like to do?" asked Caterina, the edges of her mouth curling upwards.

He raised his chin; his naked neck seemed abandoned by his collarless shirt and coat. "The people of Belnia would appreciate you keeping your airships in place until we resolve the current security matters."

One delegate applauded, immediately followed by another. Shortly thereafter, the room was full of approving nods and comments.

"As you wish, Your Majesty," said Caterina.

They watched each other as the room cleared.

Finally, she got up and walked over.

"What else do you want?" The King ground his teeth.

She placed a piece of paper before him. "I did you the honor of picking it up," she said, her voice laced with venom.

"Do you think that you can—" The look in her eyes made him stop talking.

"I'd appreciate this back within the hour. You can

formally announce it tomorrow or not at all. It doesn't matter."

He nodded.

Caterina tapped her ear. "I'm sorry, I didn't hear you? You wouldn't want there to be a misunderstanding, would you?"

"Yes, Queen Caterina."

"Clear as a bell. Maybe next time you won't bet your kingdom on the ranting of some shepherd."

CHAPTER FORTY

TO THE SKIES

"You've had the better part of an hour to look at them. What do you think?" said Abeland loudly to Amami as she joined him, Richy, Egelina-Marie, and Bakon at a metal table. A map was held down with several rocks as three Hotarus were being prepared for launch.

Amami finished wiping her hands on a cloth and threw it to the chief engineer who was right beside her. "They are less of an insult than the bloated flying pigs."

"She means the Skyfallers," said Egelina-Marie.

Richy laughed. "I think that was a compliment."

"They should not be used for extended periods of time," added Amami. "The metals the engineers say you used in the MCM engines will overheat."

"Ah, what a surprise. Something to complain about," grumbled the chief engineer. "Did you even look inside the MCMs?"

"I did," said Amami coldly.

"Hmm."

Abeland focused on the map. "They're fine. We've

flown for a few hours. Anyway, let us move on. The plan is
—"

A horn went off in the distance.

"—to focus on a more pressing problem," finished
Abeland, shaking his head. "What's going on now?" He
waved one of his soldiers over. "I want you to go directly
and find out what they're alerting us about."

"What's the horn for?" asked Richy.

"It's an alarm," said Bakon. "One's a concern. Two
horns are a warning."

Abeland smiled. "Someone was paying attention."

Egelina-Marie gave Richy a look. "I know, I was
surprised too. Abeland will even let him captain one of
these things. Mind you, after picking me, he didn't have
many other people to choose from."

"You have a natural talent for this, Egelina," said
Abeland.

"I will captain one," said Amami.

"Actually, no. You won't." Abeland stared at her. "I'm
sorry, but while I appreciate you not plunging a sword into
my chest to avenge your father's death, I'm not going to
hand you a Hotaru. Them I trust; you, not yet."

"Sir, we have reports of several Skyfallers in the area,"
said a soldier.

Abeland bit his tongue, passing on his sarcastic
comment. "Thank you."

"What's going on?" asked Bakon.

"Everything's about to change. We need Richelle to know what's going on. She's in the city." He scratched his head. "How do we get a message to her? Everything will be sealed tighter than ever."

"When did she leave?" asked Bakon.

"Hours ago. Okay, has anyone any ideas how we get a message to her before we have to run for our lives?"

"And find Tee and Elly," added Richy.

Another horn sounded, then a third.

Abeland hung his head. "Well, I hear we've come to the 'run for our lives' portion of the morning." He put two fingers in his mouth and whistled.

His chief engineer looked up from a discussion he was having with Nikolas and hurried over.

"Get those Hotarus ready to leave in two minutes, and get everyone else on the train and out of here."

"Where do we go?" asked the chief engineer.

"Back to Teuton. Get them as far away from here as possible. This is over; thank you for your service."

The chief engineer saluted him and left.

Amami stared up at the sky. "I can get into the city. I have wings."

"Are you just going to fly there?"

"No. I can jump off a Skyfaller, provided it is a few hundred feet off the ground. We hid the wings about a quarter mile before the hill."

Nikolas raised a hand as Abeland was about to protest.

"They are robust and will allow her to be agile. She can do it, I believe."

He nodded. "Go—oh boy."

Everyone stared at the sky. A Skyfaller, its bat-wings extended, was rapidly approaching.

"We probably have three to five minutes," said Abeland. "Amami, go. You'll be with Eg. Bakon, get your Hotaru off the ground."

"Richy, with me! You'll be my backup engineer," yelled Bakon.

"Nikolas—"

"Sam would tell me to prepare to receive him and the girls," he said, looking at the map and twiddling his fingers. "Where would it be? Ah, west is best. Here. Don't worry about me."

Abeland grabbed the map, and everyone took off just as a hundred yards away, flaming barrels fell from the Skyfaller and exploded.

"Grab on to something," yelled Egelina-Marie, her words lost in the sounds of the wind and the Hotaru's turbines. She pulled back hard on two levers. Her Hotaru banked sharply to the left, clipping trees and leaving her crew both clinging to the newly installed safety poles and thankful for their foot straps.

Explosions went off where they'd been as a Skyfaller continued to dog their takeoff.

As Bakon's and Abeland's Hotarus climbed into the sky,

the engineer at the back of Egelina-Marie's Hotaru sounded one of the silver bells.

"I know you're worried what the yig I'm doing." Glancing about, she held on to the levers and forced the Hotaru to complete its one-hundred-and-eighty-degree turn. "Oh great. Another Skyfaller coming in quickly. Looks like it'll be a race to the clouds."

Amami took a deep breath and held on to the pole beside her. The wings were collapsed on her back and tightly strapped over the top of her blue-white blouse.

Grabbing a silver bell, Egelina-Marie sounded a command and pumped her fist twice in the air. She could barely hear the screams of disbelief of her engineer. She sounded her bell again.

Taking a deep breath, she put both hands around a lever that came up to her shoulders. "Abeland always said in the case of an emergency—Oh!" She leaned forward and looked at the gauges. "Come on, come on…"

She looked over her shoulder at the engineer, who was in a frenzy.

Small explosions started to go off ahead of them as the Skyfaller approached.

Taking a deep breath, Egelina-Marie yanked on the lever with all her might.

The Hotaru's nose tilted sharply up, and its rear dropped down.

For a moment, it felt like the ship would fall out of the

sky. Then the turbines roared into action. Everyone's knees went wobbly, and the airship shook violently.

"Hold together. Hold together." Egelina-Marie then eased two levers forward halfway. The Hotaru banked away from the Skyfaller.

A whistle cut through the roar of the wind and the Hotaru's turbines. Egelina-Marie looked around and noticed Amami was pointing.

The first Skyfaller had doubled back.

"Those guys are back?" she said as her engineer rang his warning bell.

"Today must be Saint Heart Attack's day." Eg pushed the giant lever forward, reducing the climb angle of the Hotaru. "But now what?"

Amami whistled again.

Eg turned to see Amami with a katana out and a predatory smile on her face. She pointed at the closing Skyfaller.

"You're my kind of crazy," said Egelina-Marie with a laugh. She caught the eye of her engineer and made a circular motion with her hand.

He raised the warning bell, his eyes right on her, and he shook it.

She smiled and nodded.

He nodded and yanked a lever. A chain ladder lowered out the back of the Hotaru.

Putting one hand around the large lever again, she

raised the other one with all fingers extended. She counted them down, then pulled hard on the large lever.

The Hotaru climbed sharply in response.

Amami sprinted to the back of the airship and leaped off and on to the Skyfaller.

Egelina-Marie kept glancing at the other airship as she brought the Hotaru back around. As they passed by the Skyfaller, one of its balloons went up in flames. Amami sprang off its deck and snatched the Hotaru's chain ladder at the last second, swinging like a pendulum bob before scrambling up the ladder and onto the Hotaru's deck.

"Definitely my kind of crazy," said Egelina-Marie.

CHAPTER FORTY-ONE

BITE OF THE LIAR

"There you are, clever girl. Time to wake up," said Sam.

Tee roused as a gentle hand tapped her face. She lifted her head off her numb arms and squinted in the mid-morning light. A smiling, worried, bearded face was looking down on her.

"Hiding at the back of a dozen large barrels was good, but putting two tarps to cover the whole area was genius. It took me two passes to realize that it was out of place." He stood up and walked along the barrel to the edge. "Come on, let's get some breakfast," he said hopping down.

Tee slowly stood, holding on to the sides of the barrels. "How's Elly?"

"Sleeping in a jail cell, I think. I don't know; the last I heard was there was some confusion as to whether she was going to be executed today or tomorrow."

Tee glared at him.

"That woke you up. They've delayed it to tomorrow."

Sam looked down the alley at the marketplace. "With the sky full of Skyfallers, and no declaration of war against the Lady in Red, I'm guessing Belnia has more challenging concerns than a suspected teenage assassin."

"Pardon?" said Tee.

Sam pointed upwards.

"Oh wow... that's... that's a lot of Skyfallers."

"Last night there were three of them circling Relna, then four, then eight. This morning there were twelve by my last count. I did some shopping; word is that there are more coming. This is not going to end well. There's never been a show of force like this."

He handed Tee a worn, brown cloak. "I brought this for you."

"Is red not a popular color anymore?" she asked, attempting a smile.

"Oh, it's all the rage," said Sam as they carefully made their way towards the market. Vendors were setting up, and children were running about trading assistance for food. "After yesterday's events, soldiers and guards are stopping everyone they want. But everyone else? They've got to make a living."

He sighed and patted her on the arm. "Nikolas is safe with Richy and Amami, back at camp. Now, let's get a move on," he said, pulling his brown hood down.

"What's the plan?" asked Tee noticing three soldiers questioning a merchant.

Sam sniffed the air. "Oh, do you smell that? Fresh baked goods." He glanced about and clapped his hands together.

"Come on, let's eat.

"Now? But what about Elly?" She turned. Sam was already a dozen yards away.

"How much?" he asked the old woman standing on a folded blanket in front of a cart. There were six sections of baked goods on a wooden tray.

"Two."

Sam frowned. "Two? How many do I get?"

"Three."

"I'm in the mood for four. I think it's Tuesday."

The woman nodded, looking away. "It's Monday."

"Because there is no Saturday."

"Because there is no Sunday," she corrected.

"So we have a deal?"

"Yes," she said. "All four."

Sam handed the merchant five coins and then counted two buns over and three buns up on the first tray. He tossed it to Tee and took out a slip of paper that was underneath it. He then took three other buns at random and started walking.

"These are excellent," said Sam biting into one, its steam escaping. "The fruit filling is a Relna delicacy."

"Did we just do some shopping?" asked Tee.

"You're holding a bun, aren't you?"

She looked at the pastry in her hand and took a bit. "Mmm, this is good."

Sam stopped and opened the piece of paper.

Tee looked over his shoulder. "That isn't nonsense, is it?"

"No," said Sam, his voice serious. He tossed the paper away and walked over to another merchant. Without saying a word, he ran his hand along the inside of a crate of apples. He pulled out a wooden tile with a number on it and put it back.

"Come on," he said to Tee, walking over to a spot by a wall where a merchant hadn't shown up yet. He sat on the folded rug that was there and put his hands out.

"What are we doing?" asked Tee, copying him.

"Give it a few minutes."

Sam smiled and nodded at people as they went by. A few minutes later, a small child came by and put a small, tight bundle of papers in Sam's hands.

As if he had all the time in the world, he turned to face the wall. He casually opened the bundle, removing the five half-height pieces of paper and putting them before him. "These two are maps, likely of the first and second floors of the keep. These are notes of some kind."

"Won't someone see what we're doing?" asked Tee, looking over his shoulder.

"If we don't treat this like it's something to be worried about, then everyone will just ignore us. We look like poor people huddled in a corner, so we're invisible to most."

"To most, but not all," said a gravelly voice from behind them.

The hairs on the back of Tee's neck rose.

Out of the corner of his eye, Sam saw the fear on Tee's face.

There was a click and whirl sound behind them.

"I thought you couldn't come out."

"Well, a deal's only a deal when it can be enforced. And my dealer's very much distracted right now. But where are my manners? Who's your friend? Is it the boy who launched that sail-cart at me? I can't remember his name." LeLoup bent down, his hot breath on the back of Tee's neck. "I think it's time to get my wolf back, don't you?"

Sam turned and immediately LeLoup kicked him against the wall, winding him.

Tee spun around blindly, trying to kick LeLoup. He whacked her with his triple-barreled pistol, sending her face first into the ground.

Taking aim at Sam, LeLoup smiled.

Tee sprang into the air and punched LeLoup in the side of his head.

He stumbled backward, his balance thrown off.

Dropping to the ground, she kicked one of LeLoup's legs out from under him, bringing him crashing to the ground. Whipping a shock-stick out of her cloak, she hit him across the face with it.

As she went to charge the shock-stick, she heard him laughing and stopped. Tee looked at him, blood dripping down the side of his face and a toothy grin from ear to ear.

"Why are you laughing?"

His green eyes focused on her then slid down. "Because now we can begin."

Tee followed his gaze to his pistol, which was pointing straight behind her.

"Goodbye," said LeLoup. The pistol went off like a cannon, throwing Sam right into the wall and limply to the ground.

"Granddad!" Tee dropped her shock-stick and went to him.

"Well, it's so nice to get to meet more of the family," said LeLoup, getting up and wiping the blood from his face.

Tee rolled Sam over and searched him frantically.

"Ribs probably broken, but otherwise, I'm okay," he whispered.

Tee glared at LeLoup as he spun the barrels of the Liar.

"There's the wolf I need. Now, let's play a little game: Who can find Elly first?" With the Liar pointed at Tee's head, he backed up until he put the pistol in his hip holster and took off. "The wolf is coming out tonight!"

Sam grabbed Tee's hand and stuffed paper into them. "Palace maps," he said weakly.

"I can't leave you."

He frowned at her and waved her off, breaking into a coughing fit.

Tee stood up.

"Go."

CHAPTER FORTY-TWO
PRICE OF LEGACY

"Are you sure you want to do this?" asked Zelda, bringing out a blue and silver dress and a wig from the closet.

"You know as well as I do that we have no choice. Even if we could find Chikahn Liddel now, it's too late. No one will care if he takes back everything he said to the judicial panel. The trial is done. Now, we either press on or lose everything we have."

She went into her closet and pulled out a more subdued outfit—a jacket and pants in a similar style to Richelle's. "We believe the Piemans are weak right now, but are they? I've seen many pounce at this point, only to learn that the Piemans had a secret weapon somewhere. We won't make that mistake. Let them lick their wounds, for I know they are deep. And instead… instead, we will rain down fury on everyone else. We will push this world into chaos and take what we want when we want it."

"And what of the Tub and Eleanor?" asked Zelda.

"We need to keep an eye on her. She's becoming more desperate. Not killing Marcus in private was a warning. Maybe she wants something more public, or maybe she's swallowed her pride and is planning on double-crossing us. I don't know."

"Thus your plan," said Zelda.

"Thus my plan."

"Well?" asked the King as he stared at Marcus who was drumming his fingers on the edge of the couch. He had his hand on his hips and was pacing about the secret meeting room. "That's it. That's everything."

Marcus' eyes followed every movement of the King's. "I have to ask, how does your Prime Minister feel about this?"

"She quit. But you know that," said the King, shaking his hands. "You know that. Don't pretend you don't know everything that's happening here. We've got a parliamentary democracy. Are you going to let it fall?"

Laughing, Marcus sat on the edge of the couch. "Your Majesty, you do see the irony here, do you not? You decided to host the first Trial by Royals and then passively led the charge to dismiss it. And I just heard that you've signed an agreement with Caterina. Funnily enough, I also heard a rumor that the charges against her have been dismissed."

The King stared at him, unmoving.

Marcus covered his mouth with his handkerchief and coughed, glancing down at the new redness before putting it away. "I'm mystified. If you've allied yourself with her, why are you here?"

"Because I believe she means to betray me and to kill us all."

"Ah. And what reason do you believe I have to help you at all?" asked Marcus.

"No one can leave the city. You're trapped in here with the rest of us," said the King, his twitching fingers touching his face.

"Hmm. Debatable but let's assume that were true." Marcus leaned back, putting his arm over the back of the couch. "Does that have anything to do with the confusion about whether or not the Prime Minister quit? For the record, I had nothing to do with that."

"I can't find her. She's disappeared, as has the Deputy Prime Minister. Without them, there's no signature transferring power. The military outside of the keep isn't listening to me." The King paced about again. "I'm the king!"

"I wouldn't be surprised if Caterina had the PM and her deputy killed. No Prime Minister, no signature. No signature, no military support. You're a king without a kingdom."

"Hmm, I suppose the meeting where I was to share all the details of my railroads and Neumatic Tubes is canceled? Thank goodness, I'm not quite feeling up for it," said Marcus, touching his handkerchief.

The King sat down and stared at Marcus. "You and I both know that we cannot let Caterina bomb Relna. She'd be cutting off the heads of dozens of countries, kingdoms, and families."

Marcus raised a finger. "The important part is that it

would all be on your shoulders. There's a reason I didn't see her coming for me. She works quietly, slowly, for a long time. I've recently heard that the twins she has, Zelda and Alfrida, are the perfect advisors. Loyal, clear-headed, and without ambitions of their own. She's set everything up such that if she points the gun and pulls the trigger, everyone will agree that you are the murderer. Brilliant, truly."

"So do something!" yelled the King, his arms outstretched.

"Why?" snapped Marcus.

The King stopped, staring at him in disbelief. "What?"

Marcus shrugged. "Why should I?"

"Because you'll die. We'll all die."

"So? I'm the oldest man anyone's ever met, let alone one who's still able to hold his own. I've lived my life. What more could I want? My life isn't worth as much to me as when I was a young man." Marcus looked at the King coldly.

The King rubbed his face with his hands. "What if… if I gave you the southern half of Belnia? I once heard that you supposedly thought it should be returned to Teutonic rule."

Marcus raised an eyebrow and leaned forward. "What are you saying?"

"Stop me from going down in the annals of history as being responsible for the greatest massacre of royals and dignitaries in history"—he swallowed hard—"and I will give whomever you want sovereign rights over southern Belnia."

"Distinct and separate in every way?" asked Marcus.

"In every way," said the King, holding his head.

Marcus stared deeply into the King's eyes. "You are truly terrified, aren't you? Do you even have the authority to do that?"

The King nodded profusely. "Absolutely. Doing such a thing needs the parliament, the Prime Minister, and the King."

"So, what of the parliament?"

"As King and Prime Minister, I can dismiss it."

"Triggering an election. In the interim, with the way you have your system set up, there would be no parliamentary vote."

"Exactly," said the King, pointing at Marcus with a trembling hand.

"And now the irony of asking me to support taking the democracy away from the people. What would you expect in return?"

"Get rid of those Skyfallers." The King pointed out the window.

Marcus stood up. "Very well. Put Richelle Pieman down as the ruler, list her in the Book of Royals as the legitimate claimant, and we'll resolve titles later. Do that, and we have a deal."

"We do?" said the King, his face struck with relief. He

stood up excited.

"Understand that I make no promises about the results, only that I will commit to doing my best to salvage your legacy."

"I accept," said the King, shaking hands with Marcus.

"I expect the papers within the next fifteen minutes."

The King's eyes bulged. "What? That's hardly enough time."

"It's enough time if you run. Now go." Marcus watched as the king fled.

Marcus quietly made his way back to his room, stopping several times to lean against a wall. His breathing was becoming labored; his coughing fits, more frequent.

Opening the door to his quarters, he smiled.

"Opa, you don't look well," said Richelle, getting up and helping him to the bed.

"I am well enough to gaze upon a queen."

Richelle laughed. "What are you on about?"

"Never mind. Tell me how you are," said Marcus.

Twenty minutes later, there was a knock at the door. Richelle answered, and a page handed her a paper with several wax seals and signatures.

"What's this?"

"One man's kingdom and another's principles. It's the price of legacy."

CHAPTER FORTY-THREE
WHERE, OH WHERE

Tee reached into some bushes and pulled out the laundry servant clothes she'd stuffed in there. Glancing about, she took off her cloak, made it into a ball, and put it in the bushes. She threw the servant clothes over top of her own. With her shock-sticks stuffed up her sleeves, Tee ran off for the keep.

"How's that?" asked one of the servants as Tee walked up to an army of young girls hunched over laundry tubs, washing clothes by hand. Young boys were putting the clothes to dry on the lines in a forest of metal poles that were set up at the side of the keep.

"You, come here," said a woman in her twenties to Tee. She was wearing the same black dress with a white apron that Tee and everyone else was, and her light brown hair was done up in a bun. "I don't know you."

Tee looked at her, then at the other older women who were taking notice. "I'm..." She put her hands on her forearms. "I need to get something."

"What's your name?" asked the woman, stepping directly into Tee's path and stopping her.

"Kigmybut."

"Kigmybut?"

A cheeky smirk broke out across Tee's face. "You asked for it." She hooked her arm under the woman's and then threw her to the ground. "I need to save someone."

Gasps of astonishment broke out. One of the other women whistled.

"That's a call for help," said Tee. "Okay, we'll do this the harder way." She pulled out the small map in one hand, and a shock-stick in the other. "Out of my way!"

Tee looked up the stairs once again before creeping up to the prison door. "This shouldn't be open." She readied both shock-sticks and pushed the door open with her foot. "LeLoup, are you in there? Because I'm all ready to give you that wolf back, one smack at a time."

Squinting at the dim light, Tee cautiously entered.

A lone crank lantern was on. It was lying on the floor beside an open jail cell door, beside it was an empty crate.

Tee stepped into the jail and peered around. As she turned about, her eye caught something. Smiling, she crouched down and touched the white scratches. "The same shape that Grandpapa put on his door. You're brilliant, Elly, you know that?"

Standing up, she took a deep breath and reaffirmed her grip on her shock-sticks. "So the question is, how long ago were you here and where did you go?"

Tee chewed on her cheek as she thought. "Where would

you go? You'd go to where you'd know I'd go to look for you. And that's where no one's going to be looking."

She took out the two maps and sat down by the lantern. "Where? Where would you go? There. The ballroom. That's got to be filled with people."

With her back to the wall, Tee crept back to the stairs. "Where are you LeLoup?"

CHAPTER FORTY-FOUR
MAKING THE SKY FALL

The crate of empty milk bottles crashed to the ground.

"What in the world?" said the innkeeper, standing in the middle of the village road. She glanced at the dozen others standing in the middle of the road, with the same worried look as her.

"He's right," said an old woman. "That Chikahn was right. I knew Relna was wicked and look. The sky is going to punish them."

"No, that's not what he said," said a man holding a little girl's hand. "He said the sky saved his village. Look above us. There are a few clouds. Are they protecting us?"

A middle-aged woman shook her head. "He said the sky fell to give justice for the destruction of his village."

"What do you think he said?" someone asked the innkeeper.

She shifted her confused gaze among everyone and frowned. "I'll fetch Chikahn." She ran into the inn.

A few minutes later, she came outside with him.

In his hand was a notebook familiar to all in the village. He'd been keeping a record of his thoughts and observations of the sky.

"Are you going to write about this?" asked the old woman.

"I can't believe this," he said, staring.

"I apologize a thousand times for ridiculing you, and saying things behind your back," said the innkeeper. "I thought you were simply a madman. We get those through our village from time to time."

"Shh, I never took any offense," he said, his eyes locked on the sight. "There must be over a dozen of those Skyfallers above Relna. Has the sky taken any action against them?"

"Not yet. We couldn't remember if that's how it worked."

Chikahn frowned, folding his arms. "They look like the same airships that attacked my village. I could not have imagined that there could be so many. When did they appear above Relna?"

"It started yesterday. I... I didn't believe it at first. When more showed up, I didn't want to disturb you," said someone.

"It's okay—"

"Will they destroy our village?" asked the little girl.

He bent down and looked her in the eyes. "I believe that

the sky will protect us. We just need to watch. Maybe it was waiting for us to come so that we could all witness an even bigger miracle than I did before."

Suddenly there was an explosion in the sky, and a Skyfaller, with no balloons, fell to the ground in flames.

The crowd erupted.

"Oh, my!"

"Look! That cloud, how it moves! The sky is saving us."

"There's another!"

"It's… impossible," said the innkeeper. She gave Chikahn a sideways glance. "Isn't it?"

"Look!" yelled the little girl. "A shiny cloud's going straight down towards Relna!"

Amami held her breath as the Hotaru entered the clouds. She wiped the glass of her helmet, but to no available. The world had seemingly vanished.

Her mind was going a mile a minute, and her stomach was twisting and turning. She was crouched down on all fours, her hands clutching the safety pole tightly.

A high-pitched bell dinged off to her right; the engineer was there somewhere. Another bell went off up front.

Amami closed her eyes, thinking of what she had to do next.

Someone tapped her on the shoulder. She looked, only the dark shadow of someone was beside her. She let go of one of the foot straps and tapped the person back. "I'm ready," she yelled, stunned at how loud it was inside the brass-and-glass helmet.

The shadowy form disappeared into the haze.

Amami reached back and tugged on her wings, confirming they were ready to go. She thought of the conversation Nikolas had had with her regarding the real risks. "I will not fail. I will see Riichi again soon."

Two high-pitched dings rang out from the front, followed by two more in the back. A second later, Amami's stomach felt like it was in her mouth as the Hotaru plummeted out of the sky.

The wind roared passed, slapping her with the few parts of her blouse and pants she hadn't tied up. Her red sash shook but remained tucked into itself tightly.

Suddenly, the world reappeared in a flash of blinding blue as the Hotaru dropped out of the clouds.

The engineer rang his bell twice.

Egelina-Marie rang hers once.

Amami stared at the three-foot-long hose that connected her helmet to the body of the ship and the breathing machine below.

Shaking her head, Amami reached into her sash and pulled out the one silver bell she'd been given. She rang it but then lost her grip on it. Turning to see where it went, she caught sight of one of the other Hotarus. Two Skyfallers were on its tail. The Skyfallers' bat-like wings were out and the wind was propelling them forward in hot pursuit.

The engineer rang his bell twice.

Egelina-Marie rang hers once.

Still no.

Amami swallowed hard as she peeked over the edge at the rapidly approaching ground. Glancing about, she saw three Skyfallers turning towards them. Another fired randomly.

The engineer rang his bell twice.

Egelina-Marie rang hers twice.

Amami looked up in surprise.

Egelina-Marie was looking back at her, two fingers in the air.

Amami's body went cold as she disconnected the hose for her helmet with both hands.

The engineer started ringing his bell repeatedly.

With a deep breath, Amami removed her feet from the straps and pushed off. Once clear of the Hotaru, she extended her mechanical wings and rushed towards the ground.

Soldiers shot at Amami from the parapets of the keep as she flew over them, several bullets bouncing off her helmet.

"That small field of white, it must be laundry. I'm on the servant's side of the keep."

A shot cracked the glass window of her helmet.

"I must go past the keep. I can come back. There, the market." She eyed a building with a large, flat roof and landed, running along the roof until she could bring herself to a stop. In the blink of an eye, she discarded the helmet, cut the straps of her wings, and scaled down the side of the building to the ground.

Turning, she saw dozens of servants, merchants, and others staring at her. She pulled a small knife from her boot, cut the leather straps that bound her blouse and pants to her body, and untucked her sash.

"That feels better," she said as her clothes billowed in the breeze. Raising her head, she could hear a wave of chaos approaching as soldiers yelled for people to get out of their way.

Just as she was about to bolt, a grey-robed, bald man rushed over. "I feel I know who you are looking for. Come with me."

Amami nodded and followed. They went down many narrow streets, doubling back a few times to lose their pursuers and entering an abandoned building.

"Are you looking for the Piemans?" he asked, peeking through the slats of the broken door.

"Yes. I am seeking Richelle Pieman," said Amami.

"I know where she is. In exchange for telling you, you must agree to get me out of the city. I have tried several times, but can't. My life is in danger. I had almost regained riches, only to have them taken away again." He glanced at her. "You're from over the Eastern Mountains, aren't you?"

"My mother was," answered Amami.

"Good, then I can trust your word." The man peeked through the door once again, a hand running over his sweaty, bald head. "It looks like we lost them."

He straightened up and offered her a well-practiced smile. "I'm assuming that you aren't suicidal and have an equally ingenious plan for getting out of Relna. If I tell you where to find Richelle Pieman, will you get me out of the city?"

"Yes, I will free you from the city. Where is she?"

The man licked his lips and nodded nervously. "At a tavern two blocks from here called the Dancing Horse. She stays at one of the tables on the second floor. She doesn't know that I know she's there, but I do. I like to know as much as I can."

Amami studied the man's robes. "You don't act like a peasant."

"Oh, this?" he said, pointing. "No. It's simply a momentary humbling. I'll rise again, I always do. When you're ready to guide me out, you'll find me at the same place you find Richelle." He opened the door. "You should go now."

Amami nodded and put a foot out the door when a chill ran through her. "What's your name?"

"Silskin. Lord Ron-Paul Sil—"

He fell to the ground, a katana through his heart.

"Whaa...?" He feebly pawed at the blade. "Your oath."

With tears in her eyes, she tugged on the blade, but it

was stuck between two floor stones. "My first oath is to my family, to my brother. You stole my life!" She stared at him as the light went out from his eyes.

Shaking, she stood up and took a calming breath. "You are all of my revenge. From here, I am free."

Tapping the other sword on her back to ensure it was there, she pushed the door aside and left.

CHAPTER FORTY-FIVE

Unleashing The Wolf

From the shadows of the ballroom balcony, Elly stared down at the ballroom full of royals and dignitaries.

"I was wondering if you were going to arrive," said her grandmother from the archway to the main hallway. "I have to say that I'm pleased you were able to get out on your own, though it took you long enough."

"There were guards," said Elly, her voice unfeeling and distant.

"All of this speaks even more to you not needing Tee. You might become the youngest Tubman yet. We'll fetch you a proper black cloak in a moment. That red one is rather garish."

"It allowed me to slip past some guards." Elly shook her head. "How did you know I'd be here? There are four balconies." She motioned to the other corners of the ballroom.

"This is the best vantage point, with its view of the entrance. Everyone comes through there, stands on that platform for a moment, then descends the four steps to the ballroom floor."

"How can all of these people be here with everything that's going on?"

Eleanor gestured. "Do you see any windows? Any signs of the real world? No. Here they can pretend everything is as they wish it. The musicians over there will start playing in a moment, and over there will be an endless stream of food—enough to feed the entire city. Instead it will bloat the bellies of a few. It's the way of the world."

"I just want to get out of here and go home."

"Your home is gone. If it's about visiting your parents, then we can arrange that. I'm sure I can locate them."

"But it'll take weeks, right?" asked Elly, glaring over her shoulder at Eleanor.

"In all likelihood."

"You're just trying to manipulate me. You know where they are already, don't you?"

Eleanor gave Elly a steely look. "You are being unnecessarily emotional. It serves no purpose here. I need you to keep your eyes peeled. Today will be the day that the Tub rises again." She pointed with the head of her cane.

Elly looked down and saw the King enter. "That's Marcus Pieman behind him."

"Hmm, I didn't think you knew Marcus. Who's that in the corner over there where the stir is starting?"

Elly shrugged. "The one in the shiny blue-and-silver

dress? I don't know."

"That's Queen Caterina of Staaten and Elizabetina. She's the one who undercut everything from Marcus. The war of the Fare, in one room," said Eleanor.

The musicians played their trumpets as the King stood, waiting for everyone's attention.

"Please, I have an important, and difficult, announcement to make," he said.

"He looks like he's in pain," said Elly, leaning over the railing.

"What's this?" Eleanor reached for something shiny sticking out from the side of Elly's red cloak. "How could you have gotten this?" She pulled out the long-barreled pistol and checked it. "It's loaded with all four shots."

Elly turned and stared blankly at her.

"How did you get this? You didn't free yourself, did you?" She glared at Elly, her teeth grinding. "Are you working for Marcus Pieman? Is that why you recognize him? Is that why you stopped me from killing him?"

"What? No," said Elly, her hands raised. "You don't understand."

"It's you who doesn't understand how this world works," snapped her grandmother. "How can you allow yourself to be so weak? Even your mother was stronger than this."

Elly took a swing at her, but Eleanor knocked Elly to the ground with the back of her cane.

"Don't make me shoot you, Elly. Stay right where you are. We will resolve this in a minute." Eleanor glanced at the crowd. "Time to right the ship of society before they tip it over."

She fired at Marcus then immediately turned to fire at Caterina.

Elly kicked at her grandmother's legs just as the second shot went off. As Eleanor came tumbling to the ground, Elly snatched the pistol from her and headed into the corridor.

Looking both ways, the pistol firmly in hand, she saw a woman in a red cloak with guards approaching from the south.

As Elly fled north, the woman said, "That girl, that's one of the ones I'm looking for. Elly! I'll have to go after her in a minute."

Rounding a corner, Elly spotted two guards about to turn around. "No doors or stairways, so no choice," she muttered.

Planting a foot on the wall, Elly threw herself into the guards, knocking them aside. A second later, she was back up on her feet and tearing off, her red cloak little more than a streak.

"Excuse me, Captain?" Eleanor stared at the captain of the guard who was blocking her from exiting the balcony.

"I regret to inform you that you are under arrest," he said, his eyes lowered.

"Oh please," scolded Eleanor. "Now get out of my way.

If you want an assassin, she ran off. That girl you allowed to escape was just here." She looked past him and saw three guards and a woman waiting in the corridor.

"It hasn't been as long as I would have liked, Eleanor," said Richelle.

The captain looked up at Eleanor. "You will need to come with us."

"No," she said, stepping backward, her cane in her hands.

"You're under arrest for the attempted assassination of those under the king's protection," said the captain, his face pained.

"You work for me," said Eleanor, glaring at him. "Shoot her, and let's be done with it."

Richelle shifted her gaze between Eleanor and the captain.

"I'm sorry, I can't do that. By order of the King, the Tub and their agents are no longer given any protections or amnesties," he said in a deep voice.

Eleanor glared at Richelle. "How could you do that?"

"The final moves of the Grand Game are always the most painful, are they not, Aunt Eleanor?"

"Don't you dare call me that."

Suddenly everything shook. Dust fell from the ceiling. The chandelier in the middle of the ballroom swayed from side to side.

Eleanor slammed her cane into the ground and then

shocked the captain.

"What happened?" yelled one of the other guards as they rushed in.

"A piece of the ceiling hit him," said Eleanor, staring at Richelle. "You were watching me from another balcony."

"Yes." Richelle's eyes narrow as the two women circled each other.

"That means Marcus is unharmed, and—"

The room shook again.

Richelle swiped Eleanor's cane and shocked her with it. "Your part in the Grand Game is over." She turned to the guards. "Get her and the Captain out of here."

———————

As the building shook, Tee slipped. She banged into the wall, falling to the floor. A figure stepped out of a balcony archway several feet away.

"The balcony right by the northern staircase. It's almost like I knew you would be here," said LeLoup, the Liar resting against his shoulder.

Tee scurried backward.

Two shots rang out.

"Oh, someone's excited," he said, glancing around. He winced at the sound of the crowd breaking into hysteria.

Getting to her feet, Tee looked behind her, worried.

"Even if you managed to make it to the corner, I'll shoot you in the back down that next long stretch. I know. Not very sportsman-like, but that's life."

Tee turned and faced him. LeLoup's eyes were wild and big.

"But I'm not all bad, I brought you something," he said, throwing her a yellow cloak. "I found it in the bushes. Some people have no respect for nature these days."

Her eyes locked on his; she bent down to pick up the cloak.

LeLoup pointed his triple-barreled pistol at her. "I think that's good enough. I don't need you wearing it; just it being near you will suffice. I can't have you accidentally surviving because of it. I'd never forgive myself." A toothy grin grew from ear to ear.

The building shook again. Tee leaped at him.

She landed a punch to his face, but LeLoup managed to knock her backward with his free hand.

He snarled, stepping back a yard, his pistol trained on her. "Vigorous to the end. I like that."

A Red Cloak turned the corner and stopped. "LeLoup?"

Surprised, he looked up. "Elly? Well, what a wonderful surprise. Now it's your turn to see what it was like for Tee to watch me shoot you."

"NO!" screamed Elly.

A shot rang out. LeLoup hit the floor.

Tee opened her eyes, her hands still up protecting her face. "He's… he's dead." She stared at Elly. "What did you do?"

Elly's arm was slack at her side, Eleanor's long-barreled

pistol still smoking. Her face was blank other than her brow, which kept twitching.

"Can you hear me?" Tee walked over, waving her hand in front of Elly's face.

"I… I couldn't let him. I couldn't…" Her head kept shaking back and forth.

Tee hugged her. "You saved my life, Elly."

"I couldn't let him. I couldn't," she repeated, her head still shaking.

"You must be Tee and Elly!" yelled a woman in a red cloak running down the corridor.

Tee let Elly go. "Who are you?"

Elly stepped away, muttering to herself.

Another shot rang out.

Tee spun around and stared.

Elly was standing over LeLoup's body. The Liar was firmly in her grip, smoking.

"Mother of Mercy, Elly! Stop!"

"He can't hurt us anymore, Tee," she said, turning. Her face was a mix of sorrow and pain. "No one's going to tell me you make me weak. No one's going to haunt my dreams. No more."

"Tee, Elly, we have to leave before this place collapses."

Tee stared at her. "I know you. Wait, you're—"

"Nikolas Klaus and Sam Baker sent me to get you," interrupted Richelle.

"You helped kidnap him! Why should I believe you?"

"Because… because Nikolas doesn't like coffee."

Tee shrugged. "What's that supposed to mean?"

"He only likes tea."

Tee's face changed. "You really are with him."

Richelle nodded.

A chunk of the ceiling dropped nearby and shattered on the floor.

"We have to get you both out of here. An airship is waiting. We must get to the roof. My grandfather should already be there."

Tee shook Elly. "Elly, we have to go."

"No more," she repeated, her eyes big and wild.

Tee tore off Elly's red cloak and tugged the pistol out of her hand, throwing them both aside.

"Elly, you have to go with her. Now." Tee turned to Richelle. "She's not listening. It's like she's not there."

"Fine." Richelle hefted Elly over her shoulder and started walking.

Tee grabbed her yellow cloak.

"Where are you going?" asked Richelle.

"There's something I have to do. I'll find my way. Save Elly."

The building rattled, and the sound of a section of the keep caving in somewhere echoed through the halls.

CHAPTER FORTY-SIX
TO PIECES

The locked, double doors of Caterina's chambers burst open. The four guards tossed aside the battering log as the King and his elite guards stormed in.

"Caterina, I demand—Where's Caterina?" said the King to the woman standing in the middle of the room.

Zelda looked at the wig and blue-and-silver dress that lay on the table of the parlor. "She has already left for Staaten, Your Majesty. She had decided it was time to end the Grand Game. She asked me to remain to deliver you a message."

The King pointed at the dress. "That was you at the ball?"

"It was," she said pointing at the dented metal plate at her neck, her white leather armor otherwise unblemished. "Luckily the assassin was a bad shot."

He stomped past her, opening the door to the map room and scanning about. "Where is Caterina? She couldn't have left. She must be hiding somewhere. Every exit is sealed. I couldn't get out of here if I wanted." He turned and glared at Zelda.

She pointed upwards.

"What are you talking about?" said the King.

"She left on a Skyfaller. It picked her up from the garden while everyone else was at the ball. She wished you well as you go down in history with the blood of dozens of royals and leaders on your hands. You are the man who played both sides of the Grand Game and lost everything."

He glared at her. "I will have you executed."

"Your threats are idle, particularly given that your daughter's a guest on one of the Skyfallers. Once I am safely away, she'll be released, alive and well."

The room shook, and loud cracks appeared in the walls.

"This bombing is a betrayal of our agreement! To speak nothing of taking my daughter!"

"And what of your deal with the Piemans? She learned of it shortly before leaving. You might say that it was the spark that led to the bonfire of your legacy."

He froze, his eyes big and wild. "How… how could she have known? How?"

Zelda stared at him blankly.

"I… I didn't announce it in the ballroom, so no one knows. I can take it back. You can have those lands," said the King, his hands waving.

An explosion went off in the distance.

"You must stop this madness!"

Zelda forced the stuck doors to the balcony open. "You were never a player in the Grand Game, Your Majesty, just a piece." She stepped out and closed the doors behind her.

One of the guards rushed forward and opened it.

She was gone.

The King looked about, terror in his eyes. "What have I done?"

———————⌒———————

Bakon pulled as hard as he could on the Hotaru's largest lever and watched in horror as it bent and then broke off. He looked back at the engineer, who was staring straight back at him.

The engineer sounded one of his bells.

"I bet you're worried," said Bakon.

He sounded it again and pointed.

Bakon glared at him. "What are you pointing at? Oh no…"

Smoke streamed out from the engine room below.

His crew and Richy were continuing to reload their magnetic coil cannons. Their heads were bowed; their faces, red from their tireless efforts. He didn't know how much more he could ask from them.

Bakon waved at the engineer.

The engineer picked up a bell and rang it.

"Get over here!" Bakon waved at him more insistently.

Carefully the engineer walked over.

"Is there another way to get lift? This lever's done," said Bakon, showing him the piece.

"No. Between that and the hit we took to the engine

room, I think our steam engine is going to go critical before too long. We're going to continue losing altitude and speed, sir. I think… I think we're done."

Bakon scratched his head furiously and then adjusted his goggles. "Okay, fine. I'll bring us down there, in that field."

"What are your orders?" asked the engineer.

"Reduce our altitude, reduce our speed, but give us as long in this fight as you can. Any signs of the boiler or anything getting angrier, drop us and we'll have to make do. Go it?"

The engineer returned to his station and rang a bell.

"Yeah, yeah," said Bakon, as he shot Richy a look of disappointment.

Richy shook his head and gestured to his cannon.

Clearing his throat, Bakon turned to his crew. "We're going down, but we're going to give Abeland and Egelina-Marie as much help as we can on the way! There are still four of those stinking Skyfallers in the air, and that's too many!"

———————

Tee stood at the entrance to the ballroom. The room was packed with royals, ambassadors, and delegates, chatting in tight groups.

Tapping several fancily dressed people, Tee pointed at the swaying chandelier. "Why are you still here? Get out! This whole room could cave in."

"Nonsense! Marcus Pieman and Queen Caterina have

just been shot. We have been told by the King that this is the safest place for us to be," said a finely dressed man, yanking his arm away from her.

"I need to get all of these people out of here," said Tee, taking in her surroundings. "Oh great, guards. Can't I have five merciful minutes without guards?"

A guard was moving through the crowd towards her.

Tee crouched down and pushed through the crowd in the opposite direction.

"What are you doing? Get out of here!" yelled someone.

"A girl in pants? What is this place coming to?"

"Tee?"

She looked up. It was Alex.

Pulling back to punch him, she paused when Alex put his hands up. "I'm sorry! Please, I... it was arrogant of me."

She pointed at the ceiling. "Everyone has to get out of here, or it's going to be Kar'm all over again."

"But the King said—"

Tee punched him in the shoulder. "There are airships outside! Airships!"

There was another explosion nearby; screams broke out through the crowd and were quickly followed by laughter.

Tee glanced up at the chandelier as it swung wildly. "That's going to come down before we know it. I'll stop it from killing people, you get up to the balcony and make people listen to you."

As she started to move, he grabbed her hand. "One day,

I hope you come to see me, and we can become friends again."

Tee nodded and plunged into the crowd, weaving herself through the endless array of well-dressed people until she finally came to the beige, fabric-covered wall. She stared up at where the chandelier's rope was tied, a few feet out of her grasp. "That's looking pretty frayed."

The building shook and a loud crack filled the room from overhead.

"Get out!" yelled Tee through the momentary silence.

There a laugh and then the silence was swallowed up by renewed chatter.

A guard appeared in front of Tee. At her belt was both a pistol and short sword.

"You're exactly what I need," said Tee, pulling the short sword. "Sorry about this." She smacked the guard's knee with the hilt of the sword, bringing her down on all fours.

Tee scrambled onto the woman's back and jumped. Planting one foot on the wall and pushing off, she caught the chandelier's rope with both hands.

"What's that yellow-hooded girl doing?" yelled someone, drawing the crowd's attention.

The guard grabbed at Tee's legs.

"The rope's going to give way, grab it! Grab it!"

"Listen to her!" yelled Alex from the balcony. "She's a Yellow Hood, and that chandelier is going to come down."

"I bet she did this," someone yelled back.

"There are airships outside that are bombing the keep. It is not safe," said Alex.

"Who are you? He sounds like that Liddel fellow. Everything is falling, falling. Nonsense," said someone in the crowd.

"I am Prince Alex of Endeara, and… and I'm a friend of the girl in the yellow cloak. We must get out of here."

Several guards took hold of the chandelier's rope and allowed Tee to step away.

The building rumbled again.

Chatter started again.

"Uncle! This Yellow Hood, she's the one I told you about, the one that saved my life at Kar'm. I trust her. Our lives are in danger."

The crowd turned to the tall, thin man with the highest of collars. He glanced up at the chandelier and squinted at the cracks in the ceiling.

Smoothing his long, blue coat, Alex's uncle let his gaze sweep over the room. "The air in here has a stuffiness to it, what with all of this commotion. I'm certain the weather outside is more amenable to our character. And this… this chandelier is in need of some repair," he said in a deep, baritone voice.

The crowd muttered in agreement and started flowing out behind Alex's uncle.

"My job's done here," said Tee.

CHAPTER FORTY-SEVEN

ONE ORDER FOR PICK UP

"Abeland's going down. That's not good," said Egelina-Marie as she watched the smoke billow out the back and sides of the Hotaru ahead of and below her. "I don't remember them being directly hit. Maybe their engines went?"

She looked back at her engineer, who seemed to be monitoring the gauges in front of him happily.

"Maybe Amami did something to them? Could she have sabotaged all the engines?" She thought back to the remarks that Amami had made.

A shot ripped across their bow.

"Eyes open!" she yelled, the image of her father telling her to pay attention vividly in her mind. Her hands were cold and sweaty beneath her brown gloves.

She looked over at the magnetic coil cannons on that side of the ship the Skyfaller was approaching from. One cannon was broken. Another was stuck pointing downwards and had the last two crew members working hard to fix it.

Eg ran her hand along the series of silver bells and their cryptic labels, chewing on her lip. Taking a steadying breath, she grabbed a bell and shook it, bracing for the engineer's response.

A second later, she heard the expected reply challenging the order.

She rang it again, looking over her shoulder at the rapidly approaching Skyfaller. "If they had guns up front, we'd be dead already."

The engineer rang back his disagreement.

Egelina-Marie turned around and pointed the bell at him, then threatening to throw it at him. All of the crew stared at her, everyone waiting anxiously.

He put his hands up and nodded.

Putting the bell back, she grabbed on to two levers and looked at the gauges. "This is such a bad idea." Glancing over her shoulder to make sure the engineer was ready with his levers, she pulled hers. "Everyone grab on to something!"

The Hotaru rolled up and around in the air, coming down behind the Skyfaller as it sailed past them.

"FIRE!" she yelled, ringing a bell. The cannons on the other side of the Hotaru let loose, and the Skyfaller blew apart.

Egelina-Marie put her head against the gauges. "Mother of Mercy, that was stupid. I bet Bakon's being the sensible one."

With a steadying breath, she looked at the crew, counting them. Everyone was there, though parts of the cannon that had been getting fixed were now missing.

Suddenly the Hotaru listed to one side; everyone grabbed on to something.

Eg stared at her gauges, several of which were now broken. She looked back terrified. Her engineer's mouth was moving, but she couldn't hear him. She watched as he worked furiously until finally the airship righted itself.

He smiled and offered her the two fingers.

She nodded, wiping the sweat off her face. Out of the corner of her eye, she noticed a flash of light followed by two more. Someone was signaling them from the corner of the keep.

"That's Amami, and it looks like she's got two Skyfallers keeping her company."

Eg picked a bell and shook her head. "He's going to hate me," she said, laughing. She turned and looked at the engineer and shook it.

He waved his arms in protest.

She shook it again. "Going down," she said with an evil grin.

A minute later, the Hotaru raced towards the ground.

Amami climbed onto a roof, her eyes glued to the strange painted cloud that was heading straight down towards her. The two older Skyfallers had already stopped their bombings and were lumbering forward to engage the Hotaru.

"Bloated flying pigs," said Amami with disgust. She flashed with the mirror one more time before tossing it aside. She pulled tightly on the replacement belt holding her collapsed wings on.

"Now, Egelina. Now! Now! Now! Now!" said Amami as her voice became more panicked. Suddenly the Hotaru leveled off and started swooping across the landscape towards her. Amami ran as fast as she could and leapt into the air as the Hotaru went by.

Grabbing on to the chain ladder, Amami held on tight as Egelina-Marie brought the ship up from its dive. The Skyfallers fired their cannons, narrowly missing each other and blowing apart one of the keep's towers.

Amami let go as the Hotaru sailed over one of the Skyfallers. Using her wings, she nimbly landed on the enemy deck and pulled out her remaining sword. She pointed it at the crew as they reached for their pistols.

"You have lost this day. Either—" said Amami.

One of the balloons of the other Skyfaller exploded.

Everyone threw their guns on the floor and put their hands up.

"Surrender or die!" yelled Amami.

"We surrender!"

Amami frowned and shook her head, disappointed.

CHAPTER FORTY-EIGHT

CAMPED

Tee stepped into the deserted marketplace. One of the nearby buildings had crumbled, and several of the nearby kiosks were smoldering.

"There you are," said a warm and familiar voice.

She looked up, a nervous laugh escaping. "Grandpapa!" She ran into Nikolas' arms. "How did you know I would be here?"

He kissed her forehead and hugged her. "If there is one thing that I know, it is my Tee. Sam told me where he found you before. Knowing that you were by yourself, I was most certain that you would return here. It was simply luck that it was now."

She laughed and stepped back. "But how did you get into the city?"

Nikolas' smile warmed her heart. "I just walked up to the gate and said I was an old man looking for his granddaughter and she was inside."

"That's it?"

He shrugged. "They might have been having trouble

opening the portcullis, so I provided some advice, and we got it open. A lot of them ran away, and I walked in."

"Where's Granddad?" asked Tee.

"Sam's safe and with Elly." Nikolas' expression became somber. "She did not look well."

"She's tough. She'll be okay," said Tee, wiping her nose.

He kissed her on the head again. "So, shall we go home? But it burned to the ground."

"Home is where I leave the picture of Grandmama, and that right now is our little camp.

"Tee's here!" said Richy. He was huddled over the camp fire with Egelina-Marie, Amami and Bakon and a series of pots and pans.

"Hey, guys. Where's Elly?"

Nikolas glanced about. "Sam's not here either. This is odd."

"Actually, I am," said a voice from a tree.

Everyone turned, laughing.

"How long have you been there?" asked Bakon.

"A while. After everything calmed down, I did a bit of shopping before coming here. I like watching the afternoon melt into the evening," he said, climbing down.

Tee frowned. "But Richelle told me you were on the airship."

He shook his head. "She'd say anything to get the job done." He glanced over at Elly's tent. "When Abeland dropped her off, I was a little worried about you, but not much. I knew you'd show up."

"What about Elly?"

"I put her in her tent; she's been there ever since," said Sam, scratching his beard.

Nikolas turned and shook his head at the columns of smoke rising from Relna. "That was a beautiful city."

"It was." Sam rubbed his eyes.

"Well, I could use a cup of tea, yes?"

"Already got one ready... Nikolas," said Bakon, holding it up.

"Ah, excellent." Nikolas joined him at the fire.

"So, what now?" asked Tee.

Sam looked at her, pride written all over his face. "Well, you and Elly managed to disrupt Eleanor's secret plan to assassinate Marcus and Caterina, and you saved some of the most important people across the continent. The Tub might not mean much anymore, but the Yellow Hoods? That's a legend that's just starting."

"Really?" said Tee, her nose wrinkled and eyes wide in surprise.

"Really." Sam gazed at the city of Relna. "There's a war coming, I can feel it, but it won't be today. You put that bear back to sleep for a bit." He gave her a sideways glance. "Good job. We'll need to talk in a while about what's next."

"Can I go see Elly right now?"

Sam nodded. "Sure."

Nikolas returned, offering Sam a cup of tea.

Accepting it, he scratched the edge of his mouth.

"You are worried about Elly, yes?"

Sam nodded. "I've seen that look more than a few times. I'm sure she'll be okay, but it's going to take time."

"Ya. So then, what is next?" asked Nikolas.

"Tomorrow morning, we head out for the Pointy Stick Inn. That's where they're expecting us."

CHAPTER FORTY-NINE

FAREWELL, LADY IN RED

Knocking on the door to the courtroom, Alfrida stood waiting.

"Alfrida, it's good to see you."

"And you, my Regent—I mean, my Queen."

Caterina smiled. "It will take some getting used to."

Alfrida nodded. "I have received word that Zelda has returned the Princess of Belnia to her home."

"Did the King's agreement with the Piemans get registered? Will Belnia be divided?"

After a hesitation, Alfrida replied, "It will."

"Then... then we will have two small enemies to crush when we so choose."

Alfrida straightened up. "I didn't expect that reaction."

"I am a woman unchained. This,"—she gestured at the room—"this destiny is mine. I never realized how much relief this moment would bring me." Touching the white china bowl filled with apples that stood beside the throne on a humble stand, she laughed. "Until now, this has been the only change I've been allowed to make to this room. But now? Now we will reshape the world."

"Marcus Pieman still lives."

"The man, yes, but the legend? No. The Piemans will struggle in Teuton, and the new kingdom they have been granted has no legitimacy to it. It was hard enough for me to govern when I became regent; it will be a nightmare for the Piemans. While we have lost many Skyfallers, they have lost all of their Hotarus—save maybe one or two? Their secret facility is gone, thanks to Eleanor. And her failed attempt to kill me and the others landed her in prison, with all the anger of the continent waiting for someone to blame, they will grind her to dust at her trial."

Caterina smiled and picked up a red apple. "Sometimes victory is focusing on what you've gained, and not on what you'd wished for." She took a bite.

"Wise words," said Alfrida. "Another success for the Lady in Red."

Caterina pointed the apple at Alfrida. "I think it's time to retire that moniker."

Alfrida put her arms behind her back. "Oh?"

"I became the Lady in Red the day that I left behind the life I was given and fought to create one of my own. And here I am, with a destiny my father would have seen as beyond the realms of possibility."

She stood up and stared at the paintings of past monarchs on the walls. "He often spoke of important days in history, but I can't help but think that we know not the day that the land fell to our will because of the wheel. Nor do we know when the sea fell because of ships." She pointed a finger at Alfrida. "But we know the day the sky fell to our will."

"And it will be your name written beside it," said Alfrida. "You must be delighted."

"I also feel like I have two hearts: one bursting with pride and the other with anticipation."

"Well, then, may I call you the Queen of Hearts?"

Caterina laughed. "Oh, yes. I like that. I can only imagine what they will say one day about the reign of the Queen of Hearts."

───────

"High Conventioneer, you seem particularly happy," said Alfrida, passing Simon in the grand corridor coming from his study.

He spun on his heels and smiled. "It is a particularly good day. The Queen has returned, the Tub is gone, and I have extinguished the last remnants of that pretender, Franklin Watt."

"I'm glad to hear it," said Alfrida.

"Oh, what time is it?"

Alfrida pulled out a pocket watch and glanced at it. "Seven thirty. You really should wear one of these. They are most convenient."

"I forgot to attend to something. I wish you a good night."

"Good night." Alfrida watched Simon return to his library, her eyes narrowed and lips tight.

Simon closed the door to his office and looked at the new clock sitting on his desk. "Any moment now."

The Neumatic tube rumbled, and a cylinder arrived.

"Happiness almost made you careless," he scolded himself, picking up the cylinder and opening it.

Glancing to check that his door was closed, he pulled out the letter and read it. "Dear High Conventioneer St. Malo... yes, yes, on with it... ah, there we go. We have confirmed your designs for airships as workable and genuine. Please note we hold you in the highest regard and will keep secret, until the time of your choosing, the granting of your requested title. We have issued payment, as per your instructions."

He tore the note into small pieces and put them on an ash covered disk on his desk. Then he set it ablaze and watched the dancing little flames.

"Another kingdom pays, and more chaos is sown. Never again will I be caught without friend or funds. So, come for me when you will Abeland, and be careful of turning on me again, Caterina, for I will have a war to wage back on you."

CHAPTER FIFTY

REUNIONS AND GOODBYES

"Is this the place?" asked Tee, pointing out the window of the carriage as it slowed.

Up ahead was a large, friendly-looking building with a gradually sloped, thatched roof. Lanterns hung along its periphery and pushed back the darkest of the night. Music streamed out of it and brought a vibrancy and life to the surroundings.

Nikolas looked up and put his book away. As he turned down the small crank lantern in their carriage, a warm smile spread across his face. "Ah, this is it, my Tee. The Pointy Stick Inn is a wonderful place, and though it has changed hands several times, it has never changed spirit." He scratched his trimmed beard. "I cannot believe that it was not long ago that Marcus and I stopped here, and yet, it feels like an eternity ago. Time's a funny thing, yes?"

Tee squeezed his hand.

"Elly, we're here," said Tee, giving her a nudge.

Elly looked up from her book. "Already?"

"How can you say already?" asked Tee.

"It was a good book." Elly stretched, a yawn escaping.

Tee pointed to the spine of the inch-thick book. "That was a series, Elly."

Frowning, Elly turned it. "Fair enough. Good thing we stopped at that Owl's Nest bookstore on the outskirts of Relna on the way."

"Come girls, we must go. Your parents will be excited to see you," said Nikolas, opening the door and climbing out of the carriage.

Elly glanced at Tee. "I'm sorry I haven't spoken much since…"

Tee put her hand on Elly's forearm. "You don't have to apologize for anything, with me. Ever."

Her eyes welling up, Elly gazed down at her trembling hands.

"I think you're already going into withdrawal."

"Huh?" asked Elly, looking up.

"Your hands, they need a new book," said Tee, a smirk on her face. "Let's see if there's still one you haven't read in the trunk. They should have it down by now," said Tee. She climbed out.

With a steadying sigh, Elly followed suit.

Nikolas watched as the girls nearly knocked Sam Baker aside as they opened the trunk and pulled out a book, before heading inside. He chuckled as he noticed his foot tapping along to the music.

"It feels good, doesn't it?" asked Sam as he climbed down from the roof of the carriage.

"It does. Everyone will be together and safe. This is all that is important, yes?"

Sam nodded.

The driver of the coach came over, and Sam handed him a small bag of coins.

"A room's covered for you, your guard and your crew driving the other carriage if you want it. Stay or go; it's your choice," said Sam.

"We'll get going, if that's okay," replied the driver.

Sam looked back down the trail. The jiggling lanterns of their other carriage told him it was only a few minutes away. "That's fine by me."

The driver nodded and left.

Tapping his brown and gold vest pockets, Sam shook his head. "Well, I think I'm pretty much tapped out."

"I've never heard of a poor spymaster," said Nikolas with a wry smile.

"Neither have I," replied Sam with a wink.

The music coming from the Pointy Stick Inn was suddenly overwhelmed by a roar of delight as Tee and Elly entered.

"That should lift their spirits a bit," said Sam.

"And theirs," said Nikolas as the second coach pulled up. He opened the door.

Egelina-Marie stepped out and gave Nikolas' arm a

squeeze. Her face was still scratched up from the hard landing her Hotaru had taken, but she wore it well.

She turned and helped Bakon out, his arm in a sling.

"Do you need a hand?" asked Sam.

Bakon frowned and then laughed. "I like her to feel important."

Handing Bakon his cane, Eg scoffed. "And apparently you wanted me to feel like a better pilot than you. Though next time? You don't have to crash something to get my attention."

"Noted," replied Bakon, grimacing as he took a step.

Nikolas looked inside the carriage. "Where are Amami and Richy?" He looked at Sam who shrugged. "They were riding with you, yes?"

Egelina-Marie lowered her gaze and scratched the end of her nose. She opened her long, brown coat and took out a letter. "Richy gave this to me at the last minute. It's for his adopted parents."

"Oh no," said Nikolas, his face falling. "This is very sad."

Bakon winced, shifting his weight uncomfortably. "He and Amami are going to pay their respects to their mother's grave, and then... well, they'll be back. Maybe not right away, but they'll be back."

Nikolas nodded.

The front door flew open, and a voice boomed, "BAKON!"

They all turned to catch the sight of a hulk of a man running at them.

"Bore!" said Bakon, his face lighting up in delight.

The youngest of the Cochon brothers grabbed his eldest brother and lifted him straight up. "It's you! It's really you!"

"Aargh!" screeched Bakon.

"Ease up there, big guy," said Egelina-Marie with a laugh. "You don't want to see your big brother cry. It's not pretty."

"Hi Eg," said a man emerging from the shadows.

"Squeals! Come here," she said, waving him over and giving him a hug.

"So, is it true you guys were flying around before crashing down?" Squeals twirled a finger.

"Yeah. Though, I think my airship might still have some life left in her," she said with a smile. "But keep that to yourself."

He smiled and nodded.

"You look good, Squeals," said Bakon. "Kept out of trouble?"

A smile cracked across the middle Cochon brother's lips. "Didn't get caught."

"Even better." Bakon put his arm around Squeals' neck and gave him a squeeze.

Nikolas wiped a tear and clapped his hands. "Come. Let's go inside. I must hear about everything that's happened. Everything."

Sam watched as everyone left and the coaches departed. He stood there in the chilly night, listening to the music and enjoying the serenity of the moment.

"Hi, Sam," said a woman approaching from the far side of the tavern, an apron around her waist.

"Alice, what a wonderful surprise," he replied with a big grin.

"Liar," she said with a laugh.

"Spymasters are."

"I thought you'd like to know that Chikahn's doing well. He's got a following now, going from village to village."

Sam chuckled. "I'm glad. He was the key to unlocking everything."

"You helped save the world," she said with a smile.

"They did all the work, and though all their good work won't last, it feels good. I'm getting too old for this."

Alice tilted her head towards the inn. "Celebrate over a beer? I'm sure the victory's worth at least one."

"Sure. It's worth a beer," said Sam.

"You guys are squeezing the life out of me," said Tee to her parents. They'd pounced on her the second the inn's doors had opened.

William and Jennifer continued to rock their sandwiched daughter back and forth.

"I'm not done yet; are you, William?" asked Tee's mother, Jennifer.

"Not yet," he replied, his tired face already sore from smiling so much.

"I'm dying. Dying, I tell you." Tee flailed her arms about.

"Just a bit more," said Jennifer.

"Elly and I have a no-dying rule. Oh, oh! Now you've done it. I'm dead." Tee's arms drooped down to her sides. "Completely dead. See what you did?"

William and Jennifer laughed, finally letting their daughter go.

"I missed you guys too," she said, an awkward, shy smile on her face.

Jennifer squeezed Tee's shoulder. We know."

Tee glanced around the packed tavern. "Is this everyone from Minette and Mineau?"

"Oh no," said Jennifer, leading Tee and William to the only empty table and sitting down. "A lot of people have fled or moved on."

"Or died," added William.

Jennifer nodded. "These are the people who refused to give up. And a few wanted to meet these Yellow Hoods they'd heard whispers about."

"Did you know there are stories as far as Caixa about Yellow Hoods?" William scratched his stubbled neck.

"Spread by all sorts of unsavory characters," said

Jennifer with a playful glare.

William laughed.

A hand patted Tee on the shoulder. She looked up. "Captain Archambault!"

"I've heard you've done some great work. I just wanted —" He lost his words and choked up as Egelina-Marie entered the tavern. "Excuse me," he said, wiping his eyes.

"She's a real hero, that Egelina-Marie." Tee sighed. "I hope to be like her when I grow up."

"From what I hear, almost riding a sail-cart off our little cliff's nothing for you these days."

Tee stared at her dad, a cheeky look on her face. "Oh, I don't know. I think that's about all the excitement that I can handle right now."

Jennifer squeezed Tee's hands. "On our way to Aunt Gwen's, you're going to tell me everything. I want to hear absolutely everything."

"You sound like Grandpapa." Tee laughed and scanned about, finally finding Nikolas laughing with the Cochon brothers. Suddenly her face fell, and she stared at her mom. "Aunt Gwen's?"

Tee took a moment to have a genuine look at her parents. Her father's face looked thinner than she remembered, and his beard was greyer. Her mother's eyes looked pained and tired, but happy. "We aren't going back to Minette?"

William licked his lips and shook his head.

"Everything's gone. There's not much left in Mineau either. It'll take a long time to rebuild it properly."

Jennifer sat on the edge of her chair. "We think it's best to move on, start again. Some of the reasons we were in Minette don't apply anymore." She looked at William.

He nodded.

Rubbing the back of her head, Tee sighed. She nodded at her other grandfather, Sam, as he walked into the tavern with a woman she didn't recognize.

"I can't believe our home's gone," said Tee. "We're all going to live out near Westria? At least we'll have Aunt Gwen and good chocolate."

William turned his face away as he squirmed. "We have a friend there, already setting things up. She saved your mother's life."

"Oh?" Tee stared at her mother.

"Her name's Gretel. You'll like her. She's tough like Eg, but… had a harder life."

Pointing about the tavern, William sat forward. "Little did I know when I met Gretel and her companion here, that she'd be the difference between life and death for your mother." He shook his head and patted Tee's knee. "But that's a story for later."

"Okay."

Nikolas arrived at their table, his cheeks rosy from much laughter. "I have not found Richy's parents. Are they here?"

Jennifer stood up and hugged her father. "Do you even know how much danger you were in?"

"Ah, I had Grandmama and Tee looking after me; there was no danger," he replied, making her laugh. He frowned down at the seated William.

"They aren't here," he said, rolling his shoulders.

"Oh." Nikolas tapped the edge of the letter on the table. "Then what do we do with this?"

"We can get it to them. They're in Palais, hoping he'll show up someday. They went through a lot with everything that happened and didn't want to come with all of us. They hope he'll return home one day."

"He is home; he's with Amami," said Tee.

"You knew?" asked Nikolas.

"Not exactly, but yes." Tee's eyes went wide as something went off in her head. She turned to her parents, her brow tight in worry. "You said we're going to Aunt Gwen's. Where's Elly going?"

Elly rubbed her face and nose, the tears having subsided for a minute. "Ah… I hate this."

"Another lap around the tavern?" offered Tee. She could hear the faint sounds of Sam creeping along the roof, keeping an eye on them.

The late-night air was chilly, and the music was half of what it had been a few hours before.

"Palais is beautiful," said Tee, sniffing. "They've got fantastic dressmakers there. You always wanted to try one."

Elly laughed piteously. "Yay. I'll finally get to have a dress... and no you."

"That institute sounds like an amazing place," said Tee. "You're going to do amazing there."

"If I get in," said Elly, her feet dragging.

"You'll get in. I doubt anyone knows half as much about chemistry as you do. And if they claim to, make it a contest. The first one to build a working rocket-pack wins."

Elly chuckled and wiped her nose again. "Yeah." She sat down on a log. "How can you be so upbeat?"

"I'm a wreck inside," said Tee with a sad smile. "But you need me, and I will always be your rock."

"And me yours."

"That's what best friends are, right? No amount of distance is going to change anything." Tee sat beside her.

Elly put her head on Tee's shoulder.

"I just... I can't imagine you not being there every day," said Elly, her voice cracking again and tears streaming down.

"I'll visit, lots."

"I know, but still. Gah!" Elly stared up at the night sky. "I hate this."

Tee nudged Elly with her shoulder. "You're going to love it. This is just the beginning of something new. Plus, Richy's bound to show up in Palais sooner or later. You know he's going to drive Amami crazy."

Laughing, Elly nodded. "Yeah, completely."

"Totally crazy."

They stared at the stars for a while.

"Are you okay?" asked Tee. "From the whole... thing?"

Elly tried to answer. Failing, she bowed her head. "Let's go with a big fat no."

"You'll be okay. I know it. Hey, you know who I was thinking of?" asked Tee.

"Mounira."

Tee nodded. "I hope she's okay."

"I'm sure she's driving Christina up the wall."

"I wonder whose shins she's kicking these days."

They laughed.

"That's a story I need to hear," said Tee.

"Yeah, me too," replied Elly, wiping her eyes. "I'm going to miss you, Tee."

"I'm going to miss you too, Elly." Tee's voice finally cracking.

CHAPTER FIFTY-ONE
Farkees Or Bust

"You have no idea how good it is to have you here," said Emery, leaning on his broom.

Alice smiled. "Well, I did make a promise. Sorry it took me longer than expected to return."

"What's a few months between friends?"

"Quite a bit, I think," she replied with a wink.

Emery gazed about the empty tavern. "I tell you, Alice, I used to feel this place was cursed. But now? I feel like everything strange that is going to happen first comes in through those doors, for good or ill."

"Delivery!" yelled someone at the door.

"Mother of Mercy," said Emery, putting his hand over his heart. "You'll kill an old man... have some sense."

"I love this old place," said Alice, running up and picking up the crate of fresh vegetables. "Is he new?"

"Will it convince you to stay?" asked Emery.

She frowned at him and lowered her gaze.

"I appreciate that you've been here for a month, especially having your help with that lot from Minette and

Mineau. But I know that you can't stay. I see it in your eyes. Whatever it is that you do, wherever it is that you need to be, I want you to feel free to go." He rubbed his nose. "Just promise an old man one thing?"

"I haven't even said I was going." She sighed. "Anything."

"Come and see me; let me know what you're up to. It'll fill the holes in those rare moments of boredom."

She put the crate down on the bar and walked over to him. She gave him a kiss on the cheek. "That promise I can fulfill with all my heart."

He smiled. "I'll take care of everything from here."

"What? I don't even get to finish my shift?" She raised an eyebrow.

"It's okay. Whatever strangeness is going to come through that door, I'll be able to handle it. The help that I have isn't great, but it'll do."

Alice stared at the floor. "Are you sure?"

"I am," said Emery. "Go do whatever it is you do in the world."

She glanced about the tavern. "Okay." Taking off her apron, she walked up to the front door and stopped. She turned and smiled at him. "You never asked me where I went or who I really am."

He laughed. "Don't think I wasn't curious, but I felt it only right not to ask. I've met people from the fabled Tub and Fare, even some from societies whose names are just whispers in the night. I've learned never to tread where I'm not invited."

"My real name is Alice, well, Allison."

Emery smiled as he reached over a table and picked up the rags he'd piled there.

"And if you should ever hear of the Baker's Dozen, well, you can say you met one," she added.

He turned around, bewilderment on his face, only to find she was gone.

Sighing, he dumped the rags in a dry, wooden bucket. "It was best to let her go."

"Hey, are you open?" asked a deep voice from the doorway.

"Ah, not really," said Emery as two burly ruffians stepped into the room, flanking a younger, lanky man. Each of them had a brass tube slung over his shoulder. They had clearly been in the rain recently.

"What do you think, Franky?" said the one on the left, scratching his heavily grizzled face.

"Hang on a sec, Ruffo. Do you know how to keep your mouth shut?" asked the other ruffian, pointing at Emery.

Emery casually took his broom. "Have you ever heard of anyone important coming through here before?" he asked, sweeping.

"No," said Ruffo.

"Then there's your answer."

"I'm starving, guys," said Franklin, walking down to

the main floor. "Do you have any food?"

"I can make something," said Emery looking at them. "It'll take me a bit to get the oven fired up, but if you're not in a hurry, then we're fine. That's assuming that you gentlemen have the coinage to cover such an expense."

Stephano tapped his pocket. "Yeah, we're good. We're catching a horse and cart this afternoon, so we've got some time."

Emery leaned the broom against the wall. "Do you mind if I ask where you gentlemen are headed? It always makes me feel connected to the world."

"Farkees," said Ruffo.

"This man, Franky, he's a genius," said Stephano. He tapped one of the brass tubes. "He's going to make us flying ships, and we're going to take over."

"Are you now?" asked Emery. "That's some mighty big ambition."

"It won't be quick, but it will happen," said Franklin.

A chill ran down Emery's spin. "Well, I'll get to work on those breakfasts then."

CHAPTER FIFTY-TWO

LEGACY

Tee pulled back her yellow hood and ran her hand along the symbol on the charred door of the old three-floor treehouse. Taking a deep breath of the cool autumn air, she gazed about, taking in the familiar sights. The dusting of snow made it feel all the more like home. "Thanks for bringing me back here, Dad."

William smiled. "How could I refuse to let you say goodbye to this place?"

"Grandpapa thought that you might be trying to delay being surrounded by Auntie Gwen and her army of kids." Tee had a smirk on her face.

"Your grandfather is a wise, wise man. Never mind I heard that there's another baby."

"What?" said Tee with a laugh.

"As your mother says, her sister is a baby machine. Anyway, given that the pulley system seems intact, are you okay to get down by yourself?"

"I'll be fine."

He chuckled and stroked his chin. "It doesn't matter

what you've done or will ever do, kiddo, you'll always be my little girl," he said putting his arm around her. "I love you."

"I know." Tee sighed. As he turned to go, she called out, "Hey Dad. Did you guys make this? I mean the whole treehouse and pulleys. Did you guys make them for us?"

To her surprise, his face tensed. "It's not as simple an answer as you might think. I'm going to help Nikolas salvage anything he can from his lab. Come find us when you're done."

Tee nodded.

After he had left, she pushed open the door. Its last hinge did its best to keep the door level. Stepping onto the creaky, snow-covered floor, Tee stared at the flame-licked interior of the treehouse. It was scarred but had survived. Most of the surrounding trees had burned down.

"It feels like I haven't been here in a hundred years."

She scratched her face and gingerly made her way up to the lookout. Taking in another breath of the cool mountain air, she thought back to the first encounter with LeLoup's horsemen and their first showdown. Her throat tightened and eyes welled up as she thought of Elly. She took hold of the railing only to find it wobbled and was unsafe.

With her tour of the treehouse done, Tee headed down the mountain and walked along the dirt road. She sighed sorrowfully as she passed ruined homes, the crunching of the snow her only company.

She stared at the path she'd run down a million times

and gazed at the clearing where all of her childhood moments had been taken for granted. Her home, that adorable little cabin, had lost its roof and was filled with snow. The front door was down, defeated. She could see straight through the cabin to her father's shed in the back.

Tee walked up the two front steps and stared at the fallen door and then at the black, ashen doorframe. She wrinkled her nose at the ever-present smoky smell.

Putting a foot on the door, she gave it a shove. The floorboards underneath moaned. "Probably not safe to walk around."

With a heavy heart, she made her way around the house, staring at the few items that seem to have resisted the fire, islands in a sea of destruction. Standing before her father's shed, she thought of the number of times they'd worked on little projects: her, her father, and her grandpapa.

She turned back to look at the house. The window through which her mother would watch, was now warped and blackened.

Opening the shed, she felt a twitch of childhood naughtiness.

"Tee, don't go in the shed," she said imitating her father's voice.

There were shelves along one wall, filled with gardening tools and glass jars with seeds. Against the other wall were the shovel and a spare crossbow that had seen better days.

As she was about to close the door, she stared at the floor. Something about it was off. She looked around the side of the shed. There were several pots and tools laying on the ground, which would normally be on the floor of the shed.

"That's weird."

Bending down, she noticed a groove that formed a square in the floor boards. She ran her fingers along it until she noticed that at the front, it had a little give. She pushed it down, and the panel rose up just enough to get her fingers under it.

She opened it and stared in disbelief.

"What in the world?" she said, reaching in and pulling out a folded piece of cloth from the top. She stepped out of the shed and held out her arms, baffled by the old, worn, yellow cloak before her.

"I was wondering if Will had removed it or not."

Tee spun around. "Granddad? What are you doing here?"

Sam pulled the matte, black hood back and scratched his clean-shaven face. "We have a few things we need to talk about, Teela Baker."

"Why are you calling me by my full name?" she asked, stepping back.

"Because, this isn't a grandfather, granddaughter conversation we're about to have. Walk with me."

They headed back up to the road.

"That cloak wasn't mine, was it? It looked old," said Tee.

"You're right. It was your father's, from when he was a boy." He looked at her. "I found it one day. He'd called himself the Yellow Guardian, and he'd helped some lost kids find their way home. As any worried parent, I told him to stop, but he wore it a few more times before we sat down and had the conversation we needed to.

"His mother had died about a year before, and I wasn't handling it as gracefully as I should have. The demands on me from the Tub were high. I offered to have him with me, to learn what I did. He ended up less interested in the spy side of things, but he discovered a love of adventure—until he found himself here and fell in love with your mother."

"So, it wasn't an accident that he gave me the idea for a yellow cloak?" asked Tee, a smirk on her face.

"No, it wasn't. But this brings us to the conversation we need to have. There are old agreements, and what you've done as the Yellow Hoods is excellent, but by every rule, it has been illegal."

Tee's eyes went wide, and she gulped. "Oh."

Sam stared up at the trees, dusted in snow. "Now, the Tub has been retired. And by convention, that means it cannot be brought back for ten years and ten days."

"I thought it was gone," said Tee.

He scratched his neck. "There's gone, and there's gone. When you have an institution that has been around as long as the Tub, it's more that the dragon sleeps once again, but it'll wake up."

"Dragons burn things to the ground, you know."

"Okay, bad analogy," said Sam with a laugh. "But you get my meaning."

He pulled up his sleeve.

"What are all of these?" asked Tee, staring intently.

"These are tattooed marks for the different orders and secret societies that I've been a part of. It's what allows those old agreements to apply to me. Well, part of it…"

"So, what are you saying, Granddad?"

"I'm saying you were protected when you were with Nikolas, with Christina, and with me. But you need to either go through the proper training and be inducted into an order or stop."

Tee found herself staring at the ruins of Elly's house.

"You need to think," said Sam.

Grabbing her grandfather's arm, Tee gave him a determined stare. "I'll do whatever I need to. I want to help people."

He smiled. "There are a lot of ways to help people without going through what you'd need to."

"But this is my place." She thought for a moment. "I wonder how my parents are going to feel about this."

"Who do you think asked me to come and talk to you?" he said, with a sorrowful half-smile. He took her hand.

"Why do you look sad?"

"Oh, it's nothing. Just noting a little girl gone and a

young warrior woman standing in her place." He sniffed. "I'm getting sentimental in my old age."

She squeezed his hand. "I'm going to have my own mark."

"Are you?"

She smiled. "It'll be the Mark of the Yellow Hoods."

The End

EPILOGUE

Elly glanced up at the huge clock that stood in the center of the institute's library. It was two stories high and dwarfed by the immenseness of the building.

"Oh, I better get going, my parents are going to be here soon," she said, scooping her books and papers off the table. "I'll see you all on Monday."

"Bye Elly, have a great weekend," whispered the four girls at the table.

One of the two boys raised a hand. "Aren't you going to be working with us on that chemistry research paper?"

"Already done," said Elly with a smirk. "It was easy."

Everyone at the table grumbled, shifting her smirk into a devilish smile.

One of the girls stood up. "Um, can I walk with you?" she asked, nervously touching her silver-rimmed glasses.

"Ah…" Elly glanced about, cuddling her books. "Sure. Rainey, right?"

The girl nodded and collected her things.

"Don't tell me you're done the paper too?" complained one of the girls.

"No, I'll be back," said Rainey.

Waving goodbye to their table-mates, the two headed for one of the grand archway exits.

"By the way, I love the new blue dress. The striped shirt's a good choice too," said Rainey.

Elly blushed and stared forward. "Thanks. I like your new short hair. Very pixie," she said, the words flying out so quickly they almost tripped on each other.

"So… where are you going for the weekend?"

"Oh. My parents are coming to pick me up. We're going to Herve, to the coast." Elly reached around and pulled at her ponytail.

They both stared at the shiny tiled floor until they came to the dormitory stairs, and then went down it silently, and entered one of the many high-ceilinged corridors.

"Does your family live far away?"

Elly laughed. "No, actually. They live here in Palais. We have a… what do you call it when you have rooms in a building where other people live?"

"A flat?"

"That's it. Yes, my parents have a flat. I found it… weird. I was spending all of my time here at the university anyway, so they offered to let me live here. It's been two years now, and I just feel… at home. My room's at the end of the hall."

Rainey stopped. "Do you have a roommate?"

"Bella, but she's not around this week. Why?"

"Because your door's open," said Rainey, pointing.

Elly put her books down and bit her lip. "I probably forgot to lock it when I left this morning."

"I've only known you for a few weeks, but you never miss anything."

Elly crept slowly towards the door. "There's always a first time." She pressed herself against the door and slowly pushed it open. The door was pitch dark. She reached for the gas lantern on the wall and turned it up.

The small room had two single beds, against opposing walls, and a bookcase. Standing in the middle of the room, was a black-hooded figure, a hint of yellow showing from beneath the hood and from the inside of the cloak.

Rainey screamed, scattering her books.

"It's okay!" said Elly, grabbing her hand. "It's okay. She's a friend."

"Sorry about that," said Tee removing her hood. "This is your girlfriend?"

Both girls immediately blushed.

"Ah, no," said Elly, touching the side of her head. "Not that... I mean... It's just..."

"Yeah." Rainey pulled at the tips of her hair and turned around. "I'll see you later."

Elly glared at Tee.

"Sorry, I thought..." Tee rubbed her face.

"It's okay," yelled Rainey from the corridor.

Elly looked up and shook her head.

"I got your message. What have you got for me this

time?" asked Tee.

Elly knelt and reached under her bed, pulling out an elegantly carved, wooden box. "How's training going?"

Tee let out a stressful chuckle. "I didn't nearly fall to my death this month."

"That's an improvement," said Elly, her eyebrows raised. "On my side, no lab explosions in three months! I'm off probation."

She handed the box to Tee. "I think you're going to like what I have for you."

"I always do." Tee ran a hand along the top of the box. "What's inside?"

"Smoke bombs. I figure if you need to get away or something, it could be useful. My lab mates have confirmed that my formula is highly effective." She stared at the door. "Highly."

Tee smiled. "You should come join me."

Elly stared at the ground. With a trembling hand, she reached and tugged her ponytail. Then with a calming and steadying breath, she looked Tee square in the eye, a scared smile on her face. "Not yet, but some day."

IS THIS THE END?

Yes and no. When I first started writing this book, I had an idea for books 6 and 7, potentially a book 8. Those would revolve around freeing Tee and Elly's parents from the slavers (book 6 & 7), and then reuniting Mounira with her father and venturing into the Southern Kingdoms (book 8). So, what happened?

The further that I went with book 5, the more that I realized I was going to have pushed the characters as far as I could in good conscience, and that they deserved a rest. The ideas for books 6 & 7 started to feel like I was going be dragging things out, and I didn't want that. The story arc I started in book 1, and put into serious gear in book 2, was done.

So, does this mean it's the end for Tee, Elly, Richy, Bakon, Eg, Amami and the rest of the cast? Not at all.

From the very beginning I've planned to write a sequel series, and I will be. Before you know it, you'll be hearing about me writing book 1 of The Mark of The Yellow Hoods. But that's not all. The ending of this book was written to open the doors on this universe you've helped me create. Expect a book or three with Allison Vunderlan and the War of the Queen of Hearts, maybe a book about the Baker's Dozen, and oh, perhaps a cheeky tale called something like *When Pigs Could Fly - Sky Pirating with the Cochons*.

So charge your shock-sticks, mend your cloaks, and get ready. We're not done yet.

- Adam

THANK YOU
FOR READING THIS BOOK

Reviews are powerful and are more than just you sharing your important voice and opinion, they are also about telling the world that people are reading the book.

Many don't realize that without enough reviews, indie authors are excluded from important newsletters and other opportunities that could otherwise help them get the word out. So, if you have the opportunity, I would greatly appreciate your review.

Don't know how to write a review? Check out **AdamDreece.com/WriteAReview**. Where could you post it? On GoodReads.com and at your favorite online retailer are a great start!

Don't miss out on sneak peeks and news, join my newsletter at: **AdamDreece.com/newsletter**

PLAYLIST

Every now and then I get asked what albums I listened to when writing a book. Here's what I primarily listened to when writing The Day the Sky Fell:

Lindsey Stirling - Brave Enough
Lindsey Stirling - Shatter Me
Sabaton - Carolus Rex
Jesper Kyd - Assassin's Creed 2 & 3
Lorenna McKennitt - The Mask and Mirror
Ramin Djawadi - Game of Thrones [Season 3]

Enjoy,
Adam

ABOUT THE AUTHOR

Off and on, for 25 years, Adam wrote short stories enjoyed by his friends and family. Regularly, his career in technology took precedence over writing, so he set aside his dream of one day, maybe, becoming an author.

After a life-changing event, Adam decided to make more changes in his life, including never missing a night of reading stories to his kids again because of work, and becoming an author.

He then wrote a personal memoir (yet unpublished) as every story he tried to write became the story of his life. With that out of the way, he returned to fiction, and with a nudge from his daughter, wrote Along Came a Wolf and created The Yellow Hoods series.

He lives in Calgary, Alberta, Canada with his awesome wife and amazing kids.

Adam blogs about writing and what he's up to at
AdamDreece.com.

He is on Twitter **@AdamDreece** and Instagram
@AdamDreece.

And lastly, feel free to email him at
Adam.Dreece@ADZOPublishing.com

ADAM DREECE BOOKS

Tilruna (Season #1)
ISBN: 978-1-988746-05-0

Hope is about to die, and a small group of rebels are willing to risk everything to save it.

For two hundred years, a period of unprecedented peace, a revered group of Elves, Dwarves and Orks have pushed the frontiers of the magical sciences. Their greatest accomplishment, a fleet of interstellar spaceships, is about to be revealed to the public... but the new Elven-lead government has other plans.

"Battlestar Galactica meets Lord of the Rings."

Watch for it Fall 2017

ADAM DREECE BOOKS

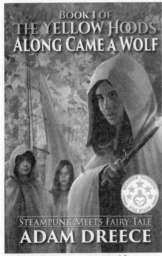

Along Came a Wolf
ISBN: 978-0-9881013-0-2

Breadcrumb Trail
ISBN: 978-0-9881013-3-3

All the King's-Men
ISBN: 978-0-9881013-6-4

Beauties of the Beast
ISBN: 978-0-9948184-0-9